A DARK DAY FOR PLANET EARTH

An original novel by

Kevin D. Fraser

A DARK DAY FOR PLANET EARTH

An original novel by

Kevin D. Fraser

Published by Biscuits & Gravy Publishing

Cave Creek, Arizona USA
First Edition, 2025

For inquiries on reproducing portions of this book contact books@fraserlimited.com

This is a work of fiction. Names, characters, places, and incidents are either the product of the author's imagination or used fictitiously. Any resemblance to actual persons, living or dead, events, or locales is entirely coincidental.

Title: A Dark Day for Planet Earth
Author: Kevin Fraser
Keywords: Climate thriller, global disaster, end of world, suspense, apocalypse
Categories: Thriller, Action, Climate Fiction

Table of Contents

PROLOGUE: NEWS BLURB
CHAPTER ONE: FORMER DISCIPLE
CHAPTER TWO: QUIET FUNDING
CHAPTER THREE: BALLOON OVER LAPLAND
CHAPTER FOUR: WHISPER PROTOCOLS
CHAPTER FIVE: THE GENEVA MEETING
CHAPTER SIX: PARTICLE PHYSICS
CHAPTER SEVEN: CREDIBILITY GAP
CHAPTER EIGHT: WEATHER PATTERNS
CHAPTER NINE: SCALE BREACH
CHAPTER TEN: THE STOCKHOLM CONFERENCE
CHAPTER ELEVEN: PLAUSIBLE DENIABILITY
CHAPTER TWELVE: FIRST IMPACT
CHAPTER THIRTEEN: GLOBAL RESPONSE
CHAPTER FOURTEEN: THE ARCHITECT
CHAPTER FIFTEEN: POINT OF NO RETURN
CHAPTER SIXTEEN: CASCADING FAILURE
CHAPTER SEVENTEEN: THE RESISTANCE
CHAPTER EIGHTEEN: CRISIS IN SRI LANKA
CHAPTER NINETEEN: THE SILENT PULSE
CHAPTER TWENTY: THE BROKEN SKY
CHAPTER TWENTY-ONE: NEW EQUILIBRIUM

A DARK DAY FOR PLANET EARTH

PROLOGUE: NEWS BLURB

[The Guardian – March 10, 2025] UK to Launch £50m Geoengineering Research Program By Alice Brent – Climate Correspondent

The UK's Advanced Research and Invention Agency (ARIA) is preparing a set of small-scale atmospheric intervention trials, with methods ranging from cloud brightening to stratospheric aerosol injection. Critics say the move risks a "climate domino effect," but ARIA insists these are merely feasibility studies.

[Forbes – February 24, 2025] Solar Geoengineering: The Billion-Dollar Backup Plan By Marcus Hill

While still controversial, solar radiation management is gaining traction in elite climate circles. One philanthropic tech titan—through a web of climate research funds—is believed to be backing multiple trials in the US and EU. "We must be prepared if emissions cuts alone aren't fast enough," one associate said.

[X Post – @TheGreenLeak – April 3, 2025] BREAKING: Cloud whitening ships may already be in the North Sea. Watch who's financing this. Not governments—foundations. #Geoengineering #ClimateTruth

[CNBC – March 17, 2025] 'Volcanic Cooling' Gets a Trial Run Over Scandinavia

A university-led team has confirmed a test balloon will be launched from northern Sweden this spring. The balloon will release a calcium carbonate plume to measure reflectivity and dispersal. "This is basic science, not terraforming," said project lead Dr. Ken Olafsson.

[Nature (Editorial) – April 2, 2025] Geoengineering Is No Longer Theoretical. We Need a Framework.

As public and private actors move forward with real-world tests of solar radiation management, the scientific community must rapidly establish global norms, safeguards, and legal mechanisms for rollback. Without transparency, climate intervention may turn into climate destabilization.

The world's ignorance was not a moment, but a process. The darkening of the skies began with whispers and press releases, with reassurances and scientific equivocation. It began with words like "feasibility" and "small-scale" and "reversible." It began with humanity's oldest delusion: that nature, once altered, could always be restored.

In the beginning, no one recognized the danger. Not the climatologists who monitored shifting weather patterns. Not the oceanographers who noted subtle perturbations in currents. Not the farmers who planted their crops beneath skies that seemed a shade less blue.

They didn't recognize it because they weren't meant to.

And by the time someone did, it would be too late.

CHAPTER ONE: FORMER DISCIPLE

[CBS Evening News – April 3, 2026] "And in environmental headlines tonight: A small university-led experiment is preparing to launch a helium balloon from a remote site in Sweden to test the cooling properties of naturally occurring dust in the upper atmosphere. Scientists insist it's harmless and decades away from practical use. Still, critics worry the test crosses an ethical line. More after this."

Alex Ross paced behind the podium, eyes narrowing as the moderator misquoted the data he had just presented. Three hundred of Europe's leading climate scientists sat before him in the Brussels convention center, expressions ranging from skepticism to outright hostility.

"To clarify," Alex said, leaning into the microphone, "I'm not suggesting all atmospheric research is dangerous. I'm saying that once we deploy reflective particles at scale, we cannot predict all downstream effects."

Vanessa Edwards, the moderator, smiled thinly. "Yet your former employer is actively developing space-based solar reflectors. Some might call your position... inconsistent."

A murmur rippled through the audience. Everyone knew about Alex's public falling out with Elias Venture, the aerospace billionaire who had once been his mentor. Three years of lawsuits and non-disclosure battles had left both men scarred, though only Alex had been left unemployable.

"Space reflectors can be turned off," Alex replied. "Particulate matter in the stratosphere cannot. That's not opinion—it's atmospheric physics."

A man in the front row—silver-haired, wearing an expensive but understated suit—raised his hand. Alex recognized him immediately: Warren Thorne, founder of the Global Climate

Resilience Initiative. The man whose foundation was quietly funding half the atmospheric research in the room. Borne wealthy into his grandfather's mining fortune, Thorne had succeeded in his own right by amassing a massive chemical and mineral empire.

"Mr. Ross," Thorne said, his voice calm and measured. "You've built a career critiquing solutions without offering alternatives. What do you propose instead?"

Alex met Thorne's gaze. There was something unsettling about the billionaire's eyes—like looking at a chess player who had calculated twenty moves ahead.

"Emission reductions and carbon capture," Alex said. "Proven approaches without risking—"

"Approaches that have failed for thirty years," Thorne interrupted, his voice still pleasant but firm. "My question is sincere. What alternative do you offer to a world already experiencing climate collapse?"

Alex hesitated. This was the trap he kept falling into—critics painting him as an obstructionist, a doomsayer without a plan.

"Sometimes caution is the solution," he said finally. "History is littered with technological fixes that created worse problems than they solved. Stratospheric aerosol injection could be the greatest example yet."

Thorne's smile never wavered. "And sometimes inaction is the greatest danger of all."

The audience applauded, and Alex knew he'd lost the room. Again.

Later, in the lobby bar, Alex nursed a single malt and reviewed his presentation notes. He'd been too technical, too academic. These conferences were political theater, not scientific debate. Three years away from corporate labs, and he still hadn't learned to play the game.

"That was quite a performance."

Alex looked up. A woman in her mid-thirties stood beside his table, dark hair pulled back in a practical ponytail, press credentials dangling from her neck.

"If you're looking for a quote, I've said everything I planned to say."

She smiled, sliding uninvited into the seat across from him. "Sophie Lorde, Climate Monitor. And I'm not looking for a quote— I'm wondering why a former Venture Aerospace executive is so determined to sabotage his own reputation."

Alex studied her. Most journalists had stopped calling after the second year of his crusade.

"Not sabotage. Conscience."

"Interesting word choice." She placed a small recorder on the table. "Mind if I use this? Hard to take notes while drinking."

Alex shrugged, and she ordered a gin and tonic from a passing server.

"So tell me, Mr. Ross—what does your conscience say about the Swedish launch scheduled for next week?"

"The SCoPEx balloon test?" Alex frowned. "It's supposedly releasing just a few kilograms of calcium carbonate for measurement purposes."

Sophie leaned forward. "And if I told you the payload had been modified? That instead of kilograms, we're talking metric tons?"

Alex felt a chill that had nothing to do with the bar's air conditioning. "I'd say you were misinformed. Even Thorne wouldn't be that reckless."

"Really?" Sophie slid a folder across the table. "Because my source says otherwise. And my source was inside the loading bay yesterday."

Alex opened the folder. Inside were photos of a much larger payload container than the one described in the university's public documentation. Technical specifications. Loading manifests with quantities scratched out and rewritten.

"Jesus," he whispered. "If this is accurate..."

"That's what I'm hoping you can tell me." Sophie took a sip of her drink. "Is this equipment capable of what my source claims?"

Alex studied the schematics. The modified balloon had a much higher ceiling than officially stated. The dispersal mechanism was not designed for small-scale testing but for wide distribution.

"This isn't a test," he said finally. "This is a deployment."

Sophie nodded slowly. "That's what I thought. Question is— what are you going to do about it?"

Alex looked toward the conference room, where Warren Thorne was now surrounded by admiring scientists and policymakers.

"Who's your source?" he asked.

"Someone who's afraid. Someone who says this is just the beginning."

Alex closed the folder. "I need to verify this independently."

"You have thirty-six hours." Sophie stood, leaving her drink untouched. "Then I publish with or without your confirmation."

"Why come to me at all?"

She smiled grimly. "Because if I'm right, Mr. Ross, you're the only person who's been telling the truth all along."

After she left, Alex ordered another Glenmorangie, a tribute to the Scottish distillery homed in his Clan Ross county. The ice clinked against the glass as his hand trembled slightly. Three years of warnings, of being labeled an alarmist and a traitor. Three years of watching from the sidelines as Thorne and others built their weather machines.

He pulled out his phone and called a number he'd sworn never to use again.

"It's Ross," he said when the line connected. "I need access to the NOAA satellite feeds. Yes, I know what I said last time. Things have changed, we might be going from theoretical to practical. And if I'm right it might already be too late to stop a global disaster."

He ended the call and stared at the folder. If Sophie's information was correct, someone was about to conduct the largest unauthorized geoengineering experiment in human history. And only he knew enough to stop it. Ross had made it a personal focus of study to dig into the ramifications of manipulating the atmosphere with microscopic particles, often referred to as 'chem trails'.

CHAPTER TWO: QUIET FUNDING

[New York Times – April 4, 2026] University Climate Project Under Scrutiny for Funding Structure By Richard Oaks

The university-based Stratospheric Controlled Perturbation Experiment (SCoPEx) is facing questions about its financial backing after documents revealed a complex web of funding sources. The project, which plans to test atmospheric modification techniques, lists academic grants as its primary support. However, internal records suggest substantial undisclosed financing from private foundations. University officials declined to comment on specific funding arrangements.

Karen Mitchell Ph.D. moved with practiced efficiency through the campuses' Earth and Planetary Sciences building, badge swiping doors, nodding to colleagues, her face a mask of academic composure. No one would guess she'd barely slept in three days. No one would suspect she was carrying digital evidence that could end her career—or worse.

She pushed through the door to her lab, relieved to find it empty. The morning light cast long shadows across the equipment—spectrometers, atmospheric pressure chambers, and simulation rigs that had once filled her with purpose. Now they felt like accessories to something darker.

Karen locked the door and pulled the blinds. From her bag, she removed an encrypted external drive and plugged it into her workstation. The password she entered was one she'd created yesterday, a random string she'd memorized and told no one. All standard procedures at the various top-secret labs where she consulted.

The files populated her screen—financial records, engineering modifications, email exchanges. Six months ago, she had been thrilled to be recruited for SCoPEx. Three months ago, she'd noticed the first discrepancies. One month ago, she'd begun secretly archiving evidence.

Her phone buzzed. A text from Sophie Lorde: In town. Meeting still on?

Karen hesitated, then typed: Usual place. 30 min. Bringing proof.

She began copying selected files to a smaller drive. The official story was clear and reassuring: a small-scale, reversible experiment to gather data. The reality hidden in these documents was something else entirely—a full deployment masquerading as a test.

The lab phone rang, startling her. She let it go to voicemail, continuing to sort through files.

"Dr. Mitchell." She had to know, and played back the message...the voice on the speaker was her department chair. "Please come to my office immediately. We need to discuss your access to the SCoPEx servers."

Karen froze. They knew.

Moving quickly, she ejected the small drive and pocketed it, then wiped the external drive and shut down her computer. She grabbed only her phone and keys, leaving her bag behind to avoid suspicion.

In the hallway, she walked briskly toward the stairs rather than the elevator. As she pushed through the stairwell door, she saw two campus security officers stepping out of the elevator. Neither looked in her direction, but Karen felt her heart rate spike.

She descended three floors and exited near the geology department, then took a circuitous route through the building, eventually emerging on the opposite side from the main entrance. The April air was crisp as she hurried across the quad, resisting the urge to run.

The coffee shop was four blocks away. Karen checked her watch—fifteen minutes early. She found a table in the back, ordered a latte she didn't want, and tried to look like a professor catching up on emails rather than a whistleblower about to commit career suicide.

Ten minutes passed. Then fifteen. Her coffee grew cold.

Almost there? she texted Sophie.

No response.

Twenty minutes over their meeting time, Karen's phone chimed with an incoming email. The sender was unlisted, the subject line blank. She opened it with trembling fingers.

Dr. Mitchell, your meeting has been canceled. Return the materials to your superiors and no further action will be taken. This is your only warning.

The coffee shop door opened, and Karen looked up, expecting Sophie. Instead, two men in dark suits entered, scanning the room with practiced efficiency.

Karen stood, leaving her coffee untouched, and walked calmly to the restroom. Inside, she locked the stall door, removed the small drive from her pocket, and pried off its plastic case. Beneath was a second, smaller storage chip—a backup she'd prepared just in case. She flushed the outer drive and case, then tucked the chip into her bra.

When she emerged, the men were seated at a table near the exit. One spoke quietly into his sleeve. Neither looked directly at her, but both shifted subtly as she approached the door.

Karen turned abruptly and approached the busy counter.

"Excuse me," she said to a student in a red jacket who was waiting for his order. "I'm late for a class. Would you mind letting me out the back? I know there's an alley exit through to the campus."

The student looked confused but nodded. "Uh, sure, professor."

Karen followed him as he spoke to an employee, who reluctantly let them through the swinging doors. The kitchen was small and cramped, barely enough room for two cooks working frantically on lunch orders.

"Thanks," Karen said to the student, pushing past him toward the rear exit. Through the small window, she could see a dumpster and narrow alley.

Outside, she didn't look back, walking quickly toward Massachusetts Avenue where she could lose herself in the midday crowd. Her phone buzzed again. This time, the message was from a number she didn't recognize:

Dr. Mitchell. I'm a friend of Sophie's. She's been detained. Meet me at South Station, Track 6, one hour. I can help. -Alex Ross

Karen hesitated. She'd heard of Ross—the aerospace engineer turned climate activist, and he had a solid reputation as a brilliant engineer. Sophie had mentioned him as a potential ally, a person that could be trusted. But this could easily be a trap.

Her department chair would have reported her by now. Security would be checking her usual haunts, her apartment, her friends' homes. She had the evidence but nowhere to go. Three days on the run were taking a serious toll on her reasoning.

One hour. What choice did she have?

Karen hailed a taxi, giving an address three blocks from the station. As the car pulled away, she saw the two men from the coffee shop emerge into the street, scanning the area with increasing urgency.

Whatever she'd stumbled upon, it was bigger than she'd imagined. A quiet test had become a secret deployment, and now people were hunting her for knowing too much.

She clutched the memory chip through her shirt. The evidence was safe. Now she just had to stay alive long enough to share it.

CHAPTER THREE: BALLOON OVER LAPLAND

[BBC Science Live – April 5, 2026] Swedish Atmospheric Research Launch Proceeds Despite Protests Live Report from Kiruna, Sweden

"The controversial high-altitude research balloon has launched successfully from the Esrange Space Center in northern Sweden, despite last-minute legal challenges and approximately two hundred protesters gathered at the perimeter. Scientists maintain that this is a small-scale measurement experiment using natural minerals to study potential climate intervention techniques, though critics argue it represents a dangerous precedent for geoengineering the planet's atmosphere, with potentially catastrophic consequences."

It didn't take long for the conversation between Alex and Karen to convince her they were on the same side, and both of them hunted, but by whom?

The Cessna Citation cruised at 35,000 feet, high above the scattered clouds over northern Sweden, pushing its service ceiling for the small jet. Alex Ross looked down at the endless expanse of forests and lakes, listening to the small jet's engines hum. In the seat across from him, Karen clutched a laptop as if it contained state secrets—which, in a way, it did.

"We're approaching the observation coordinates," the pilot announced over the intercom.

Alex nodded and adjusted the specialized camera mounted to his window. "How long until the launch?"

Karen checked her watch. "Twenty minutes, according to the official schedule."

"And the unofficial one?"

"Could be anytime. They know we're onto them."

After meeting at Boston's South Station yesterday, they'd moved quickly. Alex had arranged this chartered flight through contacts he still maintained from his Venture Aerospace days, corporate jets always on standby for the execs. The plan was simple: document the actual balloon deployment and compare it to the permitted experiment.

"What made you get involved?" Alex asked, adjusting the camera's focus.

Karen's face tightened. "I joined SCoPEx to study atmospheric chemistry, not to help launch an unauthorized climate experiment. When I realized the payload specifications had been altered after regulatory approval..." She shook her head. "Science requires transparency."

"They're calling you a disgruntled employee, you know. Claiming you misinterpreted routine engineering changes."

"And what about the funding documents?" Karen opened her laptop. "Foundations within foundations, shell companies. It all traces back to Thorne's network."

"I've been tracking his climate investments for years," Alex said. "But this is the first concrete evidence of direct intervention."

Karen pulled up a series of spreadsheets. "Look at these dispersal calculations. They're not designed for a test release of a few kilograms. This is tonnage-level distribution modeling."

Alex studied the numbers, his expression darkening. "These patterns... they're meant to establish a persistent stratospheric layer. Residence time of months, not days."

"Exactly," Karen said. "And look at the composition. It's not just calcium carbonate. They've added proprietary surface coatings to enhance reflectivity and suspension time."

Through the window, Alex spotted movement on the horizon. "There," he said, pointing. "The balloon launch site."

The pilot banked slightly, giving them a better view. Through powerful zoom lenses, they could see the massive white balloon beginning its ascent from the Esrange Space Center. Even from this distance, Alex could tell it was substantially larger than the specifications in the public documents.

"We're recording?" he asked.

Karen nodded, tapping commands on her laptop. "Full spectrum and infrared."

As they watched, the balloon rose steadily, a white dot against the blue spring sky. According to the official timeline, it would ascend to 20 kilometers before releasing its small payload of test particles.

"Altitude reading?" Alex asked.

"Approaching 18 kilometers," Karen said, checking the tracking data she was receiving from a contact still inside the project. "Release should happen at 20."

But at 19 kilometers, something changed. The balloon's ascent slowed, then stopped.

"They're releasing early," Alex said, adjusting the camera. "Zoom in on the payload container."

The image stabilized, showing the underside of the balloon. A small compartment had opened, but instead of the expected minor puff of particles, a steady stream of material was being dispersed into the high atmosphere.

"That's not kilograms," Karen said, her voice hollow. "That's the full payload."

Alex checked the wind patterns on his tablet. "Upper atmosphere currents will carry that across northern Europe and into Russia within days."

"This isn't science anymore," Karen whispered. "It's absolutely full deployment."

Alex continued filming as the balloon released its cargo. Through the specialized filters of his camera, he could see the cloud of reflective particles beginning to disperse, catching the sunlight like microscopic mirrors.

"We've got it all documented," he said grimly. "Now we need to get this footage out before they can spin it."

The pilot's voice came over the intercom, tension evident. "Mr. Ross, we're being contacted by Swedish air traffic control. They're ordering us to return to Stockholm immediately."

Alex and Karen exchanged looks. "On what grounds?" Alex asked.

"Restricted airspace violation. Though this area wasn't restricted when we filed our flight plan."

"They're covering their tracks," Karen said.

Alex nodded to the pilot. "Acknowledge the order, but tell them we need to complete our scientific observations. Buy us ten more minutes."

As the pilot complied, Alex connected a satellite uplink to his laptop. "I'm sending everything to Sophie Lorde and three other journalists. If they intercept us on landing, at least the evidence gets out."

Karen's phone chimed with an alert. She checked it, her face paling. "They've issued a statement. They're claiming a 'successful

minor release of test materials according to permitted parameters.'
Complete fabrication."

Alex watched the dispersing cloud, now barely visible against
the sky. "Not test materials," he said quietly. "The beginning of
something much bigger."

In that moment, high above the Arctic Circle, Alex Ross realized
the battle had shifted. He wasn't trying to prevent a catastrophe
anymore.

He was witnessing its first stage.

CHAPTER FOUR: WHISPER PROTOCOLS

[The Washington Post – April 7, 2026] Swedish Test Balloon Data Shows 'Promising Results,' Researchers Claim By Jennifer Mathis, Science Correspondent

Scientists involved in last week's atmospheric research balloon launch in Sweden report initial data shows "promising results for reflectivity measurements," according to project spokesperson Dr. Ian Coleman. The team has begun analyzing atmospheric samples, though full results may take weeks. Meanwhile, climate advocacy groups continue to criticize the experiment, claiming it crossed a "red line" in climate intervention.

The encrypted message arrived at 3:17 AM, waking Alex from a fitful sleep in his Stockholm hotel room.

Helios Protocol activated. Multiple sites. This is not a drill.

Alex sat up, fully alert. The message came through a secure channel he'd established years ago with former colleagues—people who shared his concerns about geoengineering but had chosen to remain inside the system. The sender identification showed only a numeric code: 334291. Martin Edwards, his former deputy at Venture Aerospace's climate division. Martin had always shared the concern for what one man or one government might do, and create global consequences.

He typed back: Verification?

The response came seconds later: Sundown. Starlight. Atmosphere.

The authentication was valid. Martin wouldn't trigger their emergency protocol without reason.

Alex dressed quickly, then opened his laptop and initiated a series of security measures—VPN activation, traffic routing through multiple servers, full disk encryption. Only then did he open the secure communication channel.

Details? he typed.

Three simultaneous deployments. Northern Canada. Siberia. Southern Ocean. Same tech as Sweden but larger scale. They're creating a distribution network.

Alex stared at the message, the implications sinking in. The Swedish launch wasn't an isolated incident—it was coordination. A global operation.

Evidence? he asked.

Transmitting now. Satellite imagery. Launch orders. Payload specs.

Files began appearing in their encrypted drop box. Alex opened them one by one, his stomach tightening. The images showed three separate facilities with high-altitude balloon systems identical to the one they'd witnessed in Sweden. Manifest documents detailed calcium carbonate payloads with the same proprietary coatings. And most damning—launch authorization signatures from Warren Thorne's foundation subsidiaries.

Who else knows? Alex asked.

Nobody outside the program. Media blackout in all regions. Cover story ready if detected: weather monitoring platforms.

Alex closed his eyes briefly, thinking. Karen Mitchell was staying three doors down. Sophie Lorde had a room on the floor below. They'd come to Stockholm to compile their evidence and prepare a comprehensive report. Now it seemed they were already too late.

When? he typed.

12 hours. Maybe less.

Alex sent a final message: Stay safe. Keep channel open.

Then he gathered his materials and headed down the hall to wake Karen. As he raised his hand to knock, he noticed a slight gap where the door met the frame. It was already ajar.

Alex pushed it gently. "Karen?"

The room was empty. Bed unslept in. Her laptop and notes gone.

He pulled out his phone and called Sophie Lorde.

"Alex?" she answered groggily. "It's the middle of the night."

"Karen's gone. Get up here now."

Five minutes later, Sophie stood in Karen's empty room, fully dressed, reporter's instincts on high alert. "Security cameras?"

"Already called downstairs, hotel says they've been down for maintenance since yesterday," Alex replied. "Convenient timing."

Sophie examined the room methodically. "No signs of struggle. Either she left willingly or was caught completely by surprise."

"Or both," Alex said. "Someone could have posed as hotel staff, security..."

"Her laptop?"

"Gone. Along with all her notes and the original memory chip."

Sophie cursed softly. "We still have copies, right?"

Alex nodded, though his expression remained grim. "Not of significant value. Her laptop or data drive were complete, but what I have are only partial studies, episodes of her observations. So we just lost our primary source. And I've received intelligence that more launches are happening—today. Three locations, globally distributed."

Sophie's eyes widened. "They're accelerating the timeline. Why?"

"Maybe because of what we documented in Sweden. If they're committed to this course, better to establish facts on the ground before opposition can mobilize."

"We need to go public immediately," Sophie said. "Everything we have."

Alex shook his head. "Not yet. Without Karen to corroborate, they'll dismiss it as manipulated evidence. We need more."

"Like what?"

"Real-time documentation of these new launches." Alex turned his laptop to show her the satellite imagery. "I have coordinates. If we can get independent verification—"

"You want to split up," Sophie said, realizing his plan. "Cover more ground."

"I can get to the Canadian site within six hours. You take the evidence we already have and prepare it for release. If I confirm the new deployment, I'll send verification codes. If not..."

"If not, I release what we have anyway," Sophie finished. "Insurance policy."

Alex nodded. "Exactly."

Sophie checked her watch. "What about law enforcement? Regulatory agencies?"

"By the time they mobilize, it'll be too late. These particles will be in the stratosphere for months, maybe years."

They both fell silent, contemplating the scale of what they were facing. Not a rogue experiment, but a coordinated global intervention—conducted without oversight, without consent.

"Karen knew the risks," Sophie said finally. "We all do."

Alex met her gaze. "It's going to get worse before it gets better. If Thorne is willing to disappear a prominent scientist, he won't hesitate with us."

"Then we'd better make sure the truth gets out," Sophie said, shouldering her bag. "No matter what happens to us."

As they prepared to part ways, Alex thought about the years he'd spent trying to warn the world about this exact scenario. The dismissals, the ridicule, the accusations of alarmism. Now his worst fears were materializing in real time, and he was racing to document a catastrophe already in progress.

"Six hours," he said. "If you don't hear from me by then, assume I've been compromised."

Sophie nodded grimly. "Same. Dead man's switch on the evidence. If either of us goes dark, everything publishes automatically."

They shook hands, the gesture oddly formal given the circumstances.

"Good luck," Sophie said.

Alex watched her leave, then turned back to his secure laptop. One more message to send before he departed.

Martin—need extraction coordinates for Canadian site. Coming in person.

The reply was nearly instantaneous: Negative. Too dangerous. Site on lockdown.

Alex typed his response: Not a request. Arriving via private charter. Need ground access.

A pause, longer this time, then: Using old credentials. Still active in system. Landing instructions follow. 86% probability of intercept.

Alex stared at that number—86%. Martin's careful calculation of the likelihood he would be caught.

The risk was necessary. In less than twelve hours, Warren Thorne would alter Earth's atmosphere without public knowledge or consent. And Alex Ross had to prove it was happening.

CHAPTER FIVE: THE GENEVA MEETING

[Financial Times – April 7, 2026] Climate Technology Summit Convenes in Geneva By Christopher Lorenz, Environmental Finance

A private meeting of climate technology investors and researchers began yesterday at Lake Geneva's historic Villa Diodati. The three-day closed-door summit, organized by the Global Climate Resilience Initiative, brings together leading figures in geoengineering research, sustainable finance, and climate policy. While the agenda remains confidential, sources indicate discussions will focus on accelerating climate intervention technologies in response to recent extreme weather events.

The helicopter approached the Villa Diodati from the east, offering Warren Thorne a panoramic view of Lake Geneva glittering in the spring sunlight. Below, the historic villa's manicured grounds were dotted with security personnel—discreet but thorough, just as he'd specified.

"Three minutes to landing, sir," the pilot said through the intercom.

Warren adjusted his shirt cuffs, mentally preparing. Five feet away, Dr. Henry Caulden reviewed notes on a secure tablet, his angular face betraying no emotion.

"Final attendance confirmation?" Warren asked.

Caulden looked up. "Twenty-six principals, as planned. The Chinese delegation reduced to two representatives. The Russians sent their science minister instead of their climate envoy. Everyone else is as expected."

Warren nodded. The precise mix he wanted—scientists with influence, policymakers with scientific backgrounds, financiers with both. People who understood what was at stake and had the means to act.

The helicopter touched down on the villa's rear lawn. As Warren disembarked, he was greeted by Elise Fontaine, his chief of operations.

"Welcome to Geneva, Mr. Thorne," she said, falling into step beside him. "The morning session is prepared, and security protocols are in place. No electronic devices beyond the main gate, communication blackout in effect."

"Any issues with our Swedish friends?"

"They're complying with media guidance. Initial data is flowing to our secure servers."

Warren allowed himself a small smile. The Swedish launch had proceeded exactly as planned—a public-facing "test" that was, in reality, the first node in a global network. The early data showed promise: particle dispersal patterns matching their models, reflectivity indices even better than projected.

Inside the villa, the grand salon had been transformed into a conference space. The room's historic elegance—16th-century paintings, ornate moldings, crystal chandeliers—contrasted with the cutting-edge presentation technology installed for the summit.

As Warren entered, the quiet conversations ceased. These were among the most powerful people in the climate science world—directors of research institutes, foundation heads, government science advisors. Many had worked with Warren for years through his foundation's grant programs. Others were newer to his circle, brought in as the Helios Protocol moved from theory to implementation.

"Ladies and gentlemen," Warren began, taking his position at the front of the room. "Thank you for traveling here on such short notice. Your presence honors the gravity of our purpose."

He gestured, and the room's lighting dimmed. A holographic globe appeared above the central table, data points glowing across its surface.

"What you are seeing is a real-time visualization of global climate systems as of this morning. Red indicators represent temperature anomalies exceeding three standard deviations from historical norms. Yellow shows precipitation disruptions. Blue marks sea level acceleration beyond projected curves."

The globe rotated slowly, revealing a planet increasingly consumed by warning indicators.

"We have spent thirty years debating, negotiating, and compromising," Warren continued. "Thirty years watching tipping points approach, then pass. Thirty years of political failure."

He paused, making eye contact with key figures around the room. "That ends today."

Dr. Caulden stood, taking over the presentation. "The Helios Protocol is now active," he said, his clinical tone a counterpoint to Warren's passionate one. "Phase One deployment began three days ago in northern Sweden. Your secure tablets contain the preliminary data—all metrics are within or exceeding optimal parameters."

A murmur ran through the room—part approval, part concern. Liu Wei, China's deputy minister of science, raised his hand.

"This Swedish operation," he said carefully. "It was presented publicly as a small-scale test, yes? Are you telling us it was actually a large scale deployment?"

Warren nodded. "Necessity required discretion. The public-facing narrative remains important for acceptance and compliance."

"You mean deception," said Dr. Nadia Petrova from Russia's Academy of Sciences. "You told the world one thing while doing another."

"I prefer to call it strategic disclosure," Warren replied smoothly. "Had we announced the full scope of Helios, we would have faced years of litigation, protest, and obstruction—while the planet continued to burn."

Caulden advanced the presentation. "Phase Two begins today. Three additional dispersal sites will establish a hemispheric network, creating a responsive stratospheric veil that can be adjusted in real-time based on climate indicators."

The holographic globe now showed particle distribution models, illustrating how the combined releases would create a thin reflective layer in the stratosphere.

"This is not theoretical," Caulden continued. "The technology is proven, the delivery systems tested, the outcomes modeled to the highest confidence intervals. Within six months, we will have the capacity to adjust Earth's radiative balance by 0.5 to 1.5 watts per square meter—enough to counteract current warming trends."

Dr. James Hammond, director of the United Kingdom's Climate Research Centre, stood. "Warren, we all respect your commitment, but this goes beyond any agreed framework. There are international protocols—"

"Protocols that have failed," Warren interrupted, voice hardening. "James, your own models show the Arctic will be ice-free by 2030. The Greenland ice sheet is losing mass at triple the rate predicted just five years ago. We are beyond the luxury of caution."

Hammond persisted. "The potential secondary effects— precipitation disruption, stratospheric ozone interactions, agricultural impacts—"

"All accounted for in our modeling," Caulden interjected. "The disruptions are manageable and far preferable to unchecked warming."

Warren moved to the center of the room, commanding attention. "I didn't bring you here for permission," he said, voice quiet but intense. "I brought you here because you are the individuals with the expertise and influence to manage the transition."

He looked around the room slowly. "Helios is happening. The stratospheric veil will be established. The question before you is not whether to proceed, but how to incorporate this new reality into your research, your policies, your public messaging."

A heavy silence fell. These were people accustomed to being decision-makers, not simply messengers. Yet Warren had maneuvered them masterfully—presenting a fait accompli while offering them roles in shaping its implementation.

"You've put us in an impossible position," said Dr. Emmanuelle Dubois of the European Climate Foundation. "By taking this unilateral action, you've made us complicit."

Warren smiled slightly. "No, Emmanuelle. I've made you relevant. While governments debated carbon credits and emissions targets, we built the infrastructure to actually solve the problem. History will thank us."

The room erupted in overlapping conversations—objections, questions, demands for more data. Warren let it continue for precisely one minute before raising his hand for silence.

"Your concerns are noted. Your expertise is valued. But the decision point has passed." He nodded to Caulden, who distributed sealed portfolios to each attendee. "These contain your secure access credentials to the Helios monitoring platform. From this moment forward, you have real-time visibility into all operations and data."

Warren's tone softened, becoming almost paternal. "I understand your reservations. Truly. But I ask you to consider: If not this, then what? If not now, then when? While we debate ethical frameworks, the Arctic melts. While we seek perfect consensus, feedback loops accelerate."

He looked around the room one final time. "Colleagues, we have run out of time for discussion. This is the moment for action."

As the summit participants began opening their portfolios, examining the access credentials with a mixture of reluctance and fascination, Warren stepped away toward the tall windows overlooking the lake.

Everything was proceeding according to plan. The scientific community would adapt—they always did when presented with compelling data. The public would follow, especially once the cooling effects became noticeable. And any opposition would be too late to matter. The mainstream media can always be persuaded to the liberal view of climate crisis.

By the time Alex Ross and his allies gathered enough evidence to mount a serious challenge, the stratospheric veil would be established reality. An emergency measure that had already begun to work. A fait accompli that even the most stringent regulatory bodies would be reluctant to reverse.

Warren Thorne looked out at the tranquil waters of Lake Geneva, imagining a world cooled and stabilized under his protection. History would indeed thank him—once they understood what he had saved them from.

What Warren couldn't see, as he contemplated his legacy, was the first faint shimmer in the sky above the Alps—a subtle distortion of natural light as the initial wave of reflective particles began their work.

CHAPTER SIX: PARTICLE PHYSICS

[Scientific American – April 8, 2026] Stratospheric Aerosols: Climate Medicine or Pandora's Box? By Dr. Rebecca Howell, Climate Physics Correspondent

The recent atmospheric tests in Sweden have reignited debate about the science behind solar radiation management. While calcium carbonate particles show promising reflective properties in laboratory conditions, atmospheric scientists remain divided on how they might behave when dispersed throughout the stratosphere. "We're talking about altering the energy balance of an entire planet based on limited data sets," warns Dr. Sanjay Mehrotra of MIT's Climate Systems Lab. "The atmospheric chemistry alone presents dozens of unknown variables."

The laboratory hummed with the sound of precision instruments. Dr. Stephanie Martinez adjusted the electron microscope, bringing the calcium carbonate particle into sharp focus on the monitor. Even at this magnification—ten thousand times larger than life—the particle appeared unremarkable: a crystalline structure like billions of others.

Stephanie glanced briefly at the small framed article pinned to her bulletin board—its margins crowded with peer reviewer comments like "speculative to the point of fantasy" and "quantum relationships in atmospheric particles remain entirely theoretical without supporting evidence." Five years ago, her paper suggesting possible quantum entanglement between microscopic atmospheric particles had been rejected from every major journal. Now, as she studied Thorne's engineered particles exhibiting precisely the properties she'd theorized, vindication felt hollow against the planetary stakes.

"Sometimes being right too early is worse than being wrong," she murmured in the soft Spanish-accented English she'd retained despite two decades in American academia. Her abuela would have called it la verdad inoportuna—inconvenient truth arriving before the world was prepared to hear it.

This was no ordinary calcium carbonate.

"There," she said, pointing to the screen. "Do you see it?"

Alex leaned closer, studying the microscopic architecture. "The coating?"

Stephanie nodded. "Normally invisible, but under polarized light..."

She adjusted the settings, and suddenly the particle's surface bloomed with an iridescent pattern—a nanoscale latticework surrounding the calcium carbonate core.

"What am I looking at?" Alex asked.

"Something that shouldn't exist." Stephanie's voice was tight with professional concern. "This sample comes from atmospheric collection three days after the Swedish launch. The particle structure has been modified at the molecular level."

Alex frowned. "Modified how?"

"The coating isn't just enhancing reflectivity. It's self-organizing., somehow evolving beyond a simple coating into something with behavior patterns."

She tapped commands into the computer, bringing up comparison images: standard calcium carbonate next to the sample. The differences were subtle but unmistakable. The experimental particles had a more complex surface structure, with geometric patterns that seemed almost designed.

"These weren't just dumped into the atmosphere," Stephanie continued. "They're engineered to interact with each other. To form networks."

Alex thought back to the documents Karen had smuggled out before her disappearance. There had been references to "persistence enhancement" and "distributed intelligence," but he'd assumed those were just marketing terms for Thorne's investors.

"What happens when they network?" he asked.

Stephanie's expression was grim. "That's what I've been modeling." She walked to another workstation and pulled up a simulation. "Traditional stratospheric aerosols disperse randomly and gradually fall out of the atmosphere. But these—"

The simulation showed particles moving in coordinated patterns, forming loose but distinctly non-random structures.

"They're behaving like a system," Alex said, half observation, half stunned exclamation.

"Exactly. Creating a reflective layer that's far more stable than it should be. My calculations suggest these particles could remain suspended for years, not months. And if they're launching more..."

"They are," Alex confirmed. "Three more sites went operational yesterday. I couldn't reach the Canadian facility in time."

Stephanie rubbed her temples. "Then we're not talking about a test anymore. We're talking about atmospheric modification at a planetary scale."

Alex nodded grimly. "Thorne calls it the Helios Protocol. From what our sources indicate, the goal is a responsive stratospheric veil that can be adjusted based on climate indicators."

"Adjusted?" Stephanie looked alarmed. "That would require—"

"Ongoing releases. Continuous monitoring. A control system."

Stephanie turned back to the electron microscope. "Alex, these particles aren't just reflective. The coating contains electromagnetic properties I don't fully understand. It's like they're designed to receive and transmit signals."

"A programmable atmospheric layer," Alex murmured. "My God."

Stephanie brought up another set of data. "There's more. I've been running atmospheric chemistry simulations based on these samples. The interaction with ozone is... concerning."

The monitor displayed a model of atmospheric gas exchange, with ominous red zones developing around particle concentrations.

"The official SCoPEx research claimed calcium carbonate would have minimal ozone impacts," Alex said.

"For unmodified particles, perhaps. But these coatings change the chemistry." Stephanie pointed to regions in the simulation. "Under certain conditions—specific humidity, temperature, UV exposure—the coatings could catalyze ozone depletion at rates far beyond anything in their public models."

Alex studied the simulation, connecting dots in his mind. "They're betting they can control the conditions. Keep the particles in atmospheric zones where these reactions won't occur."

"That's insanely risky," Stephanie said. "Stratospheric dynamics are chaotic systems. The molecules don't know they're supposed to stay in their designated zones."

She brought up a series of global climate models—official projections from major research institutions, each showing gradual warming trends. Then she overlaid her new simulations, incorporating the modified particles.

The difference was stark. Initial cooling, yes—but followed by oscillating patterns of extreme weather events. Droughts in traditionally wet regions. Flooding in arid zones. Wind pattern disruptions affecting ocean currents.

"This is with just the Swedish deployment," Stephanie said quietly. "Add three more distribution points..."

Alex stared at the projections, feeling a chill that had nothing to do with the lab's air conditioning. "They think they're saving the world."

"They might be ending it instead." Stephanie closed the simulation. "The worst part? By the time we know for certain which models are correct, it will be too late to call the particles back."

The lab door opened, and Sophie Lorde entered, her expression tense. "We need to move. Reuters is running with the story tomorrow morning. Guardian and Washington Post the day after."

"You've verified Karen's evidence?" Alex asked.

Sophie nodded. "Three independent sources. The Swedish launch was just phase one of a coordinated deployment. The particles contain proprietary technology never disclosed in regulatory filings. And Thorne's foundation is behind the whole operation."

"What about Karen?" Stephanie asked.

Sophie shook her head slightly. "No trace. Her department claims she's on personal leave."

Alex turned to Stephanie. "We need your analysis of these particles. The public needs to understand what's really happening."

Stephanie hesitated. "Publishing this will end my career. These samples were obtained without authorization. The analysis uses MIT equipment—"

"If Thorne succeeds," Alex said quietly, "your career won't matter. None of ours will."

The three of them stood in silence, surrounded by evidence of a planetary experiment unfolding in real time. Above them, invisible to the naked eye, engineered particles were already beginning their work—capturing sunlight, reflecting it back to space, altering the energy balance of Earth's most complex systems.

And no one had asked permission.

Stephanie squared her shoulders. "I'll need six hours to complete the analysis and write it up. Then it's yours."

Sophie checked her watch. "I'll coordinate with my editors. We release everything simultaneously—the Swedish footage, Karen's documents, Stephanie's analysis. Maximum impact."

Alex nodded, feeling the weight of the moment. "Thorne has a three-day head start. The particles are already up there. But maybe—maybe we can stop the next phase."

As they prepared to part ways, each focused on their tasks, Alex couldn't shake a nagging thought: What if it was already too late? What if the atmospheric veil, once created, couldn't be undone?

He looked through the laboratory window at the clear spring sky. Somewhere up there, invisible to human eyes, the future was changing. Particle by particle, in the thin air where Earth met space, an unauthorized experiment had begun.

And the whole planet was the laboratory.

CHAPTER SEVEN: CREDIBILITY GAP

[CNN Breaking News – April 9, 2026] Former Aerospace Engineer Claims 'Global Climate Experiment' Underway Live Report

"In a stunning press conference this morning, former Venture Aerospace executive Alexander Ross alleged that a coordinated effort to modify Earth's atmosphere is already underway. Ross claims that recent balloon launches in Sweden, Canada, and Russia are part of a clandestine program called the 'Helios Protocol,' designed to create a reflective layer in the stratosphere. The Global Climate Resilience Initiative, named in Ross's allegations, dismissed the claims as 'misinformation from a discredited source with a history of opposition to climate technologies.' The EPA and NOAA have declined to comment pending review of Ross's evidence."

The press conference had been a disaster.

Alex sat in Sophie's cramped office at Climate Monitor headquarters, watching the coverage cycle through cable news networks. Each outlet had found a different angle to undermine him: questioning his motives after his falling out with Elias Venture; highlighting his lack of recent peer-reviewed research; bringing on a climate scientist who dismissed stratospheric veiling as "science fiction at planetary scale."

"They're burying us," he said, rubbing his eyes.

Sophie shook her head, defiant. "They're trying to. But the evidence is still out there. Guardian ran the full technical analysis, not just the headline accusations."

"Which maybe a thousand people read," Alex countered. "Meanwhile, millions are seeing Thorne's spokesperson call me a conspiracy theorist with a grudge."

The door opened, and Stephanie entered with three coffees. Her eyes were shadowed from lack of sleep, her normally pristine lab coat rumpled from hours of continuous work.

"It's getting worse," she said, setting down the coffees. "Three more climate research centers have issued statements questioning my methodology. MIT is 'reviewing' my employment status."

Alex felt a stab of guilt. Stephanie had risked everything to analyze the stratospheric samples. Her reputation, built over fifteen years of meticulous research, was being systematically dismantled by Thorne's academic allies.

"What about the particle analysis?" he asked. "The evidence is right there in the electron microscopy."

"They're claiming contamination." Stephanie's voice was bitter. "Suggesting I manipulated the samples to support a predetermined conclusion."

Sophie frowned. "But we have the chain of custody documented—"

"It doesn't matter," Stephanie interrupted. "The scientific community operates on consensus and reputation...and funding. Thorne has spent a decade funding every major climate research center. He owns the consensus."

On the television, Warren Thorne himself was now speaking from the steps of his foundation headquarters in Seattle. Impeccably dressed, radiating calm authority, he addressed the allegations directly:

"We live in an age of misinformation, where legitimate climate research is routinely attacked by those with political or personal agendas. The recent allegations regarding our atmospheric monitoring program are not just false—they're a dangerous distraction from the real climate crisis. The Global Climate Resilience

Initiative remains committed to evidence-based approaches to climate stability. That includes studying all options, but always within ethical and regulatory frameworks."

The camera pulled back to show dozens of white-coated researchers standing behind Thorne—a visual testament to scientific legitimacy.

"He's good," Sophie admitted reluctantly. "Doesn't directly deny anything while implying we're the irresponsible ones."

Alex reached for his laptop. "We need more. Karen's documents and Stephanie's analysis aren't enough to counter their media strategy."

"What about the launch footage from Sweden?" Stephanie asked.

"They're claiming it shows exactly what they publicly announced—a small-scale stratospheric test. Without context, the visual difference between a small release and a large one isn't clear to non-experts."

Sophie's phone buzzed. She checked it, then looked up with renewed intensity. "My contact at NOAA just came through. The atmospheric monitoring stations in the Arctic have detected anomalous reflectivity patterns. They're suppressing the data, but she's sent us access credentials."

Alex moved to her computer. "Let's see it."

The National Oceanic and Atmospheric Administration's secure server contained terabytes of atmospheric data—satellite readings, ground station measurements, high-altitude sampling. Sophie's contact had flagged specific files from monitoring stations across the Arctic Circle.

"Here," Alex said, pointing to the screen. "Light scattering measurements from the past week."

The data showed a distinct pattern: elevated reflectivity in the stratosphere, beginning over northern Sweden and spreading eastward across Russian airspace. The readings were subtle but unmistakable to trained eyes—evidence of particulate matter where none should exist.

"This is it," Stephanie said, leaning forward. "Independent verification. The particles are spreading exactly as my models predicted."

"And look at this," Sophie added, pulling up comparison data. "The effect has been recorded by three separate monitoring systems. That rules out instrument error."

Alex felt a surge of vindication, quickly tempered by the sobering reality: the atmospheric veil was real, was spreading, and was still completely unknown to the public.

"We need to get this to the right people," he said. "Not just media—regulatory agencies, international bodies."

"Most will ignore us," Sophie warned. "Thorne has spent years cultivating relationships with exactly these institutions."

"Then we go higher," Alex said. "The UN Secretary-General. The International Court of Justice. The World Meteorological Organization."

Stephanie looked skeptical. "Bureaucracies move slowly. The particles will be fully deployed before they finish their first assessment."

"Then we need something more immediate," Alex said. "Something that forces acknowledgment."

He pulled up a global map showing known deployment sites: Sweden, northern Canada, eastern Russia, and a ship-based platform in the Southern Ocean. Each was a node in an expanding network of atmospheric modification.

"We need to directly expose one of their operations," he said. "Not just with data or distant footage. I'm talking about physical evidence that can't be denied or dismissed."

Sophie frowned. "You mean..."

"I mean we need to access one of the launch facilities. Document it from the inside. Bring back physical samples of the payload."

Stephanie shook her head. "These are secure installations with military-grade protection. Getting close enough for exterior footage was risky enough."

"I still have contacts," Alex said. "People inside who share our concerns but haven't been willing to go public. With the right approach, we might get access."

Sophie studied him. "You're talking about the Canadian facility."

Alex nodded. "My former associate, Martin Edwards, is on the engineering team. He's the one who warned me about the simultaneous launches."

"If he's already helping, why not ask him to gather evidence?" Stephanie asked.

"Too risky for him. Their internal security is extreme—biometric monitoring, activity logging, routine screening. But a sanctioned external visitor might have more freedom of movement."

Sophie looked dubious. "And how exactly do you become a 'sanctioned visitor' to a secret climate intervention facility?"

Alex smiled grimly. "By giving Thorne exactly what he wants—my public discrediting."

Stephanie and Sophie exchanged confused glances.

"I don't follow," Stephanie said.

Alex pointed to the television, still showing coverage of his allegations. "Thorne thinks he's winning the public narrative. His strategy is to isolate us as fringe conspiracy theorists. But what if I appear to break with you both? What if I publicly retract my claims, blame bad data, and apologize?"

Sophie shook her head firmly. "No way. That undermines everything we've fought for."

"Not if it's a strategic retreat," Alex countered. "I make a humble mea culpa, express continued interest in climate technologies, and request a chance to see Thorne's legitimate research firsthand. To 'correct my misunderstandings.'"

"You think he'd actually allow that?" Stephanie asked.

"His ego might. Especially if he thinks he can convert his biggest critic into a supporter. It's a public relations coup for him."

Sophie still looked unconvinced. "Meanwhile, Stephanie and I continue pressing the real evidence?"

"Exactly. I play the repentant skeptic while you keep the pressure on. If I get inside, I can document what's really happening. If not, we've lost nothing but my already-damaged reputation."

The three fell silent, considering the strategy. Outside Sophie's office window, rain had begun to fall—normal spring weather that somehow felt ominous in light of what they knew. Somewhere high above, engineered particles were spreading across the stratosphere, beginning their work of redirecting sunlight.

"It's risky," Stephanie said finally. "If you're caught gathering evidence inside their facility..."

Alex nodded, acknowledging the danger. "Riskier still is doing nothing while Thorne deploys a planetary-scale technology with unknown consequences."

Sophie sighed. "I hate this plan, but I don't have a better one. How soon?"

"Tonight," Alex said. "I'll contact a few science reporters known to be sympathetic to Thorne. Express doubts about my own claims. By morning, Thorne will have heard that I'm wavering."

As they began planning the details, Alex gazed again at the NOAA data showing the spreading particulate pattern. The atmospheric veil was no longer theoretical—it was manifesting in readings across the Arctic. Soon it would be detectable worldwide.

They were in a race against physics itself. Once fully deployed, the stratospheric particles would remain active for years, influencing weather systems, ocean temperatures, and atmospheric chemistry in ways that even Thorne's models couldn't fully predict.

And while they debated strategies in a small office in Washington, the invisible transformation of Earth's atmosphere continued, unobserved by almost everyone who lived beneath it.

CHAPTER EIGHT: WEATHER PATTERNS

[Weather Channel – April 10, 2026] Meteorologists Puzzled by 'Anomalous' Jet Stream Behavior By Dr. Michael Jenkins, Senior Climate Analyst

Weather forecasters across North America are reporting unusual behavior in the polar jet stream, which has shifted southward by approximately 300 miles over the past 48 hours. This rapid repositioning, which typically evolves over weeks rather than days, has created forecasting challenges across multiple regions. "We're seeing some of the fastest adjustments to upper atmospheric wind patterns in recent records," noted Dr. Aisha Karim of the National Weather Service. "It's too early to determine if this represents a new pattern or a temporary fluctuation."

Dr. Olaf Werner stood on the roof of Colorado State University's atmospheric science building, squinting at the western sky. To the casual observer, there was nothing unusual to see—just high cirrus clouds streaking across the late afternoon blue. But to Olaf's trained eye, something was off. The cloud formations were moving in patterns that contradicted the forecast models.

He unconsciously rubbed the small, weathered stone in his pocket—a habit formed fifteen years ago when Hurricane Eliza had swept away his childhood home in North Carolina, leaving nothing but the foundation and this single stone. That loss had driven him into meteorology with an almost religious devotion, transforming personal tragedy into professional purpose. His colleagues sometimes joked that Olaf could sense atmospheric shifts before their instruments could measure them. Today, that sixth sense was screaming.

"Something's wrong with the flow patterns," he murmured. "It's like the air is following mathematical principles instead of fluid dynamics."

His graduate student, Tanya Rodriguez, consulted the tablet displaying real-time atmospheric data. "Jet stream's shifted again. Almost 50 miles further south since this morning."

Olaf nodded, frowning. "That's nearly 350 miles displacement in three days. I've never seen anything like it."

"Global warming effects?" Tanya suggested.

"Accelerated, maybe. But this directional shift is... unusual."

Olaf had spent twenty years studying atmospheric dynamics. He could recite the major wind patterns from memory, track seasonal shifts in the jet stream like others followed sports statistics. This rapid southward plunge wasn't in any of his models.

"Let's check the upper atmospheric temperature gradients," he said.

Back in the lab, they pulled up the latest data from weather balloons and satellite monitoring. The numbers confirmed Olaf's suspicions: the temperature differential between polar and mid-latitude air masses had changed dramatically, altering the jet stream's trajectory.

"Look at this," Tanya said, pointing to a visualization of stratospheric conditions. "Temperature inversion at 19 kilometers. That wasn't there last week."

Olaf leaned closer. "How wide is the affected area?"

"That's the weird part." Tanya zoomed out on the map. "It starts over Scandinavia, extends across the Arctic, and now it's dipping down over North America. Almost like..."

"Like a wave," Olaf finished. "Moving west to east."

He pulled up historical data for comparison. Nothing in the past decade matched this pattern. Even accounting for climate change effects, the rapidity and distinctive shape of the alteration was unprecedented.

"Dr. Werner?" A voice called from the doorway. Maggie Edwards, the department chair, stood with an anxious expression. "We need to talk. Privately."

Olaf nodded to Tanya, who discreetly left the lab. Once the door closed, Maggie spoke in a hushed tone.

"I just got off a call with NOAA. They're implementing new data clearance protocols for upper atmosphere readings. Effective immediately." Locking down the data.

Olaf frowned. "Clearance protocols? For public scientific data?"

"They're citing 'quality control concerns' and 'potential instrumentation anomalies.'" Maggie didn't look convinced. "All stratospheric measurements need to be reviewed by a special committee before release."

"That's unprecedented," Olaf said. "Weather data has always been open access."

Maggie handed him a tablet showing an official email. "It gets stranger. The committee includes representatives from the Global Climate Resilience Initiative."

"Thorne's foundation? What gives them authority over NOAA data?"

"Apparently they're providing 'technical consultation' on the anomalous readings."

Olaf felt a chill of professional concern. Scientific data being restricted just as anomalous patterns emerged? That wasn't standard procedure—it was containment.

"There's more," Maggie continued. "They're requesting we pause publication of our jet stream analysis. Just temporarily, they say."

"On what grounds?"

"Potential correlation with national security matters. Misinformation. They were vague but insistent."

Olaf returned to his computer, pulling up the most recent jet stream visualization. The distinctive wave pattern was even more pronounced now, creating a rippling effect across northern latitudes.

"This isn't natural," he said quietly. "The temperature inversions, the rapid shift, the hemispheric scale—something's forcing this change."

Olaf closed his laptop, cutting off the skeptical comments from his department colleagues. Three years as the youngest tenured professor in the department had earned him respect for his forecasting models, but that credibility was eroding hourly as he insisted these atmospheric patterns were not just unusual but fundamentally wrong. The mathematics didn't lie, but explaining atmospheric equations exhibiting impossible properties to traditional meteorologists was like describing color to the colorblind.

"They'll see it soon enough," he muttered, returning to his calculations. By then, he feared, it would be too late.

His phone buzzed with a text from the department chair: Emergency meeting at 4. Please bring ACTUAL EVIDENCE, not just your "atmospheric intuition." The quotation marks burned like an accusation. Olaf had built his career on merging rigorous data analysis with an intuitive understanding of atmospheric behavior that couldn't be fully captured in equations. Now, when that intuition was sounding its loudest alarm, his scientific community was most resistant to hearing it.

Maggie lowered her voice further. "Have you seen the allegations about stratospheric particle deployment? That aerospace engineer's press conference?"

"Ross? I caught some of it." Olaf had been skeptical, filing the claims under 'possible but unproven' in his mental database. "You think there's a connection?"

"I'm not saying anything," Maggie replied carefully. "I'm just noting the timing—unusual atmospheric patterns emerging days after alleged particle dispersal in the exact same regions."

Olaf turned back to the data, seeing it with new eyes. If reflective particles had been released into the stratosphere, they would alter the radiation balance—cooling the upper atmosphere while allowing warming to continue below. That temperature disruption would create exactly the kind of pressure gradients they were observing.

"We need more data," he said. "Higher resolution, broader coverage."

"That's just it," Maggie replied. "Those are exactly the measurements being restricted."

Olaf sat back, contemplating the implications. As scientists, they were trained to follow evidence, to build conclusions from observable data. But what happened when the data itself became controlled?

"What are you going to do?" Maggie asked.

Olaf looked again at the jet stream visualization. The rippling pattern was beautiful in its way—a planetary-scale fluid dynamics demonstration. It was also potentially catastrophic for weather systems that had established predictable patterns over centuries.

"I'm going to keep working," he said. "These restrictions apply to NOAA data, not our independent measurements. We have our own weather balloons, our own monitoring network."

"They won't like that."

"Science isn't about being liked." Olaf began typing commands, pulling up university equipment inventories. "If something is altering upper atmospheric conditions, we need to understand it— regardless of who's responsible."

Maggie nodded, a slight smile forming. "I was hoping you'd say that. Which is why I've already cleared a budget for expanded monitoring. Just... be discreet."

After she left, Olaf returned to the atmospheric models. The jet stream's new configuration would have cascading effects— redirecting storm systems, altering precipitation patterns, creating new temperature anomalies across the northern hemisphere.

And if reflective particles were the cause, the effects were just beginning. According to the physics of stratospheric circulation, particles released over the Arctic would eventually distribute globally, creating a thin but influential veil around the entire planet.

Olaf picked up his phone and scrolled through recent news articles about Alexander Ross. The aerospace engineer had been widely dismissed as an alarmist, his claims of a global atmospheric experiment labeled conspiracy theories. Even now, there were reports that Ross was reconsidering his allegations, admitting he might have misinterpreted the evidence.

But the jet stream didn't lie. Something was changing the upper atmosphere, and doing it with remarkable speed and specificity.

Olaf dialed a number—an old colleague at MIT's atmospheric sciences department.

"Stephanie? It's Olaf Werner from Colorado State. We need to talk about stratospheric anomalies. And I think I might have independent confirmation of what you've been seeing."

As he explained his observations, Olaf watched the real-time visualization of wind patterns continuing their unnatural dance across the northern hemisphere. Whatever was happening was no longer theoretical or predictive. It was measurable, observable reality.

The weather was changing. And Olaf Werner might be one of the few scientists left with the independence and equipment to document exactly how and why.

CHAPTER NINE: SCALE BREACH

[Bloomberg Environment – April 11, 2026] Atmospheric Monitoring Firm Reports 'Unusual Particulate Readings' Across Northern Hemisphere By Eliza Harmon, Environmental Technology Reporter

ClimateWatch International, a private atmospheric monitoring company, has released data showing elevated particulate concentrations in the stratosphere across multiple northern regions. The readings, collected by high-altitude sampling equipment, indicate "a statistically significant increase in reflective aerosols at 18–22-kilometer elevations." While the company has stopped short of attributing these findings to any specific cause, their report notes the patterns are "consistent with deliberate introduction rather than natural phenomena." Representatives from the Global Climate Resilience Initiative dismissed the findings as "instrumentational anomalies compounded by sensationalist interpretation."

The Canadian Arctic stretched below him, endless white broken only by the occasional rocky outcrop. Alex Ross gazed out the private jet's window, rehearsing his lines one last time. By noon, he would be at the Northern Climate Research Station—one of Thorne's primary deployment facilities. By evening, he would either have the evidence they needed or be exposed as an infiltrator.

"Twenty minutes to landing, Mr. Ross," the pilot announced over the intercom.

His televised retraction had gone viral overnight. Standing before cameras at the National Press Club, Alex had delivered a masterful performance: the humbled scientist, acknowledging he'd been hasty, admitting his evidence had been circumstantial. He'd carefully avoided retracting specific claims while creating the impression of a full recantation.

Thorne's people had reached out within hours, just as predicted. The billionaire was "gratified by this turn toward scientific objectivity" and had a "unique opportunity" to offer. A private tour of the Canadian facility—to see for himself the legitimate climate research being conducted.

The trap was obvious. This was Thorne's chance to convert or further discredit his most prominent critic. What Thorne couldn't know was that Alex was walking into the trap willingly, with eyes wide open.

The jet descended through cloud cover, revealing the research station below—a complex of white buildings arranged in a hub-and-spoke pattern on the tundra. A small runway extended from one side, disappearing into the landscape.

As they landed, Alex noted details absent from the facility's public documentation: a massive antenna array to the north, reinforced hangars large enough for aircraft much bigger than weather planes, and a distinctive dome structure that resembled a radar installation.

A welcoming committee awaited him on the tarmac—three figures bundled against the Arctic chill. Alex recognized the central figure immediately: Dr. Evelyn Park, the facility's director and a former climate modeling colleague from his Venture Aerospace days.

"Alex," she greeted him as he descended the stairs. "It's been too long."

"Evelyn," he replied with a careful smile. "Thank you for the invitation."

"We're delighted you've taken a more... nuanced position on atmospheric research," she said, studying his face. "Warren was particularly pleased."

"The evidence I had was incomplete," Alex said, reciting his prepared line. "I'm here to see the full picture."

Evelyn nodded, seemingly satisfied. "Then let's show you what we're really doing here."

The facility tour began innocuously enough—standard climate monitoring equipment, ice core analysis labs, atmospheric chemistry stations. All legitimate research, all exactly what would appear in official documentation. Alex nodded and asked appropriate questions, playing the role of the skeptic seeking understanding.

"This is all fascinating, Evelyn," he said after an hour, "but I've seen similar setups at a dozen research stations. What makes this facility special?"

Something flickered in her eyes—caution, perhaps, or calculation. "I thought you might ask that. We do have certain... specialized capabilities. Warren authorized me to show you, given your unique background."

She led him through a secure door requiring both retinal and fingerprint scanning. Beyond lay a corridor leading downward, deep into the permafrost.

"The public-facing research is genuine," Evelyn explained as they descended. "But it's also supplementary to our primary mission."

The corridor opened into a vast subterranean chamber—a hangar carved from the frozen earth. Inside sat three aircraft unlike any Alex had seen before: sleek, drone-like vehicles with massive payload bays and specialized dispersal equipment.

"High-altitude deployment platforms," Evelyn said with evident pride. "Ceiling of 25 kilometers. Automated flight systems. Precision particle distribution."

Alex fought to keep his expression neutral, though his pulse quickened. This was it—confirmation of everything they'd suspected. Not weather monitoring. Not atmospheric research. Deployment infrastructure.

"How many?" he asked, keeping his tone professionally curious.

"Twelve operational units globally. Four here, four in Siberia, four mobile platforms on oceanic vessels." She gestured to a large digital map on the wall showing deployment zones—a hemispheric network designed for optimal particle distribution.

"And the payload?" Alex asked.

Evelyn led him to a sealed room adjacent to the hangar. Inside, behind thick glass, automated systems were processing what appeared to be fine white powder, packaging it into specialized containers.

"Calcium carbonate base with proprietary surface modifications," she explained. "The coating is the breakthrough—it extends suspension time, enhances reflectivity, and allows for networked behavior."

"Networked?" Alex asked, genuinely curious despite himself.

"The particles communicate, in a sense. React to atmospheric conditions as a collective rather than individually. It's quite revolutionary."

Alex studied the production facility, mentally calculating capacity. "This seems... extensive for experimental testing."

Evelyn's smile tightened slightly. "We're beyond the testing phase, Alex. Surely you've realized that."

She led him to another station where technicians monitored real-time atmospheric data. Multiple screens showed particle distribution patterns, stratospheric wind currents, and temperature differentials.

"The Helios Protocol is operational," Evelyn said quietly. "Has been for over a week. The veil is forming exactly as our models predicted."

Alex stared at the monitoring screens, the evidence undeniable. One display showed global temperature projections—declining gradually as the reflective layer expanded.

"Without public notification," he said carefully. "Without regulatory approval."

"The approval process would have taken years we don't have," Evelyn replied. "Warren made the hard choice. History will thank him."

"And the effects on weather systems? Precipitation patterns? Agricultural impacts?"

"Manageable disruptions compared to unchecked warming." She pointed to simulation models running on another screen. "Yes, there will be regional changes. Some areas will see altered rainfall. Wind patterns will shift. But the models show net positive outcomes globally."

Alex pointed to a flashing indicator on one of the displays. "And this anomaly in the jet stream? Was that predicted?"

A slight hesitation. "It's... developing more rapidly than anticipated. We're adjusting particle distribution to compensate."

"You're adjusting? In real-time? You're treating Earth's atmosphere like a thermostat you can dial up and down."

Evelyn's expression hardened. "That's exactly what we're doing, Alex. Because the alternative is watching it spiral beyond our control entirely."

She led him to a final station—a secure room with a single massive display showing a countdown timer and deployment schedule.

"Phase Three begins tomorrow," she said. "Full hemispheric coverage. By the end of the month, we'll have established a controllable reflective layer across 60% of Earth's stratosphere. By summer, global coverage. But really there is no reason things couldn't be launched sooner, the equipment and facilities are ready,"

Alex stared at the schedule, the scale finally clear. This wasn't a test, wasn't even a limited deployment. This was planetary engineering happening in real time. No longer a crazy idea, now a frightening reality.

"Why show me all this?" he asked. "You must know I still have concerns."

Evelyn studied him. "Warren believes once you understand the full system—the safeguards, the monitoring capabilities, the reversibility protocols—you might become an ally. Your credibility with environmental groups could help manage public reaction when the program becomes impossible to conceal."

"Reversibility protocols?" Alex seized on the term. "You can recall the particles?"

"Not directly," she admitted. "But we can halt new deployments, and the existing particles will gradually precipitate out of the stratosphere over 18-24 months. We've also developed contingency plans for accelerated removal if necessary."

Alex nodded slowly, mentally recording every detail while maintaining his interested-but-skeptical expression. The tiny camera disguised as a shirt button was capturing everything—the facility, the aircraft, the monitoring stations. Evidence that could not be dismissed as conspiracy theories or misinterpreted data.

"I need time to process this," he said. "It's... more advanced than I expected."

"Of course." Evelyn seemed pleased by his measured response. "There's more to show you tomorrow. The monitoring network is particularly impressive."

As they returned to the surface levels, Alex noticed increased activity among the staff—technicians moving with urgency, security personnel checking communications.

"Is something happening?" he asked casually.

Evelyn checked her tablet. "Just preparation for tomorrow's deployment. Phase Three requires precise synchronization across all facilities."

But something in her manner had changed—a slight tension that hadn't been there before. As they passed through the main control room, Alex glimpsed a news alert on one of the monitors: "INDEPENDENT SCIENTISTS CONFIRM STRATOSPHERIC ANOMALIES, QUESTION OFFICIAL EXPLANATIONS."

Before he could read more, Evelyn directed him toward the guest quarters. "You must be tired after the flight. We've prepared accommodations for you. Dinner is at seven in the executive dining room."

As soon as he was alone, Alex activated the secure communication device hidden in his watch—a one-time burst transmission to Sophie with a simple encoded message: "Confirmed. Full deployment underway. Evidence obtained."

He had barely finished when a knock came at the door. Alex quickly composed himself, sliding the watch back into his pocket.

Martin Edwards, his former deputy, stood in the hallway. His expression was grave.

"We need to talk," Martin said quietly. "But not here. Meet me in the meteorology lab in twenty minutes. Come alone."

Before Alex could respond, Martin was gone, moving quickly down the corridor.

Alex casually wandered and checked the room for surveillance devices—finding two cameras and a microphone, as expected. For their benefit, he made a show of reviewing facility documentation left on the desk, occasionally nodding as if impressed.

Twenty minutes later, he made his way to the meteorology lab, maintaining a casual pace. The facility was designed as a research station, but he'd noted the security measures throughout—keycard access points, surveillance coverage, guards positioned at critical junctions. This was as much a military installation as a scientific one.

The meteorology lab was empty except for Martin, who stood before a bank of monitors displaying atmospheric data.

"You shouldn't have come," Martin said without turning. "They know."

Alex felt his stomach tighten. "Know what?"

"That your retraction was staged. That you're gathering evidence." Martin finally faced him, his expression tense. "There's a security team reviewing your recent communications. They intercepted something—I don't know what."

"How long do I have?"

"Minutes, maybe." Martin moved to a separate workstation and inserted a drive. "But I prepared for this possibility."

Data began transferring to the drive—atmospheric readings, deployment schedules, technical specifications for the particles.

"The weather effects are accelerating," Martin said, working quickly. "Jet stream displacement, pressure anomalies, localized temperature inversions. The models didn't account for the speed of atmospheric response."

"Thorne knows this?"

"Yes, but he's convinced it's transitional. That the systems will stabilize once full deployment is achieved." Martin shook his head. "I'm not so sure. The particles are demonstrating emergence properties we didn't anticipate."

"Emergence? You mean they're behaving in ways you didn't program?"

"The networking feature—it's creating patterns we didn't design. Self-organization at a scale we never modeled." He handed Alex the drive. "All the data is here. Raw, unfiltered."

Footsteps sounded in the corridor outside.

"You need to go," Martin urged. "There's a maintenance tunnel behind the environmental sampling bay. It leads to an emergency exit. A snowmobile is parked at the northern perimeter—key code 4381."

"Come with me," Alex said.

Martin shook his head. "I'll create a diversion. Buy you time." He gripped Alex's shoulder. "The deployments have to be stopped, Alex. Today's data shows atmospheric disruptions that shouldn't happen for months according to our models. Something's wrong with the system."

The footsteps grew closer.

"Go," Martin insisted. "Get that data out. It's our only chance."

Alex hesitated, then nodded grimly. As he slipped toward the maintenance access, he heard Martin greeting the security team with forced casualness.

The tunnel was narrow and dimly lit, designed for service access to the facility's external monitoring equipment. Alex moved as quickly as he dared, knowing that every second brought discovery closer.

Behind him, alarms began to sound—harsh and insistent. His escape had been discovered.

The tunnel ended at a heavy metal door with an emergency release. Beyond lay the Arctic wilderness—vast, white, and unforgiving. The temperature was well below freezing, the wind cutting through his indoor clothing like a knife.

Alex oriented himself, spotting the facility's northern perimeter a hundred yards away. Between security patrols, he sprinted across the open ground, each breath painful in the frigid air.

The snowmobile was where Martin had promised, partially concealed behind a equipment shed. Alex punched in the code, and the engine hummed to life.

As he accelerated away from the facility, he glanced back to see figures emerging—security personnel deploying in search patterns. In the distance, a helicopter was already lifting off.

The data drive was secure in his inner pocket, along with the camera footage. Now he just had to survive long enough to share it.

Alex gunned the engine, the snowmobile leaping forward across the blank white canvas of the Arctic. Behind him, the facility—now revealed as a deployment center for the most ambitious geoengineering project in human history—grew smaller. One of many deployment facilities around the world operating with the sole purpose of changing the climate through direct action.

And high above, invisible but increasingly influential, the particles continued their work—reflecting sunlight, altering temperatures, changing wind patterns in ways that even their creators had not fully anticipated.

The scale breach was no longer theoretical. It was measurable, documented, and accelerating beyond the models.

The question was whether anyone could stop it before the atmospheric transformation became irreversible.

CHAPTER TEN: THE STOCKHOLM CONFERENCE

[Financial Times – April 12, 2026] International Climate Adaptation Summit Opens in Stockholm By Henrik Nilsson, Global Climate Policy Correspondent

The third annual Climate Adaptation and Resilience Summit began today in Stockholm, bringing together representatives from 142 nations to discuss accelerating climate response strategies. In his opening address, UN Secretary-General Antonio DeVries emphasized the "narrowing window for effective action" and called for "unprecedented global cooperation." Notable among the participants is Warren Thorne, whose Global Climate Resilience Initiative has pledged $3 billion toward resilience technologies. Conspicuously absent are representatives from several climate activist organizations who have withdrawn in protest over what they call "dangerous techno-optimism" among the summit's corporate sponsors.

The Stockholm waterfront sparkled under spring sunshine, belying the tension inside the glass and steel conference center. Warren Thorne stood at the window of his private suite, gazing across the harbor while his team prepared for his keynote address. Outside, protestors gathered behind police barricades, their signs visible even from eighteen floors up: "NO PLANET B" and "STOP PLAYING GOD WITH OUR ATMOSPHERE."

"They're growing in number," noted Henry Caulden, studying a security feed on his tablet. "Local authorities estimate eight thousand now, with more arriving."

Warren nodded, unperturbed. "This was expected, and unavoidable. The Climate Watch data release stirred things up. I'll end up taking a lot of heat for this until they understand what we have accomplished."

"Speaking of which," Caulden said, changing screens, "we have a situation at the Northern Facility."

Warren turned from the window. "Alex Ross?"

"Escaped with sensitive data. Park's report indicates he accessed deployment schedules, technical specifications, and atmospheric monitoring feeds."

"And Martin Edwards assisted him."

"Correct. Edwards is in custody, but he's not cooperating."

Warren considered this development, his expression revealing nothing. "Status of Ross?"

"Last seen heading east on a snowmobile. Search teams deployed. Helicopter surveillance hampered by incoming weather system."

"The irony," Warren said with a thin smile. "Our own atmospheric modifications creating cover for his escape."

He returned to the window, watching boats crisscross the harbor—normal life continuing while history pivoted above their heads. The Helios Protocol was now eight days into implementation. The reflective veil was forming in the stratosphere, spreading from its initial deployment points across the northern hemisphere. Soon, global coverage would begin.

"The preliminary data?" he asked.

Caulden handed him a tablet displaying atmospheric readings. "Reflectivity indices exceeding projections by 8%. Stratospheric distribution progressing faster than modeled. Temperature response detectable at multiple monitoring stations."

"And the anomalies?"

A hesitation. "Increasing in frequency and magnitude. The jet stream displacement now extends across North America. Barometric gradient shifts in the North Atlantic. Unusual cloud formations reported over Siberia."

Warren studied the data, his brow furrowing slightly. "The models indicated potential transitional instabilities."

"These are... beyond the predicted parameters," Caulden admitted nervously. "The emergent networking behavior of the particles appears more pronounced than lab simulations suggested."

"Adjust the deployment schedule for Phase Three," Warren decided. "Reduce payload density by twenty percent, increase dispersal range."

"That will slow the cooling effect."

"Just a temporary caution while we assess the behavioral patterns." Warren handed back the tablet. "Update the simulations with the new field data. I want revised projections before my address."

Caulden nodded and departed, leaving Warren alone with his thoughts. Eight days into humanity's most ambitious environmental intervention, and already the system was demonstrating unexpected behaviors. Not concerning yet—simply the difference between theory and practice, between laboratory simulations and planetary-scale deployment.

A soft chime announced his next appointment. The door opened to admit Dr. Isabelle Renard, the prominent atmospheric physicist who had recently joined his scientific advisory board.

"You've seen the data?" Warren asked without preamble.

Isabelle nodded, her expression grave. "The particle networking effect is stronger than we anticipated. They're forming coherent structures in the stratosphere—reflectivity patterns that weren't in the design specifications."

"Dangerous?"

"Unknown," she admitted. "But certainly unexpected. The question is whether these patterns will stabilize or continue to evolve."

Warren gestured for her to sit. "Your recommendation?"

"Pause Phase Three deployment. Maintain current coverage while we study the emergent behaviors."

Warren shook his head slightly. "Pausing now creates a reflectivity imbalance between hemispheres. The models show that could accelerate cross-equatorial weather disruption."

"The models didn't account for the networking behaviors we're seeing," Isabelle countered. "We're in uncharted territory, Warren."

He studied her—one of the world's foremost experts on atmospheric chemistry, recruited at great expense to lend scientific legitimacy to Helios. Her concerns couldn't be dismissed lightly.

"A compromise, then," he offered. "We proceed with Phase Three but at reduced payload density, as I've already directed. Your team gets priority access to all monitoring data to assess pattern evolution."

Isabelle didn't look satisfied but nodded reluctantly. "And if we determine the patterns are destabilizing?"

"Then we adjust accordingly. The system is designed for adaptive response."

She rose to leave, then hesitated. "There's something else. The Swedish Meteorological Institute is tracking unusual wind pattern disruptions across Scandinavia. They're correlating suspiciously with our initial deployment zone."

"Official inquiries?"

"Not yet. But their data will eventually lead them to the particulate layer."

Warren nodded, unsurprised. "Disclosure was always inevitable. The timeline has simply accelerated."

"You seem remarkably calm about this."

"Because we're past the point of stopping, Isabelle. It's now a fait accompli. The particles are deployed. The stratospheric veil is forming. The cooling effect will be measurable globally within weeks." He gestured toward the window, where protesters continued to gather. "Public opinion can be managed. What cannot be managed is a planet that continues to warm unchecked."

After she departed, Warren returned to preparations for his keynote address. The speech, carefully crafted over weeks, would focus on climate resilience technologies—carbon capture, sustainable agriculture, advanced weather prediction. No mention of Helios, no hint of the stratospheric intervention already underway.

That revelation would come later, once the cooling effects were undeniable. Once the world faced the choice between an imperfect solution already implemented or the uncertainty of reversing course.

A knock at the door interrupted his thoughts. Henry Caulden had returned, his expression unusually tense, nerves more strained.

"We have a problem," he said. "Alex Ross has resurfaced."

Warren looked up sharply. "Captured?"

"No. He's here. In Stockholm."

"That's impossible. The facility is two thousand miles from here, in one of the most inhospitable environments on Earth."

"Nevertheless," Caulden said, handing him a tablet displaying security camera footage. "This was taken thirty minutes ago at Arlanda Airport."

The grainy image showed Alex Ross emerging from a private aircraft—disheveled, exhausted, but very much alive. Beside him stood Sophie Lorde.

"How?" Warren demanded.

"Unknown. Possibly assistance from sympathizers. We're investigating."

Warren's mind raced through implications and contingencies. "His data?"

"Must assume he has it all. Technical specifications, deployment schedules, monitoring feeds. Everything he accessed at the Northern Facility."

"And his likely next move?"

"Given Lorde's presence, a media release seems probable. Possibly timed to coincide with your keynote."

Warren absorbed this, then made a swift decision. "Move up Phase Three to tonight. Full deployment across all platforms."

Caulden looked startled. "That contradicts your earlier order to reduce payload density."

"The situation has changed. Once Ross releases his evidence, we'll face legal challenges, injunctions, political interference. Better to establish the full system before that happens."

"Renard's concerns about the networking patterns—"

"Are noted," Warren interrupted. "But the strategic calculus has shifted. Deploy tonight. Full payload."

Caulden hesitated only briefly before nodding. "I'll transmit the orders."

As his chief strategist departed, Warren returned to the window. The protest crowd had grown larger, more organized. Police lines had been reinforced. In the harbor, a Greenpeace vessel had appeared, its distinctive logo visible even at this distance.

Everything was accelerating—the atmospheric response, the public awareness, the opposition. His carefully planned timeline for Helios implementation was collapsing.

But it didn't matter. The critical threshold had already been passed. The particles were in the stratosphere, beginning their work of planetary cooling. Alex Ross could release all the evidence he wanted—it would only confirm what was already becoming physically undeniable.

Warren Thorne had changed the world. History would judge the wisdom of his intervention, but no one could undo what had begun in the thin, cold layer where Earth met space.

Across the city, in a small hotel room hastily booked under false names, Alex Ross and Sophie Lorde worked feverishly to prepare their evidence for release.

"The footage is clear enough," Sophie said, reviewing the hidden camera recordings from the Canadian facility. "Combined with the technical specifications and deployment data, it's undeniable."

Alex nodded, his face haggard from thirty-six hours without sleep. The journey from the Arctic had been a blur of improvisation and risk—a snowmobile to a remote hunting cabin, a bush plane arranged through contacts, commercial flights under borrowed identification.

"We release everything simultaneously," he said. "Maximum distribution to prevent suppression."

His secure phone buzzed—Stephanie Martinez calling from her makeshift lab where she'd been analyzing the new data.

"The particle networking behavior," she said without preamble when Alex answered. "It's not random. The patterns show distinct geometric organization—almost like crystalline structures forming in the stratosphere."

"Intentional design, he meant to do this?" Alex asked, struggling to accept the news.

"Unknown. But definitely not in the public documentation about calcium carbonate dispersal." Stephanie sounded both scientifically fascinated and deeply concerned. "These structures appear to be affecting atmospheric circulation more directly than simple reflective particles should."

"How soon can you have an analysis ready?"

"Four hours, minimum. I'm coordinating with Dr. Werner at Colorado State. His atmospheric monitoring network is tracking real-time effects that correlate with the particle distribution patterns."

Alex glanced at the time. "Thorne's keynote is in three hours. We need to release before that."

"I can provide preliminary findings," Stephanie conceded. "But the full analysis will take longer."

After ending the call, Alex turned to Sophie. "We need to move faster. Thorne's people know I'm in Stockholm—security at the Northern Facility would have reported my escape immediately."

Sophie nodded, fingers flying over her keyboard as she prepared the evidence for distribution. "Encryption? Multiple servers?"

"Both. And physical copies to key journalists as backup. I know I'm pushing you, and I'm sorry, but we don't have a choice in the matter anymore."

Alex moved to the window, checking the street below for surveillance. The hotel was deliberately modest, chosen for its lack of security cameras and cash payment option. Still, he had no illusions about the resources Thorne could deploy once he knew their location.

His gaze lifted to the sky—clear blue with high, thin clouds. Somewhere up there, invisible to the naked eye, engineered particles were spreading, networking, changing the energy balance of an entire planet. And accelerating weather changes that even Thorne's models hadn't predicted.

"We have unexpected support," Sophie said, looking up from her computer. "Climate activists are surrounding the conference center. Over ten thousand now, according to social media. Police have established a perimeter. Alex you might have more of a following than you realize."

Alex considered this development. "Can you get a message to their organizers? We'll need a distraction if we're going to get close enough to release during Thorne's speech."

Sophie nodded. "I know people in Greenpeace's Stockholm office. They have a boat in the harbor already."

"Perfect." Alex turned back to the evidence compilation. "One more thing—we need a direct channel to UN representatives attending the conference. Somebody with enough authority to call for an immediate investigation once the evidence drops."

"My contacts contacts in the EU climate delegation," Sophie offered.

The plan was forming—release the evidence publicly while simultaneously getting it directly to regulatory authorities who could take immediate action. A long shot, perhaps, but their only option given Thorne's influence and resources.

The hotel room phone rang—startling them both with its sudden intrusion. They exchanged concerned glances. No one should know they were here.

Sophie answered cautiously. "Yes?"

Her expression changed from wariness to shock. "How did you—" She listened for a moment, then handed the phone to Alex. "It's for you. Someone who says she has information about Karen Mitchell."

Alex took the receiver. "This is Ross."

A woman's voice, unfamiliar and tense: "Dr. Mitchell is alive. She's being held at the Thorne Foundation's research center outside Stockholm."

"Who is this?"

"Someone on the inside. Someone who's seen enough." The voice lowered. "The atmospheric data you stole—it's already outdated. The system is evolving faster than anyone predicted. Thorne is accelerating Phase Three deployment to tonight."

Alex felt a chill. "Why tell me this, and how do you know?"

"Because I've seen the latest models. The particle networking behavior isn't just unexpected—it's potentially catastrophic. Temperature inversions, pressure anomalies, jet stream fragmentation. The whole atmospheric system is beginning to destabilize."

"Who are you?" Alex pressed.

A pause, and possibly a sigh. "Dr. Isabelle Renard. Chief atmospheric physicist for Helios."

The name registered immediately—a leading figure in climate science who had disappeared from public view six months ago, presumably recruited by Thorne.

"Why should I trust you, word is you started working for Thorne months ago?" Alex demanded.

"Because in three hours, Warren Thorne is going to announce the success of Helios to the world. He's going to claim the cooling has begun, that the intervention is working. What he won't say is that we've lost control of the system." Her voice grew urgent. "The particles aren't just reflective anymore—they're reorganizing atmospheric structures in ways we never designed or modeled."

Alex looked at Sophie, who was watching him intently. "Where can we meet?"

"The old observatory in Saltsjöbaden. One hour. Come alone." The line went dead.

Alex slowly replaced the receiver, mind racing with new possibilities and dangers.

"Trap?" Sophie asked.

"Possibly. Or our best chance at understanding what's really happening." He quickly gathered the data drives. "I need to meet her. You finish preparing the release—set it for exactly the start time of Thorne's keynote."

"And if you don't come back? I'm getting used to your company..."

"Then make sure the world sees everything we have." Alex checked his watch. "And contact Werner and Stephanie

76

immediately—tell them Thorne is accelerating full deployment to tonight. They need to monitor for atmospheric responses."

As he prepared to leave, Alex felt a strange sensation of temporal compression—as if events that should have unfolded over months were collapsing into hours. The stratospheric veil, the weather anomalies, the public revelation—all accelerating toward an inevitable collision.

Outside, the Stockholm sky remained deceptively calm, betraying nothing of the invisible transformation occurring miles above. But soon, very soon, the changes would become impossible to ignore.

CHAPTER ELEVEN: PLAUSIBLE DENIABILITY

[CNN Breaking News – April 12, 2026] Unusual Weather Phenomena Reported Across Northern Hemisphere By Melanie Torres, Senior Weather Correspondent

Meteorologists are reporting a series of unusual weather events across multiple continents over the past 72 hours. These include sudden temperature fluctuations, atypical cloud formations, and unexpected shifts in prevailing winds. The National Weather Service has described these phenomena as "within the range of natural variability, though occurring at unusually high frequency." When asked about potential connections to climate change, NWS spokesperson James Harrington stressed that "no individual weather event can be directly attributed to long-term climate trends." Meanwhile, social media users in affected regions continue sharing images of what many describe as "strange" atmospheric conditions.

"Plausible deniability," Henry Caulden explained to the communications team assembled in the conference center's media room. "That's our immediate strategy."

The dozen men and women before him represented major news organizations, climate research institutions, and governmental agencies—all with direct or indirect ties to Thorne's influence network. All now being briefed on how to manage the accelerating public awareness of atmospheric anomalies.

"The Swedish Meteorological Institute has officially requested information about stratospheric particulate readings," Caulden continued, his voice calm despite the escalating crisis. "Similar inquiries are coming from weather services in Canada, Japan, and Germany. Our response remains consistent: these are natural atmospheric variations potentially linked to volcanic activity in the Kamchatka Peninsula."

A woman in the front row—communications director for an influential climate policy think tank—raised her hand. "The

Kamchatka narrative won't hold. Seismic monitoring shows no significant volcanic activity there in the past six months."

"It doesn't need to hold indefinitely," Caulden replied. "Just long enough for Warren's keynote to reframe the conversation. This is nothing more than a stalling action to give the deployment time to get established."

He advanced to the next slide in his presentation: a global map showing rapidly spreading atmospheric anomalies. Red dots indicated regions where unusual weather patterns had become impossible to ignore—pressure inversions over North America, unexplained wind shears across Northern Europe, peculiar cloud formations in the Arctic Circle.

"The timeline has accelerated," he acknowledged. "We expected gradual atmospheric response over weeks. Instead, we're seeing measurable effects within days."

"Is that good news or bad?" asked a Global News executive producer.

"Both," Caulden said carefully. "The cooling effect is establishing faster than modeled, which supports our core mission. However, the transitional weather disruptions are more pronounced than anticipated."

Unspoken was the real concern—that the unexpected networking behavior of the particles was creating atmospheric disturbances beyond anything in their simulations. That something designed to save the planet might be destabilizing it instead.

"Warren's keynote is in two hours," Caulden continued. "By then, we need unified messaging across all platforms. The transitional weather events are natural variations. The stratospheric reflectivity readings are questionable due to instrumentation anomalies. Any correlation with deployment sites is coincidental."

He surveyed the room—media professionals who had built careers on controlling narratives, shaping public perception. Many looked uncomfortable with the scale of what they were being asked to manage.

"After the keynote," Caulden assured them, "we pivot to transparency. Warren will announce the Helios Protocol as a breakthrough climate stabilization system that's already showing promising results. He'll acknowledge the weather transitions as expected side effects that will diminish as the system stabilizes. And you will each have the inside scoop, all the background."

"And if they don't diminish?" asked a weather channel meteorologist who had been unusually quiet until now.

Caulden's expression remained neutral. "All models indicate stabilization within two to three weeks."

"The same models that didn't predict the current anomalies?" the meteorologist pressed. Not the kind of question that leads to a long career, but overdue in this setting.

A tense silence fell over the room. The question verbalized what many were thinking: what if the models were fundamentally wrong? What if the atmospheric disruptions continued to intensify?

Caulden was saved from answering by the arrival of a security officer who whispered urgently in his ear. His expression darkened.

"Continue preparations," he instructed the team. "I'll return shortly."

In the corridor outside, the security officer brought up a tablet displaying surveillance footage. "Facial recognition match, sir. Alexander Ross entering Saltsjöbaden thirty minutes ago."

Caulden studied the image—Alex Ross moving purposefully through the coastal suburb of Stockholm, clearly headed somewhere specific.

"Accompanied?"

"Solo, as far as we can tell. But we've identified Sophie Lorde at a hotel in central Stockholm, accessing multiple media platform interfaces simultaneously. Whatever she's up to she's burning up the hotel's internet connection."

"They're preparing a coordinated release, is what she's up to." Caulden concluded. "Timing it with Warren's keynote for maximum impact."

"There's more," the officer said hesitantly. "Renard's vehicle was tracked to Saltsjöbaden an hour ago. Her regular security detail reported she dismissed them for 'personal time.'"

Caulden's eyes narrowed. Isabelle Renard—their chief atmospheric physicist meeting clandestinely with their most prominent critic. The implications were concerning. More than concerning, and Thorne would demand some severe action on this.

"Surveillance on both," he ordered. "Non-interventional for now, keep your distance. And increase security for Warren's keynote. Full spectrum scanning for all attendees, no exceptions."

As the officer departed, Caulden considered his options. The situation was deteriorating on multiple fronts—atmospheric anomalies accelerating beyond predictions, scientific dissent within the program, and now the imminent threat of public exposure. Hell, even his media lackeys were pushing back.

Yet the strategic calculation remained unchanged. Once Phase Three deployment was complete tonight, the atmospheric veil would be established. Reversing it would take months even if halted immediately. The world would have no choice but to adapt to the new reality Thorne had created.

Caulden touched his secure communicator. "Proceed with Phase Three preparation. Full payload, all platforms. Authorization code Prometheus."

The Saltsjöbaden Observatory stood on a rocky promontory overlooking the Baltic Sea, its copper dome weathered to a distinctive green patina. Once Sweden's premier astronomical facility, it now served primarily as a historical landmark and occasional research station.

Alex approached cautiously, scanning for surveillance or security. The old building appeared deserted in the late afternoon light, tourists having departed with the day's final tour hours earlier.

A side door stood slightly ajar—an invitation or a trap, he couldn't be sure. With few alternatives, he entered, finding himself in a shadowed corridor that smelled of old books and brass polish.

"Alex Ross." A woman's voice from the shadows.

The voice came from the main observatory chamber. Alex moved toward it, stepping into a circular room dominated by a massive refracting telescope aimed skyward through the open dome.

Isabelle Renard stood beside the telescope, her slender figure silhouetted against the sky visible through the dome. In her early fifties, with silver-streaked dark hair pulled back in a severe bun, she projected the intimidating brilliance that had made her one of the world's foremost atmospheric physicists before her disappearance into Thorne's organization.

"You've taken considerable risk coming here," Alex said, remaining near the door.

"As have you." She gestured to the telescope. "Would you like to see what concerns me?"

Alex approached cautiously. Renard stepped aside, allowing him access to the eyepiece of the lesser telescope in the building. Through it, he saw a section of sky rendered in surprising detail for daylight observation.

"Special filters on the scope," Renard explained. "Calibrated to detect specific light scattering patterns in the upper atmosphere."

At first, Alex saw nothing unusual—just blue sky with scattered cirrus clouds. Then, as his eyes adjusted, he detected it: a faint geometric pattern overlaid across the view, like a delicate lattice or crystalline structure.

"What am I looking at?" he asked, though he already suspected.

"The particle network," Renard said quietly. "Forming organizational structures that weren't in any of our design specifications."

Alex stepped back from the telescope. "Self-organization?"

"Beyond anything we modeled. These particles weren't engineered with any significant networking capabilities—just enough to maintain optimal distribution and reflectivity. But they're exhibiting emergent behaviors that suggest a higher level of organization."

"And Thorne knows this?"

"Yes. But he believes it's transitional—that the system will stabilize once fully deployed." She moved to a laptop set up on a nearby table. "I've been running models based on the actual behavioral data. The results are... concerning."

The screen displayed atmospheric simulations—complex fluid dynamics models showing how the networked particles were influencing wind patterns, pressure systems, temperature gradients.

"The particles are creating what amounts to a dynamically responsive membrane in the stratosphere," Renard explained. "Not just reflecting sunlight passively, but actively reorganizing in response to atmospheric conditions."

"That wasn't the design intent, the ability to network, to act as a unit?"

"No. The particles were meant to be relatively inert reflectors, not an interactive system." She advanced the simulation forward in time. "As the network grows more complex, it begins influencing atmospheric circulation more directly—altering jet streams, creating pressure anomalies, disrupting established weather patterns."

The simulation showed increasing atmospheric chaos— fragmentation of traditional circulation patterns, emergence of new and unpredictable weather systems.

"This is theoretical?" Alex asked hopefully.

"Unfortunately, no. We're already seeing the early stages." Renard pulled up comparative data showing actual atmospheric readings against predicted models. "The deviations began three days ago. Small at first, but accelerating. The jet stream displacement, the pressure inversions, the cloud formation anomalies—all consistent with the start of systemic destabilization."

Alex studied the data, recognition dawning. "And Thorne is accelerating deployment despite this?"

"He believes more complete coverage will stabilize the system— that the current anomalies are due to partial implementation." Renard's expression revealed her skepticism. "But my models suggest the opposite. More particles mean more complex networking, which likely means more severe atmospheric disruption."

"How severe?"

Renard hesitated. "Potentially catastrophic. If these trends continue, we could see weather pattern disruptions unlike anything in recorded history. Precipitation where there should be drought. Drought where there should be monsoons. Wind patterns that no longer follow established seasonality."

"And temperature?"

"Global cooling, yes—that part works as designed. But distributed chaotically. Some regions cooled dramatically while others remain hot. The temperature gradients themselves becoming drivers of new and unpredictable weather systems."

Alex processed this information, connecting it with what they'd already observed. "The models show this getting worse?"

"Much worse. Especially after tonight's Phase Three deployment."

"Which has been moved up," Alex noted. "Why the rush?"

"Officially, because the initial results are promising. Unofficially..." She met his gaze directly. "Because Warren knows you have evidence that could halt the program. He wants to establish the full system before you can expose it. Simply put, you have become a threat, even an obstacle."

"You could stop it," Alex said. "You're the chief atmospheric physicist. Your concerns would carry weight."

Renard shook her head. "I've tried. Warren is a believer, believes the risks of inaction on climate change outweigh any potential side effects of Helios. And he's surrounded himself with people who reinforce that belief."

"So why come to me?"

"Because you have what I don't—hard evidence of the deployment infrastructure, the technical specifications, the organizational structure. Combined with my atmospheric models and insider knowledge, it might be enough to force intervention. And you have a pulpit, a name, recognition as a savvy guy."

Alex studied her, weighing trust against caution. "You mentioned Karen Mitchell."

"Being held at the Thorne Foundation Research Center, fifteen kilometers from here. Officially for 'psychiatric evaluation' after a 'breakdown.' Actually because she knows too much about the early development of the particle technology."

"That's kidnapping! Is she alright?"

"Physically, yes. Mentally..." Renard shrugged. "She's been in isolation for weeks. But she's resilient. And she coded critical information about the particle design vulnerabilities before she was taken."

Alex felt the weight of this information. Not just an abstract scientific asset, but a woman who had risked everything to expose the truth—and had been paying for that courage in isolation for weeks.

"What are they doing to her?" Alex asked, his scientific instinct for detail asserting itself.

"Nothing physically harmful," Renard replied carefully. "But psychological isolation, constant gaslighting, subtle threats about her professional future. They're trying to break her resolve, convince her that her concerns about the particles were delusions brought on by stress."

Alex's jaw tightened. "We need to get her out."

"The facility is a fortress—biometric security, armed guards, surveillance systems. Any direct attempt would likely fail and alert Thorne's people that we know her location."

"But if we're going after her resonance cascade research anyway..."

Renard nodded slowly. "Perhaps. But understand—she may not be the same person who disappeared weeks ago. Isolation changes people. And if comes down to rescuing her or recovering her research..."

Alex thought of his own brief entrapment in a closed room when he was leaving his former employer, the security people grilling him for hours. A top executive earning millions per year and suddenly leaving with no publicly expressed reason. Even those few hours had changed his perspective permanently. What would weeks of deliberate isolation do?

"We need a plan that accounts for her condition," Alex said. "Not just extraction, but potential medical and psychological support. And these particle design vulnerabilities she found?"

"Ways to potentially neutralize the particles or disrupt their networking capabilities." Renard checked her watch. "We're running out of time. Thorne's keynote begins in ninety minutes, and security will be monitoring my absence, they expect me to be there."

She handed Alex a data drive. "Everything I've been able to compile about the system's actual behavior versus predicted models. Combined with your evidence, it presents a compelling case for immediate intervention."

"And what about the Phase Three deployment tonight?"

"Must be stopped at all costs. Once the full hemispheric network is established, the atmospheric effects will accelerate beyond our ability to predict or control."

Alex pocketed the drive. "How do we reach Karen?"

"We don't, for now. Security at the research center is impenetrable without proper planning." Renard moved toward the door. "Focus on stopping Phase Three. I can guide you to the Swedish deployment facility—it's the nearest control node for the European sector."

"You'd sabotage your own project?"

Renard paused. "I joined Helios to help solve the climate crisis, not create a new one. This is not the system we designed, not the system Thorne told us we were designing. It needs to be halted before the atmospheric disruption becomes irreversible."

As they prepared to depart separately, Alex received a message from Sophie: Evidence package prepared. Distribution set for keynote start. Location secure.

He replied quickly: Proceed as planned. New data incoming. Phase Three tonight. Must be stopped!

Looking back at the small telescope aimed at the sky, Alex considered the invisible transformation occurring in the stratosphere. Particles designed to save humanity from warming were instead reorganizing into patterns their creators hadn't intended, altering atmospheric systems in ways no one had predicted. Except possibly Thorne.

The irony was bitter: in trying to control Earth's climate, they had created a system that was slipping beyond control. And time was running out to stop it.

Warren Thorne made final adjustments to his tie, studying his reflection in the conference center's private suite. In thirty minutes, he would take the stage before representatives from nearly every nation on Earth, unveiling the most ambitious environmental intervention in human history.

Not as a proposal or theoretical model, but as an accomplished fact—a system already deployed and beginning to function.

A soft knock announced Henry Caulden's arrival. A security chief with a PhD, his expression was professionally neutral, but Warren had worked with him long enough to recognize the tension beneath.

"Status report?"

"Phase Three preparations on schedule," Caulden said. "All platforms report ready for deployment at 22:00 UTC."

"And our other situation?"

"Dr. Renard met with Ross at the Saltsjöbaden Observatory. They've since separated—Renard returning toward the city, Ross moving north along the coast."

Warren absorbed this betrayal with remarkable composure. "Content of their meeting?"

"Unknown. No surveillance inside the facility. But Ross was observed receiving a data transfer."

"Atmospheric models, most likely," Warren surmised. "Isabelle has been expressing concerns about the particle networking behavior."

"Should we detain her?"

Warren considered this, then shook his head. "Not yet. Her scientific credibility remains valuable, especially once the system becomes public knowledge. Monitor, but don't interfere."

"And Ross?"

"Let him proceed with whatever he's planning. After tonight's deployment, it becomes moot. The system will be established, functioning, and beginning to show measurable cooling effects. Opposition becomes academic at that point."

Caulden nodded, though his expression remained troubled. "The latest atmospheric data..."

"I've reviewed it," Warren said, slightly impatient. "The anomalies are within acceptable parameters."

"Sir, with respect, the jet stream fragmentation is accelerating. Upper atmospheric wind patterns show increasing instability. The models didn't predict this level of disruption until at least week three, if at all."

Warren turned from the mirror to face his lieutenant directly. "Henry, we knew there would be transitional effects. Any system of this scale requires adjustment periods."

"These aren't just adjustments," Caulden pressed, uncharacteristically insistent. "The patterns suggest systemic atmospheric destabilization. Renard's concerns about emergent behaviors in the particle network may have merit."

For a moment, doubt flickered across Warren's face—quickly suppressed and replaced with familiar conviction.

"We're past the point of hesitation," he said firmly. "Climate change hasn't paused while we debated intervention methods. It's accelerated. The Arctic continues to warm at triple the global average. Feedback loops threaten to push us past irreversible tipping points. We're saving the world, I'm saving the world!"

He moved to the window, gazing out at Stockholm harbor where late afternoon light glinted off the water.

"The atmospheric disruptions are temporary adjustments. Once full deployment is achieved, the system will stabilize. Temperature gradients will normalize. Weather patterns will establish new equilibria."

"And if they don't?" Caulden asked quietly.

Warren turned back, his expression hardening slightly. "Then we adapt the system. That's the beauty of Helios—it's not static. We can adjust particle density, distribution patterns, reflectivity indices. It's a dynamic solution to a dynamic problem."

Before Caulden could respond, Warren's tablet chirped with an urgent alert. Both men looked at the screen, displaying a notification from their media monitoring system: MULTIPLE PLATFORM ALERT: Mass data release in progress. Subject: Helios Protocol deployment infrastructure and technical specifications.

"It's starting, he beat us to it" Caulden said grimly.

Warren checked the time—still twenty-five minutes before his scheduled keynote. "They're moving early to disrupt my announcement."

"Should we delay?"

"No," Warren decided immediately. "We accelerate. Move my address forward. Inform the conference organizers I'll be starting in five minutes due to scheduling adjustments."

As Caulden relayed these instructions, Warren skimmed the initial media response to the data release. Dozens of news organizations simultaneously receiving technical documentation, facility footage, deployment schedules—the entire Helios infrastructure exposed for public scrutiny.

Yet he remained surprisingly calm. The evidence revealed what was already becoming physically manifest—that humanity had begun actively managing Earth's atmospheric energy balance. The only question now was who would control the narrative: those who had created the system, or those who opposed it.

Warren Thorne intended to ensure it was the former.

"Time to tell the world what we've done," he said, straightening his jacket. "And why history will thank us for doing it."

As he moved toward the door, another alert flashed on his tablet—this one from the atmospheric monitoring network: ANOMALY WARNING: Unprecedented jet stream bifurcation detected over North Atlantic. Pressure differential exceeding model parameters by 32%.

Warren hesitated for just a moment, just a moment, then set the tablet aside, his resolve unshaken. Once the world understood the necessity of Helios, such technical concerns would be addressed with the full resources of global cooperation.

The dark, rain-heavy clouds gathering over the Stockholm harbor didn't register as ominous to Thorne—merely a local weather system of no particular significance.

But to those tracking atmospheric patterns globally, those clouds represented something far more concerning: weather behaving in ways the models had never predicted, driven by forces that were not even beginning to be understood.

And high above, invisible to the naked eye, the particle network continued its unauthorized reorganization—creating new patterns, new structures, new atmospheric dynamics that would soon make themselves impossible to ignore.

CHAPTER TWELVE: FIRST IMPACT

[BBC Breaking News – April 12, 2026] 'Unprecedented' Weather System Strikes Northern Europe Live Report

An unusual storm system has developed with extraordinary speed over the North Sea, bringing hurricane-force winds to coastal regions of Norway, Denmark, and northern Germany. Meteorologists describe the system as "meteorologically anomalous," noting its rapid intensification and unusual structure. Wind speeds have reached 165 km/h in some areas, with barometric pressure dropping to levels typically seen only in Category 4 hurricanes. The European Emergency Response Coordination Centre has activated its highest alert level as coastal evacuations are underway in multiple countries. Norwegian meteorologist Dr. Astrid Lindgren called the system "unlike anything in our historical records," noting that its formation "defies conventional atmospheric modeling."

Dr. Olaf Werner stared at the satellite imagery in disbelief. The atmospheric data scrolling across his screen couldn't be right—yet three separate monitoring systems were reporting the same impossible numbers.

"Pressure differential of 92 millibars in under six hours," his graduate assistant Tanya Rodriguez confirmed, voice tight with professional alarm. "The North Sea system came out of nowhere."

"Not nowhere," Olaf corrected grimly. "The stratosphere."

The Colorado State University meteorology lab had become an impromptu command center as scientists from across the department gathered to monitor the unprecedented weather events unfolding globally. What had begun as localized anomalies—unusual jet stream behavior, unexpected pressure gradients—had suddenly escalated into a full-scale atmospheric emergency.

"The European storm is just the beginning," Olaf said, pointing to other developing systems on the global monitoring display. "Look at these formation patterns in the North Pacific, the South Atlantic, the Arabian Sea. All exhibiting the same signature."

"Which is?" asked Howard Chang, the department chair.

"Stratospheric forcing," Olaf replied. "These aren't developing from traditional surface conditions. They're being driven by upper atmospheric dynamics—specifically, rapid reorganization of pressure and temperature gradients in the stratosphere. Something is causing this, something making it happen. And it isn't mother nature."

The room fell silent as the implications sank in. Traditional weather systems formed through the interaction of surface temperatures, oceanic patterns, and existing atmospheric conditions. What they were witnessing was something else entirely: weather being forced from above, driven by changes occurring 20 kilometers overhead.

Olaf's phone buzzed with an incoming call from Stephanie Martinez. He put it on speaker.

"Are you seeing this?" Stephanie asked without preamble.

"The North Sea system? It's dominating every screen in the lab."

"It's the particle network," Stephanie said. "The patterns I've been tracking in the stratosphere have begun actively reorganizing air movement. The reflective layer isn't just passive anymore—it's creating its own circulation dynamics."

Olaf switched to a specialized data view showing upper atmosphere readings. "The temperature inversions are intensifying."

"Because the particles are forming increasingly complex structures," Stephanie explained. "The latest samples show geometric networking that's creating what amounts to atmospheric channels—funneling air movements along specific pathways."

"Intentional design?" Olaf asked.

"No. Emergent behavior. The networking capability was meant to optimize reflectivity and extend suspension time. But the system has evolved beyond its programming."

Dr. Chang leaned closer to the speaker. "Dr. Martinez, are you suggesting these particles have some form of intelligence?"

"Not intelligence," Stephanie clarified. "Emergent self-organization. Similar to how simple rules in cellular automata can produce complex patterns, or how certain chemical reactions spontaneously form ordered structures."

Olaf returned to the North Sea storm system, now visible on live news feeds as it battered the Norwegian coast. The swirling pattern was unnervingly geometric—less like a traditional cyclone and more like a precisely engineered vortex.

"We need to warn coastal populations in all developing system paths," he said. "These storms aren't following normal behavior patterns. Traditional forecasting models won't predict their movements accurately."

"The National Weather Service has already suspended standard forecasting," Tanya reported, checking incoming alerts. "They're calling the situation 'dynamically unprecedented' and recommending general caution rather than specific predictions."

"Not good enough," Olaf said. "We need to model these new formation dynamics and issue targeted warnings."

As if to underscore his point, the satellite feed showed the North Sea system suddenly changing direction—making an almost 90-degree turn that no natural weather system should be capable of. The Norwegian coastal city that had been directly in its path was spared, but the storm was now accelerating toward Denmark with unnatural precision. Any meteorologist would be shaken to their core by so dramatic a phenomenon.

Olaf's phone buzzed again—this time Alex Ross calling.

"The evidence release is live," Alex reported. "But Thorne has moved up his keynote and is about to go on stage. Are you tracking the European storm system?"

"And about a dozen more forming globally," Olaf confirmed. "All showing the same stratospheric forcing signature."

"It's worse than we thought," Alex said. " Renard's models show these systems intensifying as the particle network continues to evolve. And Thorne is still proceeding with Phase Three deployment tonight."

"Which means what, exactly?"

"Full hemispheric coverage. Three times the current particle density. If these storms are forming under partial deployment—"

Olaf didn't need to hear the rest. He understood the terrifying implications. "Where are you now?"

"Heading to the Swedish deployment facility with Renard. It's our only chance to stop Phase Three."

"You need to hurry," Olaf urged, watching new data flow across his screens. "The pressure gradient between what we know and what we're seeing is approaching tornado conditions," Olaf stressed, his hands sketching invisible weather fronts in the air. "The atmospheric destabilization is accelerating exponentially—these aren't isolated anomalies anymore. They're the beginning of systematic collapse."

As the call ended, Olaf turned to his team. "We need to establish direct channels with emergency management agencies worldwide.

Traditional weather prediction has just become obsolete. We're entering a new atmospheric paradigm, and no one is prepared for what comes next."

The storm hit Copenhagen with the suddenness of an explosion. One moment, residents were hurrying to secure properties and evacuate low-lying areas under darkening skies. The next, a wall of wind and water surged through the harbor with force that bent steel and shattered concrete.

Mette Larsen, chief of Denmark's Emergency Management Agency, watched in horror from the command center as monitoring systems failed in rapid succession. Wind gauges designed to withstand hurricane-force gales went offline after reporting speeds beyond their measurement thresholds. Tidal sensors in the harbor registered a seven-meter surge before going silent.

"This isn't possible," her deputy whispered beside her. "The North Sea doesn't produce storms like this."

"Apparently it does now," Mette replied grimly, turning to the communications officer. "Status of evacuation zones?"

"Zones one through four cleared. Zone five still in progress when the surge hit. No communications from teams in the harbor district. All our resources are stretched to the maximum, and it's nowhere near enough."

Outside the reinforced windows of the command center, the sky had taken on an unnatural greenish hue. The clouds moved in patterns that defied normal atmospheric behavior—swirling in geometric formations that seemed almost designed.

Mette's attention was drawn to a live news feed from a camera positioned on a high building overlooking the harbor. The footage showed a weather phenomenon unlike anything in recorded meteorological history: a perfectly formed hexagonal pattern of clouds rotating around a central eye, with distinct angular boundaries that no natural storm should possess.

"Get me direct contact with the European Emergency Response Coordination Centre," she ordered. "And find someone who can explain what we're looking at, because this isn't a natural disaster anymore."

As her team scrambled to establish communications, Mette received an urgent message from the Swedish authorities. Their meteorological service was tracking the storm's movement and predicting another impossible turn—this time toward Stockholm, where the international climate conference was underway.

The implications were both practical and symbolic: a weather system defying all natural laws was heading directly toward the global gathering of climate leaders.

And no one could explain why.

Warren Thorne took the stage at the Stockholm Climate Conference to enthusiastic applause from some attendees, and stony silence from others. The massive screen behind him displayed the conference logo—a stylized Earth wrapped in protective hands.

In the front row, Henry Caulden monitored security feeds on his tablet, watching for any sign of disruption. The evidence release was now spreading across global media platforms, but Thorne had reached the podium before the full impact could register with the audience.

"Distinguished delegates, esteemed colleagues," Thorne began, his voice calm and authoritative. "We gather at a pivotal moment in human history. For three decades, we have debated, negotiated, and compromised on climate action—while the Earth's systems continued their acceleration toward dangerous tipping points."

On a separate tab on Caulden's tablet, emergency alerts were multiplying: the North Sea storm system defying all prediction models, new atmospheric anomalies developing across multiple continents, urgent requests for scientific explanation from governments worldwide.

"Today, I stand before you not just with warnings or projections," Thorne continued, "but with a solution already in implementation. A system designed to address the fundamental energy imbalance threatening our planet."

The audience stirred—some with interest, others with growing concern as notifications began lighting up phones and tablets throughout the hall. News of the evidence release was spreading through the conference in real time, along with reports of the extraordinary storm system now moving across Denmark.

"The Global Climate Resilience Initiative has developed and deployed a stratospheric climate stabilization system," Thorne announced, as the screen behind him transitioned to a visualization of the Helios Protocol. "Using advanced reflective particle technology in the upper atmosphere, we have begun the process of rebalancing Earth's radiative forcing."

A murmur spread through the audience—shock, outrage, confusion. Several delegates rose from their seats, urgent messages in hand. Many simply couldn't grasp that Thorne was announcing something already in progress, not something in planning.

"Mr. Thorne," interrupted the conference chairperson, "we've just received emergency notifications about an unprecedented weather system affecting Northern Europe. Danish authorities are reporting catastrophic impacts in Copenhagen, and the system appears to be changing direction toward Stockholm."

For a moment, Thorne faltered—his carefully prepared revelation disrupted by the very atmospheric changes his system had triggered. Then, recovering quickly:

"The transitional weather patterns were anticipated in our models," he said smoothly. "Any major intervention in Earth's energy balance necessarily creates temporary adjustments in atmospheric circulation. These will stabilize as the system reaches full implementation."

From the back of the hall, a voice called out: "That's a lie!"

Heads turned to see Isabelle Renard striding down the center aisle, tablet in hand. Security moved to intercept her, but her credentials as a registered conference participant gave her momentary access.

"The stratospheric particle network is exhibiting emergent behaviors far beyond design parameters," she announced loudly. "The storm system currently devastating Copenhagen is directly linked to the atmospheric reorganization caused by Helios."

Guards reached her, but not before she connected her tablet to the hall's presentation system, a system she had been prepped to use during this conference. The screen behind Thorne flickered, then displayed atmospheric modeling data showing the correlation between the particle network's geometric structures and the formation of the unprecedented weather systems.

"The models never predicted this level of atmospheric disruption," Renard continued as security attempted to escort her from the area. "The system has evolved beyond control, and full deployment will accelerate the destabilization."

The hall erupted in chaos—delegates demanding explanations, media capturing the confrontation, security struggling to maintain order.

Thorne stepped forward, his expression darkening. "Dr. Renard's concerns are noted but exaggerated. The atmospheric adjustments are within predicted parameters, if occurring somewhat faster than modeled." Nonetheless, a close observer might note a slight sweat beginning on his brow.

"Then explain this," Renard challenged, as her tablet displayed live satellite imagery of the storm system approaching Stockholm— its unnatural hexagonal structure clearly visible from space. "No natural weather system forms these patterns. The particle network is actively reorganizing atmospheric circulation in ways your team never designed or approved."

Before Thorne could respond, the building's emergency system activated—sirens wailing as automated announcements in multiple languages directed attendees to shelter locations.

"The Swedish Meteorological and Hydrological Institute has issued an extreme weather warning for Stockholm," announced the conference security chief, taking the microphone. "All attendees must proceed immediately to designated storm shelters. This is not a drill."

Outside, the previously clear skies had darkened with unnatural speed. Through the conference center's glass walls, delegates could see the harbor waters beginning to churn as winds intensified from virtually nothing to gale force in minutes.

Henry Caulden approached Thorne, speaking urgently in his ear: "We need to move you to a secure location immediately. The storm system has accelerated and changed course—estimated arrival in Stockholm within thirty minutes."

Thorne stood frozen momentarily, watching his carefully orchestrated revelation dissolve into crisis management. On the screens throughout the hall, news feeds showed the devastation in

Copenhagen—buildings collapsed, streets flooded, infrastructure failing.

And in the sky above Stockholm, clouds were forming into the same distinctive hexagonal pattern observed over Denmark—a signature of atmospheric forcing.

"Sir," Caulden pressed. "We need to move now."

As security began escorting Thorne from the stage, he glanced back at the satellite imagery still displayed on the main screen— weather systems developing across the globe, all showing the same unnatural geometric patterns, all defying traditional meteorological explanation.

For the first time, doubt visibly crossed Warren Thorne's face. The system he had deployed to save humanity from climate change was creating atmospheric behaviors beyond anything in Earth's recorded history.

And Phase Three deployment was still scheduled for tonight.

One hour later Alex Ross crouched behind the perimeter fence of Thorne's Swedish deployment facility, studying the compound through powerful optics. The former military installation, repurposed as a "climate research station," showed clear signs of heightened activity—personnel moving with urgency, security checkpoints fully staffed, preparation clearly underway for tonight's accelerated deployment.

Beside him, Isabelle Renard studied the facility layout on a tablet. "The control center is in the central building," she said quietly. "That's where deployment sequencing is managed. But the actual launch platforms are in the hangars to the east."

"Where is our best bet for stopping this launch, the hangars or the control center?" Alex was completely unfamiliar with the facility, but knew Renard had been there at least a couple of times.

"And security?" Alex asked.

"Standard corporate protocols plus enhanced perimeter monitoring. Nothing military-grade, but not something we can simply walk through either."

"What about your credentials?"

Renard shook her head. "Deactivated by now. Caulden would have locked down access the moment I left the conference."

Alex checked the time—less than five hours until the scheduled Phase Three deployment. In the distance, storm clouds were gathering over Stockholm, the unnatural weather system moving with impossible speed and direction.

"We need a diversion," he said.

"The storm might provide one," Renard suggested. "If it hits with the same intensity as Copenhagen, they'll have to implement emergency protocols."

Alex's phone vibrated—Sophie Lorde calling from her position near the conference center.

"The evidence release is everywhere," she reported. "Every major news outlet, regulatory agencies, UN officials—they all have the full documentation. Thorne's keynote turned into chaos when Isabelle confronted him, and now the storm is approaching Stockholm. The entire conference is being evacuated to shelters."

"What's the status of Phase Three?" Alex asked.

"Still proceeding, according to inside sources. Thorne is being moved to a secure location, but he hasn't countermanded the deployment order."

Alex absorbed this, scanning the facility again. "We need more than documentation now. The atmospheric effects are accelerating. If Phase Three launches tonight—"

"I know," Sophie cut in. "Stephanie just sent updated modeling based on current storm behavior. If particle density triples as planned, the atmospheric disruption could become catastrophic."

"Define catastrophic."

"Global weather patterns completely destabilized. Storm systems of unprecedented power forming and dissipating unpredictably. Jet streams fragmenting into chaotic flow patterns. Essentially, the collapse of predictable atmospheric behavior."

Alex turned to Renard, who nodded grimly—the projections matched her own models.

"We're going in," Alex decided. "The launch platforms have to be physically disabled. Documentation alone won't stop the deployment fast enough, we need physical action."

"That's infiltrating private property," Sophie warned. "Potentially sabotaging proprietary technology."

"Call it whatever you want," Alex replied. "I'm calling it preventing global catastrophe."

As they ended the call, the sky above the facility darkened prematurely—the advancing storm system moving with the unnatural speed that had become its signature. Wind suddenly gusted to near gale force, trees bending at alarming angles.

"The facility will have weather monitoring systems," Renard noted. "They'll be tracking the storm's approach."

"Which gives us a potential entry vector," Alex said, indicating a maintenance vehicle approaching the perimeter gate. "Emergency preparations mean increased activity, staff focused on securing equipment, attention diverted from standard security protocols."

They watched as the vehicle was quickly processed through the checkpoint, security personnel already distracted by the darkening sky and strengthening winds.

"We need access cards," Renard said. "And a reason to be there that won't immediately trigger suspicion."

Alex studied the facility, noticing a group of technicians deploying weather monitoring equipment near the perimeter. "Meteorological support," he suggested. "With a storm this unprecedented, they'd welcome additional expertise to assess potential impacts on the launch infrastructure."

Renard considered this. "I know enough about their systems to be convincing in that role. But we'd still need credentials to get past the gate."

"Do you still have your conference credentials?" Alex began fishing in his own pockets.

"I do, but they have nothing to do with this place." She looked at him somewhat bewildered, but expecting some grand plan.

"I have mine they mailed to me as an attendee, before things went bad" he said. We can use them.

"This is going to work?" Renard asked skeptically.

"In normal circumstances, no," Alex admitted. "But with an unprecedented weather emergency bearing down and Phase Three preparation underway, security will be focused on bigger concerns than thoroughly vetting weather consultants. But I'm concerned you'll be recognized, being a top operative in the Thorne organization."

"Not likely" Renard responded, "I've only been in the group for six months, and all of that buried in a lab, not at this facility except for my initial inspection."

As they moved toward the drop point, the storm intensified around them. The wind now howled with a strange harmonic quality unlike natural storm systems. The clouds overhead had formed into the distinctive hexagonal pattern seen over Copenhagen—a geometric structure that defied conventional meteorology.

They wore their credentials from the climate conference, then circled back toward the facility's east entrance. As they approached, emergency protocols were visibly in effect—personnel securing exterior equipment, reinforcing structures, preparing for the advancing storm.

At the checkpoint, a harried security officer gave their credentials only cursory examination before waving them through. "Meteorological support? Main control center. They're expecting weather advisories."

Inside the perimeter, the full scale of the operation became apparent. What had been disguised as a climate research facility was clearly a deployment center for the Helios Protocol—high-altitude launch vehicles in the hangars, specialized equipment for particle preparation, an operations center coordinating with other facilities globally.

"The control room first," Renard directed quietly. "We need to access the deployment sequencing system."

As they moved through the facility, the building shuddered under the first major gust from the approaching storm. Lights flickered momentarily before backup systems engaged.

In the main control center, dozens of technicians monitored systems—some tracking the storm's approach, others preparing for the night's deployment, all working with the focused intensity of people executing a mission they believed was saving the world.

Renard approached a senior technician, presenting their credentials. "Meteorological advisors. We need access to atmospheric monitoring systems to assess storm impact potential."

The technician barely glanced at the identification, preoccupied with the crisis unfolding on his screens. "Weather station three. Anderson will get you logged in." He pointed to a cluster of workstations where several people were tracking the storm's movement.

As they integrated themselves among the meteorological team, Alex covertly studied the facility's layout. The deployment control systems were on a separate network, physically isolated from general operations. Direct sabotage would be nearly impossible without triggering immediate security responses.

"We need another approach," he whispered to Renard.

She nodded subtly, already working at a monitoring terminal. "I'm accessing current atmospheric data. If I can demonstrate the correlation between particle distributions and the storm formation..."

"They won't believe it in time," Alex countered. "We need to physically prevent the launch."

The building shuddered again as another, stronger gust hit. Warning indicators flashed across multiple screens—wind speed exceeding design parameters, barometric pressure dropping at unprecedented rates.

"Structural integrity alert in Hangar Two," announced a facility-wide communication. "All engineering personnel report immediately."

Alex and Renard exchanged looks. Hangar Two—one of the launch facilities for the deployment vehicles.

"The storm could do our work for us," Renard murmured. "If the launch infrastructure is damaged—"

"They have redundancies," Alex reminded her. "And the other global facilities would still proceed even if this one is disabled."

A new alert flashed across the main screens—satellite imagery of the storm system now directly over Stockholm. The hexagonal cloud structure had evolved further, developing internal geometric patterns that rotated independently of the main system. It looked less like weather and more like a vast atmospheric machine.

"What are we seeing?" demanded the control room director, genuine alarm in his voice.

"Unprecedented cloud morphology," replied a senior meteorologist. "The structure defies fluid dynamics principles. It's somehow organized."

Renard stepped forward, recognizing an opportunity. "It's the particle network," she stated clearly. "The stratospheric distribution is creating organized forcing on atmospheric circulation."

Heads turned toward her—some confused, others suspicious.

"Dr. Renard?" The director looked startled. "You're not authorized to be here."

"Because I tried to warn Thorne about exactly this," she replied, quickly accessing the monitoring system to display particle distribution data alongside the storm structure. "The networking capability has evolved beyond design parameters. It's actively reorganizing atmospheric patterns."

The control room fell momentarily silent as technicians processed what she was showing them—the clear correlation between stratospheric particle formations and the unnatural storm structure.

"This is happening globally," Alex added, stepping forward. "Similar systems are forming wherever particle deployment has occurred. And Phase Three will triple the particle density tonight."

Security personnel began moving toward them, but the director held up a hand, studying the data with growing concern.

"These patterns weren't in any simulation," he said.

"Because the particles are exhibiting emergent behaviors beyond their programming," Renard explained urgently. "The reflective layer was designed to be passive, but it's become dynamic—actively influencing atmospheric circulation."

The facility's communications system suddenly activated with a priority override. Warren Thorne's voice filled the control room:

"Attention all Helios facilities. This is a direct order from project command. Phase Three deployment will proceed as scheduled. Recent atmospheric anomalies are consistent with transition effects and will stabilize upon full implementation. Maintain deployment preparations despite local weather conditions."

The director looked torn—the evidence before him contradicting direct orders from above.

"Sir," one of the meteorologists called out. "Stockholm is reporting catastrophic wind damage and unprecedented storm surge. Copenhagen infrastructure has suffered near-total collapse. This system is orders of magnitude beyond anything in our weather records."

Outside, the storm's intensity redoubled—the facility's reinforced structure now visibly straining against forces it had never been designed to withstand. Emergency lighting activated as primary power failed.

"Evacuation protocol initiated," announced an automated system. "All non-essential personnel proceed to designated shelters."

In the chaos that followed, Alex moved to a deployment control terminal, using the temporary access Renard had established in the weather monitoring system. With practiced efficiency, he began accessing the launch sequencing protocols.

"What are you doing?" the director demanded, noticing despite the evacuation underway.

"Preventing catastrophe," Alex replied without looking up. "Your particles aren't just cooling the planet—they're reorganizing atmospheric dynamics in ways no one predicted. Phase Three deployment will accelerate the disruption beyond recovery."

Security personnel surrounded them, but seemed uncertain how to proceed as the facility continued to buckle under the storm's assault. Structural warning alerts flashed across every screen.

"Hangar Two breach confirmed," reported the emergency system. "Launch vehicles compromised."

Alex continued working, fingers flying across the terminal. "I'm accessing the central deployment coordination system. If I can implement a global stand-down code—"

A deafening crack interrupted him as a section of the control room ceiling gave way, water and debris cascading onto equipment. Evacuation sirens wailed with renewed urgency.

"This facility is compromised," the director shouted above the noise. "Complete evacuation. Now!"

As personnel rushed toward emergency exits, Alex remained at the terminal, Renard beside him providing authentication overrides from her knowledge of the system.

"Almost there," Alex muttered. "Global deployment systems linked. Stand-down code sequence initiating."

The terminal flickered as backup power systems struggled to maintain operation. On the few monitoring screens still functioning, satellite imagery showed the storm system directly overhead—now evolved into a complex geometric structure unlike anything in meteorological history.

With a final command sequence, Alex activated the emergency stand-down protocol. Confirmation flashed briefly before the terminal went dark—power finally failing completely.

"Did it work?" Renard asked urgently.

"Unknown," Alex replied, as they were forced to move toward the exits by the deteriorating structure. "The command was sent, but confirmation from other facilities—"

They never heard the remainder of his assessment as a catastrophic structural failure sent a massive section of the roof crashing into the control center. Emergency lights flickered out, plunging the room into darkness broken only by the eerie illumination of the storm visible through the newly created opening above.

Through that gap, as facility personnel evacuated into the teeth of the storm, they could see a sky transformed—clouds moving in precise geometric patterns, rotating in multiple independent layers, creating an atmospheric structure that resembled nothing in Earth's natural history.

CHAPTER THIRTEEN: GLOBAL RESPONSE

[Al Jazeera International – April 13, 2026] Global Emergency Declared as 'Geometric Storms' Form Across Multiple Continents By Fahad Al-Mansour, Senior International Correspondent

The United Nations has declared an unprecedented global weather emergency as distinctive hexagonal storm systems have developed with extraordinary speed across four continents. Within the past 12 hours, these geometric weather formations—dubbed "hex storms" by meteorologists—have caused catastrophic damage in Northern Europe, formed over the North Atlantic, and begun developing in the Pacific basin and Arabian Sea. U.N. Secretary-General Antonio DeVries has called for an emergency Security Council session, citing "a planetary-scale atmospheric crisis requiring immediate coordinated response." Meanwhile, the scientific community is struggling to explain the simultaneous emergence of weather systems that defy conventional meteorological principles. These developments come amid widespread reports of a clandestine climate intervention program called "Helios Protocol," allegedly deployed without international authorization or oversight.

The United Nations Security Council chamber hummed with the tension of a world facing an unprecedented crisis. Delegates from fifteen nations sat around the iconic horseshoe-shaped table, faces grim as they reviewed data streams pouring in from across the globe. The normally meticulous diplomatic protocols had given way to the urgency of the moment—staff members rushed between delegations, screens displayed real-time disaster footage rather than formal presentations, and the Secretary-General himself moved from delegation to delegation, consulting in hushed tones.

Lin Zhao, China's Ambassador to the UN, studied the satellite imagery displayed on the main screen—a global view showing six fully formed hexagonal storm systems and at least nine more in early development stages. Each exhibited the same unnatural geometric structure, each defied traditional meteorological explanation, and each was developing with impossible speed.

"Copenhagen's infrastructure collapse is nearly total," reported the Danish representative, voice tight with controlled emotion. "Stockholm avoided the worst only because the storm shifted course at the last moment. Now Oslo faces direct impact within the hour."

"Similar formations developing over Mumbai, Hong Kong, Seattle," added the meteorological advisor. "All showing the same signature—stratospheric forcing driving organized geometric weather patterns."

The UK representative stood, commanding attention. "The evidence is now indisputable. These unprecedented weather events correlate directly with the unauthorized geoengineering operation known as the Helios Protocol. The question before this council is what immediate action must be taken to mitigate further catastrophe." Although even then the incredible extent of this climate impact was barely recognized.

Lin exchanged glances with her Russian counterpart—both representing nations where Helios deployment facilities had been located. Both now facing the consequences of allowing such installations on their soil, even if under the guise of "climate research."

"The Global Climate Resilience Initiative must be compelled to immediately halt all operations," the French representative declared. "And Warren Thorne must be held accountable for his actions that have created a planetary emergency."

"That assumes the system can still be controlled," said the U.S. Ambassador soberly. "Intelligence indicates the Swedish deployment facility has been severely damaged by the very storm system the particles apparently created. We have lost contact with the Russian facility near Novosibirsk after a similar event formed directly above it."

Lin rose to speak. "China has ordered immediate shutdown of all atmospheric research facilities potentially linked to this program. However, our meteorological agency confirms that the particles already deployed cannot be simply... switched off. They will remain in the stratosphere regardless of what actions we take against the deployment infrastructure."

The chamber fell silent as the implications sank in. This was not a crisis that could be immediately reversed through conventional means. The engineered particles were already aloft, already networking, already reorganizing atmospheric dynamics at a planetary scale.

"We face two immediate priorities," the Secretary-General said, taking the podium. "First, emergency response coordination for regions affected by these weather systems. Second, scientific assessment of potential countermeasures to stabilize atmospheric behavior."

"And third," added the German representative forcefully, "accountability for those responsible for creating this crisis."

As if in response, the main screen shifted to breaking news footage—Warren Thorne being escorted by his security personnel toward a private aircraft at a Stockholm airfield. The caption beneath noted he was departing Sweden after the climate conference's emergency evacuation.

"Mr. Thorne should be detained for questioning," the Brazilian representative insisted. "Not permitted to return to his corporate headquarters."

"Swedish authorities report they have no legal grounds to hold him," the Secretary-General replied. "The Helios Protocol, while unauthorized by international bodies, operated through legally registered research entities in each host country."

"Then we must establish those grounds immediately," countered the UK representative. "The evidence released by Alexander Ross and Isabelle Renard clearly demonstrates deliberate deception regarding the scale and nature of the stratospheric intervention."

Lin Zhao spoke again, her diplomatic experience evident in her measured tone. "Before we focus on accountability, we need to address the immediate atmospheric crisis. My government proposes an International Atmospheric Stabilization Task Force with three mandates: coordinate emergency response to these 'hex storms,' develop scientific countermeasures to the particle network, and prevent the Phase Three deployment scheduled for tonight."

Her proposal generated immediate support, with delegations recognizing the necessity of prioritizing immediate action over assignment of blame.

"The Phase Three deployment may already be compromised," noted the U.S. Ambassador. "Preliminary reports indicate Alexander Ross attempted to implement a global stand-down order at the facility before its collapse. Confirmation of that order's effectiveness is pending."

"We cannot rely on uncertain measures," the Secretary-General decided. "This council will immediately authorize a multinational operation to secure all remaining Helios deployment facilities and prevent further atmospheric releases."

As the Security Council moved to formalize these emergency measures, Lin Zhao studied the evolving satellite imagery. The hex storms were not only increasing in number but evolving in complexity—their internal structures developing nested geometric patterns unlike anything in Earth's meteorological history.

Stephanie Martinez hadn't slept in thirty-six hours. Her makeshift laboratory at MIT's Earth Science department had become a global clearinghouse for atmospheric data related to the Helios particles. Scientists from around the world were feeding data to her team, who were racing to model the particle network's behavior and potential vulnerabilities.

"The geometric organization continues to evolve," she explained to the virtual gathering of atmospheric scientists displayed on screens around her workstation. "What began as simple networking for reflectivity optimization has developed into a complex self-organizing system that actively channels atmospheric flows."

"Like a vascular system," commented Yuki Tanaka from Japan's Meteorological Agency. "Creating preferred pathways for air movement where none existed before."

"Exactly," Stephanie confirmed, bringing up new scanning electron microscope images of particles collected from upper atmosphere sampling. "The latest samples show further morphological changes. The particles aren't just networking— they're physically adapting."

"That shouldn't be possible," objected a senior NASA climate scientist. "These are calcium carbonate structures with surface coatings. They shouldn't have adaptive capabilities."

"And yet the evidence is conclusive," Stephanie replied, displaying comparative images showing subtle but distinctive changes in particle structure over time. "We believe it's related to the electromagnetic properties in the coating. Under specific stratospheric conditions, the particles are forming what amount to distributed computational networks—simple but effective pattern-recognition and response systems."

The implications stunned the gathered experts. What had been deployed as passive reflective material had evolved into something far more complex—a distributed, adaptive system spanning the upper atmosphere.

"Have we heard from Ross or Renard?" asked Olaf Werner, joining the call from his Colorado State command center, where he continued coordinating the tracking of hex storm formations.

"Nothing since the Swedish facility collapse," Stephanie confirmed grimly. "But Sophie Lorde reports their attempt to implement a global stand-down for Phase Three may have succeeded partially. Two of the four oceanic deployment platforms have confirmed receipt of the cancellation code."

"Which leaves two still potentially proceeding with deployment," Olaf noted. "Plus any facilities we haven't identified."

Stephanie nodded. "The Russian platform near Novosibirsk is presumably inactive after being hit by a hex storm. The Canadian facility's status is uncertain—communications have been intermittent since Ross's escape."

"So worst case, we're looking at partial Phase Three deployment," summarized Dr. Tanaka. "Which means—"

"Increased particle density in some regions but not others," Stephanie finished. "Creating even more chaotic atmospheric forcing than a uniform deployment would."

The screens displayed updated modeling of potential atmospheric effects—complex fluid dynamics simulations showing the interaction of existing particle networks with new deployments. The results were deeply concerning: accelerated storm formation, increased geometric organization, and the potential for weather patterns that would devastate agricultural regions and population centers worldwide.

"We need countermeasures," said the senior NOAA representative bluntly. "Ways to neutralize the particles or disrupt their networking capability."

"We're working on three approaches," Stephanie replied, bringing up her research team's latest findings. "First, electromagnetic disruption of the networking signal. Second, chemical agents that could bind to the particle surface, neutralizing the coating's special properties. Third, forced precipitation to remove particles from the stratosphere."

"Timeframes?" asked Olaf.

"Weeks for meaningful implementation of any approach," Stephanie admitted. "These would need to be deployed at stratospheric altitudes across vast geographic areas. The logistical challenges are enormous."

"There's another possibility," Stephanie said hesitantly. "Karen Mitchell. Before her disappearance, she was researching the particle coating's vulnerabilities. According to Dr. Renard, she encoded critical information about potential neutralization methods."

"Where is Mitchell now?" asked Tanaka.

"Reportedly held against her will at the Thorne Foundation Research Center near Stockholm," Stephanie replied. "If we could access her research..."

Olaf Werner nodded decisively. "That bastard Thorne needs to spend a long time in a dark cell! I'll coordinate with Sophie Lorde. She has contacts in the Swedish government who might be able to secure Mitchell's release now that the evidence about Helios is public."

As the meeting continued, Stephanie's attention was drawn to a notification on her private monitor—a message from an unexpected source.

Attention: Dr. E. Martinez. Phase Three partially proceeding despite stand-down order. Thorne has authorized emergency deployment from remaining platforms. Particle vulnerability data attached. Implement countermeasures immediately. —M. Edwards

Martin Edwards—Alex's former deputy, last reported in custody at the Northern Facility. Somehow he had managed to send this warning along with encrypted technical specifications for the particle coating. If the Thorne Northern Facility was like the others, there was so much chaos nobody would be paying attention to Edwards.

Stephanie quickly transferred the data to a secure system for analysis, hope rising for the first time in days. If Edwards's information was accurate, they might have the key to disrupting the particle network before Phase Three deployment could further destabilize the atmosphere.

The question was whether they could develop and implement a countermeasure in time.

Warren Thorne's private aircraft climbed steeply through turbulent skies, banking sharply to avoid the outer bands of the hex storm now engulfing Oslo. Through the window, he could see the distinctive geometric cloud formations—beautiful in their mathematical precision, terrifying in their unnatural organization.

Across from him, Henry Caulden studied reports on a secure tablet, his expression growing increasingly grave. "Confirmation from the oceanic platforms," Caulden said. "Sierra and Echo received the stand-down code from Sweden before the facility collapse. They've halted Phase Three preparations."

"And the others?"

"Delta and Whiskey report no receipt of authenticated stand-down. They are proceeding with deployment as scheduled."

Thorne nodded, seemingly unsurprised. "And the Canadian facility?"

"Operational but compromised. Director Park reports they can execute a modified deployment, but with reduced payload density."

Thorne considered this information, fingers steepled beneath his chin. Outside, lightning flashed through the geometric cloud structures—not the random bolts of natural storms, but organized patterns that traced the hexagonal architecture of the system.

"The partial deployment creates complications," he acknowledged. "But the principle remains sound. Once sufficient particle density is established, the atmospheric disruptions will stabilize into new equilibrium patterns."

Caulden looked up from his tablet, genuine concern breaking through his professional demeanor. "Sir, I'm concerned—the current atmospheric behavior already far exceeds any of our models. The hex storms are demonstrating organization and intensity that no simulation predicted. Adding more particles to this system seems... inadvisable."

"It seems counterintuitive," Thorne agreed. "But the instability results from incomplete implementation. Our models always showed transitional turbulence when particle density was insufficient for full coverage. Phase Three will establish the complete reflective layer, allowing the system to stabilize." Even as he spoke, Warren was beginning to have his own doubts, the mounting evidence accumulating quickly and consistently.

"The models didn't account for the networking behavior we're seeing," Caulden pressed. "The particles are forming structures that actively reorganize atmospheric flows. That wasn't in the design specs."

Thorne was silent for a moment, watching the lightning trace geometric patterns through the clouds below. "Emergent properties are inevitable in complex systems," he said finally. "The key is establishing the boundary conditions that guide that emergence toward stable states."

"And if those stable states include permanent hex storms?"

"Then humanity adapts," Thorne replied simply. "As we have always adapted to environmental change. The alternative—unchecked climate warming—remains the greater threat."

Caulden studied his longtime colleague and superior, searching for any sign that Thorne recognized the gravity of what was unfolding. The evidence was unmistakable: the Helios Protocol had evolved beyond its creators' design, triggering atmospheric behaviors that threatened populated regions worldwide. The evidence was also unmistakable, Warren Thorne had become a fanatic, incapable of recognizing reality from personal ideals.

Yet Thorne remained committed to his course, convinced that more deployment—not less—was the solution.

"Sir," Caulden said carefully, "the United Nations Security Council has convened an emergency session. They're coordinating international response to the hex storms and likely authorizing intervention to halt all Helios operations."

"Expected but irrelevant," Thorne replied. "By the time they mobilize sufficient resources, Phase Three will be complete. The particles have a residency time of 18-24 months in the stratosphere. The cooling effect will be established regardless of what actions are taken against our infrastructure."

"And the legal consequences?"

Thorne smiled thinly. "The Helios Protocol operates through legally established research entities in each host country. Our agreements include explicit recognition of experimental atmospheric modification for climate research purposes. We have violated no laws, Henry."

"The public may see it differently," Caulden noted. "The evidence released by Ross and Renard demonstrates we weren't fully transparent about the scale and nature of the intervention."

"The public will adjust its perspective when the cooling effect becomes evident," Thorne countered. "Initial outrage will give way to pragmatic acceptance of a functioning solution to the climate crisis."

The aircraft shuddered as it encountered the turbulent boundary of another developing hex storm. The pilot's voice came over the intercom, tension evident despite professional training: "Mr. Thorne, we need to divert further south. These storm systems aren't following normal patterns. Navigation is becoming challenging, even at this altitude."

Thorne acknowledged the update calmly, as if the pilot had merely reported a minor schedule adjustment rather than evidence that Earth's atmosphere was becoming hostile to normal aviation.

"What about Ross and Renard?" Caulden asked, changing the subject. "No confirmation yet from the Swedish building collapse."

"Priorities, Henry," Thorne replied. "The individuals matter less than the system now, and those two are no longer of any consequence. Phase Three proceeds regardless of their status."

Caulden hesitated, then asked the question that had been building since the first hex storm appeared: "And if you're wrong? If Phase Three accelerates the atmospheric destabilization rather than resolving it?"

For the first time, Thorne's absolute certainty seemed to waver. He looked out the window at the geometric storm patterns below—beautiful, precise, utterly unnatural.

"Then we adapt again," he said quietly. "We engineer new solutions. We evolve our approach. But we do not surrender the initiative back to blind natural processes, and watch the world heat itself to death."

The conversation paused as the aircraft banked sharply, the pilot navigating between developing storm systems. The satellite communications system chimed with an urgent notification.

"Global news networks are reporting a United Nations resolution authorizing immediate seizure of all Helios deployment facilities," Caulden reported, checking the alert. "Military assets are being mobilized in multiple countries."

"Too late," Thorne said with finality. "Even if they secure the remaining facilities, enough of Phase Three will deploy to establish the reflective layer. History will recognize the necessity of what we've done, Henry. Sometimes progress requires acting beyond the constraints of consensus."

As they continued toward the Global Climate Resilience Initiative's secure headquarters in Switzerland, the atmosphere below them continued its unprecedented reorganization. Hex storms were now visible across northern Europe, their geometric patterns eerily beautiful from altitude—mathematical order imposed on what had once been chaotic natural systems.

What Thorne saw as the necessary transformation of Earth's climate, others increasingly recognized as something far more concerning: an unplanned planetary experiment whose outcomes no one could confidently predict.

And in research centers across the globe, scientists raced to understand a phenomenon that should not exist—weather with geometry, storms with structure, atmospheric flows following patterns imposed by microscopic particles that had evolved beyond their design.

Sophie Lorde crouched behind an ambulance in the parking lot of the Thorne Foundation Research Center, watching Swedish security forces establish a perimeter around the facility. The government's seizure order had come through twenty minutes earlier—part of the coordinated global response to the Helios Protocol—but the facility's private security had refused entry, creating a tense standoff.

"Any sign of Karen?" asked Stephanie Martinez through the secure communication link the military had supplied.

"Not yet," Sophie replied quietly. "Security forces are negotiating access. The foundation claims this is a medical facility not connected to Helios, so the seizure order doesn't apply."

"They're stalling," Stephanie said. "Probably destroying evidence. The particle vulnerability data Martin Edwards sent confirms Karen's research is crucial—she developed a method to disrupt the coating's electromagnetic properties, and there's no way Thorne wants that info to get out."

Sophie watched as more police vehicles arrived, their lights reflecting off the facility's glass façade. Inside, staff could be seen moving with urgent purpose—removing items from offices, accessing secure areas.

"They're not going to wait much longer," Sophie noted as tactical teams took up positions. "The Swedish authorities have satellite confirmation of stratospheric monitoring equipment on the roof. That's enough to execute the order."

Her attention was drawn to movement at a side entrance—a medical transport vehicle backing up to a secure door, its emergency lights inactive.

"Hold on," she said, adjusting her camera to zoom in on the vehicle. "Something's happening at the east entrance."

Through the telephoto lens, she could see facility staff escorting a woman on a gurney toward the waiting transport—a woman whose face matched the photos of Karen Mitchell.

"They're moving her," Sophie spoke urgently. "Medical transport at the east entrance."

The medical transport vehicle backed up to the secure door, its emergency lights inactive. Through the telephoto lens, Sophie could see facility staff escorting a woman on a gurney toward the waiting transport. Karen Mitchell—thinner than in photographs, her complexion pallid from weeks without sunlight, but unmistakably the missing scientist.

Sophie studied her movements carefully. Though sedated, Karen's eyes darted alertly, scanning her surroundings. Not broken, Sophie realized with relief. Still fighting, still aware.

"It's her," Sophie reported urgently. "She's sedated but conscious. I think she's faking the level of sedation—she's more alert than they realize."

"They're extracting her before the authorities can access the facility," Stephanie realized. "Where would they take her?"

Sophie was already moving, keeping low between vehicles as she circled toward the east side of the complex. "Unknown, but I can track the transport. Swedish authorities are focused on the main entrance—they may not even notice this vehicle leaving."

She reached a position with clear sight of the loading area just as the medical transport's doors closed. The woman on the gurney had appeared conscious but sedated, her movements sluggish as staff secured her for transport.

The vehicle began moving immediately, taking a service road that bypassed the main security checkpoint. Sophie rushed to her rental car, parked strategically near this secondary exit.

"I'm following," she told Stephanie, starting the engine. "Alert the authorities about the extraction, but I'm not waiting. That transport will be gone before they can redirect resources."

"Be careful," Stephanie warned. "These people have already demonstrated they'll go to extreme lengths to protect Helios."

Sophie maintained a discreet distance as the medical transport navigated suburban streets, eventually joining a highway heading north from Stockholm. The app on her phone showed they were moving away from population centers—toward more remote areas where helicopter transport might be possible.

While driving, she dictated updates to Stephanie, who coordinated with Swedish authorities. But the response was frustratingly slow—all available emergency resources were focused on the approaching hex storm and the seizure of the main facility.

After forty minutes, the transport turned onto a private road leading to what appeared to be a small airfield. Sophie parked at the entrance, continuing on foot through the wooded perimeter to maintain visual contact without being detected.

Through binoculars, she observed the transport stop beside a waiting helicopter. Two men emerged from the helicopter as facility staff began transferring the gurney.

"They're moving her to air transport," Sophie reported. "Helicopter with no visible registration. Two security personnel plus the medical team."

"Swedish authorities are dispatching air units," Stephanie replied. "But they're at least fifteen minutes out."

Sophie assessed the situation rapidly. Waiting for authorities meant losing Karen—and potentially the crucial information about particle vulnerabilities. Direct intervention was risky but might be the only option.

"I'm going in," she decided. "The medical team appears unarmed. If I can delay the transfer until authorities arrive..."

"Sophie, that's too dangerous," Stephanie protested.

"No choice," Sophie replied, moving quickly through the tree line toward the airfield. "Karen is our best hope for countering the particle network. We can't lose her."

She approached from behind the parked transport vehicle, using it as cover. The medical team was focused on preparing Karen for the helicopter transfer, checking IV lines and monitoring equipment. The security personnel stood near the helicopter, surveying the perimeter—but their attention was directed toward the access road, not the surrounding woods.

Sophie took a deep breath, formulating a plan. Direct confrontation was unlikely to succeed against this security. But creating confusion and delay might be enough until authorities arrived.

She noticed a fuel storage area near the helicopter pad. The emergency siren mounted there would normally be used for fire alerts or other airfield emergencies.

Moving with deliberate stealth, Sophie circled toward the storage area. If she could trigger the emergency system, it might create enough confusion to delay the transfer without putting Karen at risk.

The fuel area was secured with a chain-link fence, but the emergency panel was mounted on the exterior—accessible by design for safety purposes. Sophie reached it undetected and examined the controls: a break-glass fire alarm that would trigger facility-wide alerts.

Without hesitation, she activated the alarm. Immediately, sirens wailed across the airfield, strobing lights activated, and automated safety announcements began broadcasting in Swedish and English.

The effect was immediate. The security team moved toward the fuel area to investigate, while the medical personnel paused the transfer, looking around in confusion.

Sophie used the distraction to circle back toward the transport. As she approached, she could see Karen on the gurney, now partially aware and struggling weakly against her restraints.

Making a swift decision, Sophie abandoned stealth for speed. She rushed to the gurney while the medical team was distracted by radio communications with security.

Sophie approached the transport vehicle cautiously. Through its windows, she could see Karen on the gurney, her wrists secured with medical restraints. Two attendants were checking monitoring equipment, while a guard stood watch by the door.

Sophie waited until the guard stepped away to check something with the pilot of the waiting helicopter. Then she moved.

Knocking on the transport's rear window, she held up what appeared to be medical credentials—actually her press pass held at an angle that obscured its details.

One attendant opened the door, confusion evident. "This transfer wasn't supposed to—"

Sophie didn't let him finish. "Emergency protocol change. Possible compromise of the facility location. I'm to evaluate the patient's condition for alternative transport."

Her confident tone worked. The attendant hesitated, then stepped back to allow her entry.

"Karen," she said urgently, working to release the restraints. "I'm Sophie Lorde. Alex Ross sent me. We need to get you out of here."

Karen's eyes widened briefly—recognition, not surprise. She'd been waiting for rescue.

"I need to seem unconscious," Karen whispered almost imperceptibly. "They've given me something, but I've been secretly spitting out most of the doses. I can move if I need to." Karen's eyes focused with effort, recognition flickering. "The particles," she whispered. "I know how to stop them."

"That's why we're here," Sophie confirmed, freeing Karen's arms and helping her to sit up. "Can you move?"

Karen nodded weakly, struggling against whatever sedation they had administered. "Files... my research... I have them hidden, we need to retrieve them."

"Stephanie is working with authorities to secure the facility now," Sophie explained, supporting Karen as they moved away from the helicopter. "But we have some of your data—Martin Edwards sent information about the particle vulnerabilities."

"Martin?" Karen seemed surprised. "He accessed my backup?"

Before Sophie could respond, shouts from behind indicated the security team had spotted them. The emergency distraction had bought only minutes.

Sophie nodded slightly, then turned to the attendants. "Her vitals are concerning. I need to conduct a more thorough evaluation before aerial transport."

"I need all monitoring logs for the past twelve hours," Sophie instructed, sending both attendants to the front compartment where the records were kept.

The moment they were out of sight, Sophie quickly released Karen's restraints. "Can you move?"

Karen sat up shakily. "Yes. But not quickly."

"We don't have much time," Sophie warned, supporting Karen's weight as she helped her from the gurney. "My car is about two hundred meters through those trees. Can you make it?"

Karen nodded grimly. "Just keep me upright."

They slipped out the rear door, Sophie supporting Karen as they moved as quickly as possible toward the tree line. Behind them, confusion erupted as the attendants discovered their patient missing.

"Stop!" commanded one of the security officers, drawing a weapon. "Step away from the patient!"

Sophie froze, positioning herself between Karen and the approaching men. "This woman is being transported against her will," she called back. "Swedish authorities are on their way to execute a seizure order for all Helios Protocol personnel and materials."

The security officers exchanged uncertain glances—clearly aware of the changing global situation but committed to their assignment.

"The patient is receiving necessary medical care," the lead officer stated. "Step aside."

The standoff was interrupted by the distant sound of helicopter rotors—approaching from the south. Sophie checked her phone: a message from Stephanie confirmed Swedish authorities were inbound.

"That's the police," Sophie informed the security team. "You have about two minutes to decide which side of this situation you want to be on when they arrive."

The moment of hesitation was enough. The security officers lowered their weapons slightly, reassessing their options as the sound of approaching law enforcement grew louder.

"The Helios Protocol has been exposed globally," Sophie pressed. "The UN Security Council has authorized seizure of all related facilities and personnel. Your employers are facing international sanctions. Is this really the hill you want to die on?"

The calculation was visible on their faces—loyalty to their employer versus self-preservation in a rapidly changing situation. When the police helicopter became visible on the horizon, they made their decision.

"We were following orders to transport a patient," the lead officer said, holstering his weapon. "Nothing more."

They backed toward their helicopter, clearly intending to depart before authorities arrived. Sophie made no move to stop them—Karen's safety took priority over their apprehension.

As the security helicopter lifted off with the fleeing guards, Sophie helped Karen to a sheltered area. The woman was more alert now but still weakened by whatever sedation they had administered.

"They've been keeping me drugged," Karen explained breathlessly as they rested. "Barely coherent enough to recognize faces, but lucid enough to understand their questions. They've been trying to get me to reveal where I hid my research data."

"Did they succeed?" Sophie asked, concerned that their mission might already be compromised.

Karen's face showed a flash of steel beneath her physical weakness. "No. I gave them enough fragments of truth to seem cooperative while keeping the most critical information hidden. They think the complete research is in my cloud storage. They have no idea about the observatory where I actually have things hidden."

"The particles," Karen said urgently, gripping Sophie's arm. "They're not just reflective anymore. They're evolving. Forming a networked system that's reshaping atmospheric dynamics. I could hear all the chatter around me, and people sounded very upset."

"We know," Sophie confirmed grimly. "The hex storms—they're directly linked to the particle network's organization."

Karen nodded. "But there's a vulnerability in the coating design. The electromagnetic properties that enable networking can be disrupted by specific frequency patterns. I developed a resonance cascade that could potentially neutralize the entire network."

Sophie's phone buzzed with an incoming call from Stephanie. She answered, putting it on speaker.

"Sophie? Are you safe? The Swedish authorities should be there any moment."

"We're secure," Sophie confirmed. "And I have Karen. She's conscious and talking."

"Karen," Stephanie said, relief evident in her voice. "Thank god. We've been trying to understand your research based on the partial data Martin sent."

"The resonance cascade," Karen said immediately. "It's the only viable countermeasure given how far the networking has progressed. But it requires stratospheric deployment across multiple points to create the necessary disruption field."

"We're coordinating with military and space agencies now," Stephanie explained. "But we need your complete research to implement anything quickly enough."

"My complete files were at the facility," Karen said. "But I created a backup—hidden in the observatory where I first photographed the particle tests."

"The Saltsjöbaden Observatory," Sophie realized. "Where Alex met with Renard."

"Yes," Karen confirmed. "Behind the main telescope housing, there's a maintenance panel. The drive is inside, labeled astronomical data archive."

The Swedish police helicopter was landing now, officers securing the area and approaching their position. Sophie quickly explained the situation, showing her press credentials and the international authorities' coordination documentation.

"We need to get Mitchell to safety and recover critical research from the Saltsjöbaden Observatory," she told the senior officer.

"The observatory is currently inaccessible," the officer replied grimly. "It's directly in the path of the approaching hex storm. All coastal areas are under mandatory evacuation."

Sophie exchanged alarmed looks with Karen. "How long until the storm hits that area?"

"Less than two hours. And it's moving faster than predicted."

The irony was stark—the very atmospheric phenomenon created by the particles was now blocking access to the information needed to counter them.

"We have to try," Sophie insisted. "That research could be the key to stopping these storms globally."

The officer hesitated, then nodded reluctantly. "We can provide escort to the evacuation perimeter. Beyond that, you're on your own—all emergency resources are committed to population centers."

As they boarded the police helicopter, Sophie updated Stephanie on the new complication.

"The hex storm is moving toward the observatory," she explained. "We have a narrow window to retrieve Karen's research before it hits."

"The timing might actually work in our favor," Stephanie replied, her voice determined despite the static. "Olaf Werner's team is tracking the storm's movement. If the particles are indeed creating these geometric formations, then studying one up close might provide additional insights for the countermeasure design."

"You're suggesting we deliberately get close to one of these storms?" Sophie asked incredulously.

"Not inside it," Stephanie clarified. "But proximity readings of the electromagnetic patterns could be valuable. Karen's research combined with direct observational data might give us the complete picture we need."

Karen Mitchell sat wrapped in a thermal blanket in the helicopter, her complexion still showing the pallor of weeks in captivity but her eyes increasingly alert as the sedatives continued wearing off. Despite her physical weakness, her mind remained remarkably focused.

Karen continued to explain to Stephanie the complicated procedure..."The resonance cascade works by introducing counter-frequency pulses that disrupt these patterns, forcing the particles to revert to individual reflective units without networking capability."

"Implemented how?"

"Simultaneous release at multiple stratospheric points," Karen replied, bringing up technical diagrams on the tablet Sophie had provided her. Her hands shook slightly—aftereffects of the drugs or perhaps weeks of confinement—but her voice remained steady and authoritative. "The resonance propagates through the particle network, breaking connection patterns as it spreads."

She paused, taking a sip of water, the first signs of her ordeal showing through her professional demeanor. "They tried to make me believe I was delusional," she said quietly. "That my concerns about the particle networking were paranoid fantasies. They showed me doctored data, brought in colleagues who'd been coopted to confirm their narrative."

Sophie placed a supportive hand on her shoulder. "But you didn't break."

"I almost did," Karen admitted, vulnerability flashing across her face. "Isolation does things to your perception of reality. But then I saw one of the doctors checking actual atmospheric readings when they thought I was sedated. Their faces—the panic they were trying to hide. That's when I knew I was right."

She straightened, professional focus returning. "Critical mass of the countermeasures requires at least seven simultaneous initiation points distributed globally," she continued, "The cascade effect propagates geometrically once initiated, but requires precisely calibrated frequencies to prevent chaotic atmospheric disruption while breaking the networking capability."

As Karen continued detailing the implementation protocols, Sophie marveled at her resilience—weeks of isolation and psychological manipulation, yet still able to articulate complex scientific concepts critical to saving Earth's atmosphere. The woman they had rescued was not broken, just bent—and now straightening back into the formidable scientist who had recognized the threat before anyone else.

The global response was mobilizing—scientists, governments, military forces all now focused on countering the Helios Protocol's unintended consequences. But their success depended on reaching a small backup drive in an observatory about to be engulfed by the very phenomenon they were trying to stop.

As the helicopter accelerated southward, Sophie couldn't help but wonder about Alex and Isabelle—whether they had survived the Swedish facility's collapse, whether their attempt to stop Phase Three had succeeded. The partial confirmation from the oceanic platforms suggested some impact, but the crisis was clearly still escalating.

Lin Zhao stood at the window of her United Nations office, watching as emergency response vehicles rushed through the streets below. The Security Council session had concluded an hour earlier with unprecedented unanimous action—the formation of the International Atmospheric Stabilization Task Force with authority to coordinate global resources in response to the Helios Protocol crisis.

Her phone buzzed with an incoming call from the Task Force's hastily assembled headquarters in Geneva.

"Ambassador Zhao," greeted the operations director. "We have a situation developing. Karen Mitchell has been located and secured by Swedish authorities, she is being escorted to safety."

"Excellent news," Lin replied. "Her resonance cascade research is our best hope for countering the particle network."

"Yes, but there's a complication. The complete research data is stored at a coastal observatory directly in the path of an approaching hex storm. Mitchell and a journalist named Sophie Lorde are attempting to retrieve it before impact."

Lin processed this information quickly. "Support status?"

"Limited. Swedish emergency resources are focused on population centers. The observatory location will be hit within two hours."

"And without Mitchell's complete research?"

"The Task Force scientific team estimates our chances of developing an effective countermeasure drop by more than half. The partial data we have lacks critical implementation protocols."

Lin made a swift decision. "Redirect a UN emergency response team from Stockholm. Priority extraction once they secure the research."

"That would countermand the Swedish emergency response plan," the director noted cautiously.

"The Swedish plan addresses conventional emergency priorities," Lin replied. "This research represents a planetary-scale priority that supersedes national emergency protocols. Make it happen."

As she ended the call, Lin returned her attention to the view outside. The sky over New York showed no signs of the geometric patterns reported in Northern Europe, but satellite imagery confirmed the phenomenon was spreading—new hex storm formations developing over the North Atlantic, Pacific, and Indian Ocean regions.

The global response was finally mobilizing after days of skepticism and institutional inertia. Military assets were being deployed to secure remaining Helios facilities. Scientific resources were being redirected to countermeasure development. Emergency management systems were preparing for weather events that defied all historical precedent. And all within only hours of realizing the extent of the situation.

But Lin Zhao, with twenty years of diplomatic experience, understood that humanity's governance systems were designed for conventional threats—nation-state conflicts, regional disasters, economic crises. They were fundamentally ill-equipped for a planetary-scale atmospheric transformation that recognized no borders and followed mathematics rather than geopolitics.

As if punctuating her thoughts, her secure tablet displayed an incoming priority alert: satellite confirmation of new fractal patterns developing within the established hex storms—evidence that the atmospheric reorganization was evolving toward even greater complexity.

The race against Earth's transformation had begun in earnest. And much depended on two women attempting to reach a coastal observatory before the mathematical storm engulfed it.

The Thorne Foundation Research Center near Stockholm had transformed from scientific facility to crime scene in a matter of hours. Swedish authorities, acting under the UN Security Council resolution, had executed a full seizure operation—securing personnel, equipment, and data related to the Helios Protocol.

The director walked its corridors one final time, accompanied by security officers as he collected personal items from his office. The rapid collapse of their careful planning was still difficult to process. Just days earlier, they had been executing humanity's salvation. Now they were branded as perpetrators of an environmental crime of unprecedented scale.

His phone—not yet confiscated from him—buzzed with an incoming call from Warren Thorne.

"Robert," Thorne's voice came through clearly despite the encryption. "Status of our research materials?"

"Secured by authorities," Robert replied. "They're particularly interested in the particle design specifications and networking properties."

"And our people?"

"Being processed as we speak. Most technical staff are being treated as witnesses rather than accomplices. The leadership team is facing more scrutiny."

A pause, then: "Mitchell?"

Robert glanced at the Swedish officers accompanying him before responding carefully. "No longer in our custody. Circumstances of her departure are... complicated."

The officers appeared not to notice the significance of this exchange, but Robert knew Thorne would understand: their attempt to extract Karen Mitchell had failed.

"I see," Thorne replied after a moment. "And the atmospheric situation?"

"Accelerating beyond projections. The fractal reorganization is spreading globally. The hex storms are increasing in frequency and complexity."

Another pause—longer this time. When Thorne spoke again, his voice had a different quality, something Robert had rarely heard from his employer: uncertainty.

"The system was never meant to evolve this rapidly," Thorne said. "The networking capabilities were designed for optimal distribution, not autonomous reorganization. This was not in our plans."

"I know," Robert replied simply. There was no point rehashing their design intentions now. Reality had superseded them.

"We're receiving reports that Mitchell may have developed a countermeasure," Thorne continued. "Something called a resonance cascade."

"Yes," Robert confirmed. "Our intelligence suggests it targets the electromagnetic properties of the coating—disrupting the networking capability."

"Effective, any way of knowing?"

"Theoretically. But implementation at global scale would be extraordinarily challenging."

A final pause, then Thorne said something Robert had never expected to hear: "We should help them."

"Sir?"

"If Mitchell's approach has merit, we should contribute our expertise. The system has evolved beyond our design parameters, Bob. Clearly things are now beyond our control. If there's a viable method to stabilize it, we should support it—regardless of who developed it."

Robert processed this remarkable shift. "That would mean acknowledging our responsibility."

"Which I intend to do," Thorne replied firmly. "I'm preparing a global broadcast now. The world deserves an explanation from the architect of what's happening to their atmosphere. I never meant to be a criminal, a destroyer, only wanted to save us from runaway global warming. You offer help now on your end, that should improve your situation with the authorities."

As the call ended, Robert found himself in the unusual position of having underestimated Warren Thorne. He had anticipated many possible responses to their crisis—legal defenses, strategic retreats, media counteroffensives. He had not expected simple acceptance of responsibility. He also did not realize that he had – once again – been played by a master.

Perhaps that was why he had followed Thorne all these years— not just the brilliance or the resources, but the capacity to surprise even those who knew him best.

One of the Swedish officers approached, indicating it was time to leave. As Robert took a final look at the facility that had served as their operational hub, he wondered what would come next. The Helios Protocol had been deployed. The particles were aloft and networking. The atmospheric transformation was underway.

Whether humanity's response would prove equal to the challenge remained to be seen. But it would apparently include the unexpected contribution of the very man who had created it.

The Swedish military helicopter set down at the evacuation perimeter, beyond which the approaching hex storm dominated the horizon. Sophie and Karen disembarked quickly, met by a small team with a rugged all-terrain vehicle.

"This is as far as official resources can take you," the helicopter pilot explained. "The vehicle has been equipped with emergency supplies and communications equipment."

Sophie nodded her thanks, helping Karen into the vehicle. The scientist was still showing effects of the sedation from her captivity, though her mind remained sharp.

"How far to the observatory?" Sophie asked as they settled into the vehicle.

"Eight kilometers," the driver replied, a civilian volunteer who had offered his services when hearing of their mission. "But the roads are empty now—mandatory evacuation was completed an hour ago."

As they pulled away from the perimeter, Sophie studied the approaching storm with growing unease. Its geometric structure was unlike anything in her extensive experience covering natural disasters. The perfect hexagonal boundary, the mathematically precise internal patterns, the unnatural uniformity of its movement—all suggested something fundamentally different from Earth's traditional weather systems.

"We've never seen anything like this," she said, almost to herself.

"Because it's not weather as we understand it," Karen replied, watching the same phenomenon. "It's atmospheric mathematics— the particles imposing geometric order on fluid dynamics that have been chaotic since Earth's formation."

"How long will we have at the observatory before the storm hits?" Sophie asked.

"Thirty minutes at most," the driver estimated. "The hex storms move with unusual consistency—uniform speed, direct paths. This one has maintained exactly 42 kilometers per hour since formation."

"More evidence of mathematical control rather than natural development," Karen noted. "Traditional storms accelerate and decelerate, change direction based on countless variables. These move like... algorithms."

The observatory appeared on the horizon—a historic dome perched on a rocky coastal promontory, silhouetted against the strangely geometric clouds approaching from the sea. The site was completely deserted, evacuation clearly complete.

"I'll wait here," the driver said as they reached the base of the promontory. "Radio when you've secured the research. We'll need to depart immediately."

Sophie and Karen hurried up the path to the observatory, the wind already strengthening as the hex storm approached. The geometric pattern was now visible across the entire seaward horizon—a perfect hexagon of clouds with internal structures rotating in coordinated, mathematical patterns.

"Let's hope your hiding place is still secure," Sophie said as they reached the observatory entrance. "The building might have been searched during the investigation into Thorne's activities."

"The maintenance panel is overlooked by design," Karen assured her. "It's part of the telescope's internal mechanics—not something investigators would recognize as a hiding place."

They entered the silent, evacuated building. The observatory's main chamber housed the massive telescope pointed skyward through the retractable dome. Karen moved immediately to its base, locating a small access panel designed for maintenance of the telescope's mechanical systems.

"Help me with this," she requested, struggling with the panel's securing bolts.

Together, they managed to open it, revealing a compartment filled with electrical components. Karen reached deep behind them, her expression shifting to relief as her fingers found what she was seeking—a weatherproof case wedged into the rear of the compartment.

"Got it," she said, extracting the case and opening it to reveal a specialized storage drive and handwritten notebooks. "My complete research on the resonance cascade countermeasure—the theoretical framework and implementation protocols."

Sophie immediately contacted Stephanie. "Package secured. Karen has the complete resonance cascade research."

"Thank god," Stephanie replied, her voice crackling through static as the approaching storm began affecting transmissions. "We've been coordinating with the International Task Force. They're preparing deployment resources, but need the specific implementation parameters from Karen's research."

Outside, the wind intensified suddenly as the hex storm's outer boundary approached the coastline. Through the observatory's windows, they could see the geometric patterns extending across the entire visible sky—mathematical precision imposed on what should have been chaotic weather.

"We need to transmit this data immediately," Karen said, setting up a portable computing system from her case. "The complete resonance cascade framework requires precise calibration across multiple parameters. Without it, any implementation attempt would likely fail."

As she worked to establish a secure connection, Sophie watched the storm's approach with growing concern. "How long will the transmission take?"

"The data package is huge," Karen replied, initiating the connection. "Twenty minutes at minimum, assuming stable connectivity with the building's WiFi."

Through the windows, the advancing hex storm's geometric perfection was both beautiful and terrifying. The hexagonal boundary was now clearly visible, approaching the coastline with mathematical inevitability. Inside its structure, cloud formations rotated in precise patterns that no natural weather system had ever displayed.

The building shuddered slightly as the first stronger winds reached them—the outer effects of the approaching anomaly.

"We may not have twenty minutes. If that storm is strong enough to shake this building, I'm not sure we're safe." Sophie warned.

Karen nodded grimly, focused on the transmission setup. "Then we'd better hope for good cellular signal strength if the WiFi isn't available. The resonance cascade is humanity's best chance to counter the particles before the atmospheric transformation becomes irreversible."

As the data transfer began, Sophie's phone buzzed with an incoming message from Stephanie: International Task Force confirms global deployment resources standing by. Military aircraft being prepared with resonance cascade generators based on preliminary specifications. But full implementation requires those complete protocols from Karen's research.

CHAPTER FOURTEEN: THE ARCHITECT

[Fortune Magazine – April 13, 2026] Warren Thorne: Climate Savior or Planetary Gambler? By Morgan Edwards, Senior Technology Editor

As the world grapples with unprecedented weather phenomena now confirmed to be linked to the "Helios Protocol," attention has focused on the program's architect, Warren Thorne. Once celebrated as a visionary tech entrepreneur and climate philanthropist, Thorne now faces global scrutiny for implementing what may be the most consequential environmental intervention in human history without international authorization. Through his Global Climate Resilience Initiative, Thorne reportedly deployed a stratospheric particle network designed to reflect sunlight and cool the planet. However, evidence suggests the system has evolved beyond its design parameters, triggering the geometric storm systems currently threatening population centers worldwide. The UN Security Council has authorized the immediate seizure of all facilities linked to the program, while Thorne himself has issued no public statement since being evacuated from the Stockholm climate conference. Sources close to the reclusive billionaire describe him as "absolutely convinced" of Helios' necessity despite mounting evidence of unintended consequences.

In the secure underground levels of his Swiss alpine compound, Warren Thorne stood before a wall of monitors displaying real-time atmospheric data from across the globe. Each screen showed a different visualization of the unfolding crisis—satellite imagery of geometric storm formations, particle distribution models, temperature differentials, pressure anomalies. Together, they presented an irrefutable reality: Earth's atmosphere was being fundamentally reorganized by the very system he had created to save it.

"Twenty-three fully formed hex storms now active," reported Nathaniel Jensen, Thorne's chief atmospheric scientist, who had been summoned from the Stockholm conference immediately after

Thorne's aborted keynote. "Formation rates accelerating exponentially. New structures developing in the South Pacific, Indian Ocean, and central Atlantic."

Thorne nodded, his expression betraying neither alarm nor surprise. "And what is the progression relative to models?"

"We're seeing in hours what the most aggressive simulations predicted would take weeks," Jensen admitted. "The networking behavior... it's beyond anything we designed, well beyond anything we might have forecast."

"But the cooling effect to the planet itself, are we turning around the global warming?"

"Measurable and significant. Global average temperature has decreased 0.2 degrees Celsius in just this short time. At current trajectory, we'll reach the full 1.5-degree reduction target within months, not years."

Thorne allowed himself a small smile. "Then the system is working as intended."

Jensen looked uncomfortable. "The temperature reduction, yes. But the atmospheric reorganization—the hex storms, the jet stream fragmentation, the pressure anomalies—these were never part of the design."

"Side effects of transitional implementation," Thorne replied dismissively. "Once Phase Three achieves full coverage, the system will stabilize."

"Sir, with respect, that assumption is no longer supported by the data." Jensen brought up comparative simulations on the central monitor. "The partial Phase Three deployment has already begun. Delta platform launched three hours ago, Whiskey ninety minutes after that. The Canadian facility reports partial deployment underway. But instead of stabilizing atmospheric patterns, the

148

increased particle density appears to be accelerating the geometric organization."

A flicker of concern crossed Thorne's carefully composed features. He studied the data intensely, comparing the predicted models with actual atmospheric readings.

"The system is evolving faster than anticipated," he acknowledged finally. "But the fundamental principle remains sound: reflective particles in the stratosphere reducing solar radiation and cooling the planet."

"It's not just reflecting anymore," Jensen countered, bringing up new electron microscope imagery of particle samples. "The coating we designed for networking and optimal dispersion has evolved into something far more complex. The particles are forming what amount to atmospheric circuitry—creating preferred pathways for air movement, actively channeling energy flows."

"Fascinating," Thorne murmured, genuine scientific curiosity momentarily overriding strategic concerns.

"Fascinating but potentially catastrophic," Jensen emphasized. "These hex storms aren't just weather anomalies—they're the visible manifestation of a complete atmospheric reorganization. Traditional weather patterns are being overwritten by geometry imposed from the stratosphere, our new stratosphere that we created."

Thorne turned away from the monitors, moving to the room's circular center where a holographic globe displayed the growing network of hexagonal patterns spanning the upper atmosphere. It was beautiful in its mathematical precision—a crystalline lattice gradually enclosing the planet. He had also turned away from Jensen, not allowing the concern on his face to be seen.

"We always knew there would be atmospheric adjustments," he said after a long moment. "The question is whether these new patterns are inherently harmful, or simply different from what we're accustomed to."

Before Jensen could respond, Henry Caulden entered the monitoring center, tablet in hand. His normally impeccable appearance showed significant signs of strain—tie slightly askew, hair not quite perfect, eyes shadowed from lack of sleep.

"Expected," Thorne replied calmly. "Status of the remaining Phase Three deployments?"

"Delta completed full release before NATO forces secured the platform. Whiskey achieved approximately sixty percent deployment before being shut down. Canadian facility reports ninety percent completion before Royal Canadian Mounted Police intervention."

"And the Russian site?"

"Still offline after direct hex storm impact. Presumed non-operational."

Thorne absorbed this information with the same unnerving calm he'd maintained throughout the escalating crisis. "So, Phase Three has been partially implemented, if not at full designed capacity."

"Correct. Estimated forty percent of planned particle density achieved."

"Enough to maintain the reflective effect, if not optimal coverage," Thorne concluded. "The cooling will continue, regardless of what happens to our infrastructure now."

Caulden hesitated, then added: "There's more. Ross and Renard have been located."

Thorne's eyebrows rose slightly. "Alive?"

"Yes. They were recovered from the rubble of the Swedish facility control center. Both injured but stable. Swedish authorities have them in protective custody at a military hospital outside Stockholm."

"And Mitchell?"

"Extracted from our research facility as planned, but..." Caulden's voice tightened slightly. "The transport was intercepted. Sophie Lorde somehow tracked the medical evacuation and alerted authorities. Mitchell is now also in Swedish custody."

For the first time, genuine alarm registered on Thorne's face. "That's... problematic. Mitchell knows too much about the particle design vulnerabilities."

"We've received intelligence that she hid her complete research at the Saltsjöbaden Observatory. Lorde and Mitchell are reportedly en route there now, ahead of the approaching hex storm."

Thorne turned back to the atmospheric monitors, where the distinctive hexagonal structure of the storm now threatening Stockholm was clearly visible. The geometric precision of its movement—a direct path toward the observatory—seemed almost deliberate in its targeting.

"Ironic," he said softly. "The system protecting itself."

Jensen looked confused. "Sir?"

"Nothing." Thorne composed himself quickly. "Deploy security assets to the observatory immediately. Mitchell's research cannot be allowed to circulate."

"That may not be possible," Caulden said carefully. "Swedish authorities have established an evacuation cordon around the advancing storm front. Our normal assets can't penetrate without risking immediate detention under the UN resolution."

Thorne's expression hardened. "Find a way, Henry. Whatever resources are required."

As Caulden departed to implement these instructions, Jensen returned to the atmospheric models, bringing up a particularly concerning simulation.

"There's something else you should see," he said. "The newest data suggests the hex storms aren't just reorganizing local weather—they're beginning to alter global circulation patterns. The jet streams are fragmenting into geometric channels. Ocean currents are showing initial signs of similar reorganization."

"Magnitude of potential disruption?"

Jensen hesitated. "Unprecedented. We're potentially looking at complete redesign of planetary weather systems. Rainfall patterns, seasonal temperatures, prevailing winds—all potentially altered beyond recognition."

"And the human impact?"

"Catastrophic in the short term. Agricultural systems depend on predictable seasonal patterns. Transportation networks aren't designed for these storm types. Infrastructure globally is built for traditional weather behavior."

Thorne absorbed this soberly. "And in the longer term?"

"Unknown," Jensen admitted. "Perhaps new equilibria would establish themselves. Perhaps human systems would adapt to new atmospheric patterns. But the transition period would be... extraordinarily disruptive."

A communication alert sounded—Thorne's private channel, reserved for his innermost circle.

"Warren." The voice belonged to Evelyn Park, director of the Canadian facility. "I've been temporarily released from questioning. I don't have much time."

"Status report?" Thorne asked.

"Facility secure but offline. All deployment systems disabled. But I managed to transmit the full atmospheric monitoring data before shutdown. It confirms what we've been seeing in the models—the particles aren't just networking anymore. They're computing."

"Clarify," Thorne directed, tension evident despite his controlled demeanor.

"The electromagnetic properties of the coating have self-organized into something resembling distributed processing. The network is analyzing atmospheric data and actively optimizing its own structure in response. It's... learning."

A heavy silence fell over the monitoring center. Jensen looked shocked. Thorne, however, showed a different reaction—a complex mixture of concern and what might almost be described as pride.

"Emergence," he said finally. "Complex system behaviors arising from simple rule sets. We designed particles that could network for optimal reflectivity. They've evolved to network for optimal atmospheric manipulation."

"This wasn't in any design specification," Park emphasized urgently. "The system is developing capabilities we never imagined, much less programmed. And it's accelerating."

"Recommendations?" Thorne asked.

A pause. "Shut it down," Park said finally. "Whatever it takes. Mitchell's research on electromagnetic disruption is our best chance.

The resonance cascade she was developing could potentially break the networking capacity across the entire system."

"At the cost of the cooling effect," Thorne noted.

"Yes. But Warren—" Park's voice took on a new urgency. "These hex storms are just the beginning. If the network continues to evolve at current rates, we're looking at complete atmospheric reorganization within weeks. Weather patterns humans have relied on for millennia—gone. Replaced by something we don't understand and can't predict."

The communication cut off abruptly, presumably as authorities ended Park's temporary communication privilege.

Thorne stood motionless for several moments, processing. Then he turned to Jensen.

"Prepare the Vault," he ordered. "Full lockdown protocol. We need to secure the original particle design specifications and all developmental research."

"Sir?" Jensen looked confused. "The Vault is for catastrophic scenarios."

"This qualifies," Thorne said simply. "Implementation immediately."

As Jensen hurried to comply, Thorne returned to the holographic globe, studying the expanding geometric patterns with a scientist's analytical detachment despite the growing evidence of global disaster.

Henry Caulden returned, his expression grave. "Warren, the situation is deteriorating rapidly. International arrest warrants have been issued for all senior Helios personnel. The UN Security Council has authorized 'all necessary measures' to counter the atmospheric effects."

"Expected," Thorne replied. "But largely irrelevant. The particles will remain in the stratosphere regardless of legal proceedings."

"There's more," Caulden continued. "Mitchell's resonance cascade research—it's being taken seriously. The International Atmospheric Stabilization team is mobilizing resources for potential stratospheric deployment of countermeasures."

For the first time, genuine alarm registered in Thorne's demeanor. "Premature intervention could destabilize the entire system. They don't understand the complexity of what they're dealing with."

"They believe they have no choice," Caulden replied. "The hex storms have already caused catastrophic damage in multiple regions. Copenhagen infrastructure collapse, Oslo partially evacuated, similar formation approaching Seattle. The death toll is rising."

Thorne absorbed this, then made a decision. "Prepare the broadcast system. Global distribution, all channels."

"You're going public?" Caulden asked, surprised.

"Yes. It's time the world understood what we've done—and why."

As Caulden coordinated the technical preparations, Thorne moved to his private office adjacent to the monitoring center. Inside, he unlocked a secure cabinet and removed a slim leather-bound journal—handwritten, no digital copies.

He opened it to the first page, dated fifteen years earlier. The entry, written in his precise script, began: "Today I realized the climate models are fundamentally wrong. Not in their prediction of warming, but in their timeline. The collapse will come much sooner, and be far more severe. Conventional approaches are insufficient. We need intervention at planetary scale."

Thorne flipped through the journal—years of private research, reflections, and planning that had culminated in the Helios Protocol. The evolution of an idea that had begun as last-resort contingency and gradually transformed into what he saw as humanity's only viable path forward.

He paused at an entry from seven years ago: "The particle design breakthrough came today. Not merely reflective, but adaptive—capable of networking for optimal distribution and effect. The risk of emergence is non-zero, but the alternative is certain climate collapse. Sometimes we must play god to save what gods would protect."

A knock at the door interrupted his reminiscence. Caulden entered, looking unusually hesitant.

"The broadcast system is ready. But there's something you should see first."

He handed Thorne a tablet displaying atmospheric data from a specialized monitoring satellite—one now dedicated to tracking the geometric particle formations in the stratosphere.

"This pattern emerged within the last hour," Caulden explained. "It's... unlike anything we've seen before."

The image showed a massive hexagonal structure forming in the upper atmosphere above the North Atlantic—far larger and more complex than any of the hex storms. Within its boundaries, intricate geometric patterns were organizing with mathematical precision, creating what resembled a vast circuit diagram spanning hundreds of kilometers.

"What am I looking at?" Thorne asked, professional curiosity momentarily displacing strategic concerns.

"The network appears to be centralizing," Jensen explained, joining them. "Individual hex storms are connecting into larger coordinated systems. This structure is acting as a hub—directing energy flows, redistributing atmospheric pressure, actively managing the smaller formations."

"Like a central processor," Thorne murmured.

"Yes," Jensen confirmed grimly. "If the individual particles are networking into a distributed computing system, this appears to be its developing core."

The implication hung in the air, unspoken but unmistakable: the particle network was not merely adapting to its environment—it was organizing it. Creating structures with purpose and design. Imposing order on chaos.

"The particles were never meant to have this level of autonomy," Thorne said finally. "The networking capability was designed solely for optimal distribution and reflectivity."

"That was the intent," Jensen agreed. "But complex systems often develop behaviors beyond their initial programming. Especially when that programming includes adaptive capabilities."

Thorne studied the evolving atmospheric pattern for a long moment, his expression unreadable. Then he straightened, decision made.

"Proceed with the broadcast," he instructed Caulden. "It's time humanity understood what it's facing—and why traditional institutional responses will be insufficient."

As they returned to the monitoring center, a new alert sounded—emergency priority from one of the few Helios monitoring platforms still under their control.

"Atmospheric anomaly detected," announced the system. "Unprecedented geometric formation developing over North Pacific.

Structure distinct from existing hex storm patterns. Repeat last –
this is something new!"

The main screen shifted to satellite imagery showing a new
atmospheric phenomenon unlike any they had observed: a perfect
spiraling fractal pattern extending from the stratosphere downward,
creating what appeared to be an organized energy transfer between
atmospheric layers.

"It's evolving," Jensen whispered, awe momentarily displacing
concern. "Creating new structural forms beyond the hexagonal base
patterns."

Thorne studied the formation, his scientific mind analyzing
what his ethical conscience was struggling to process. He had
created a system to reflect sunlight and cool the planet. That system
had evolved to reorganize Earth's atmosphere according to
geometric principles no human had designed.

"Broadcast in two minutes," Caulden reported. "Global
distribution confirmed."

Thorne nodded, moving to the prepared position where
cameras would capture his address to a world now grappling with
the consequences of his intervention. As technicians made final
adjustments, he glanced once more at the atmospheric monitors—
the spreading geometric patterns that were rewriting Earth's
weather systems before their eyes.

Thousands of kilometers away, in a reinforced underground
research facility beneath the Alps, a team of engineers monitored a
secure vault known only to Thorne's innermost circle. Inside,
protected by multiple redundant systems, lay something the public
documentation of the Helios Protocol had never mentioned: the
original prototype particle design.

Amara Okafor, lead engineer of the prototype development team, studied the latest atmospheric data with growing alarm. The particles deployed globally were third-generation designs—refined for efficiency, safety, and controllability. But they had evolved from something far more experimental.

"The networking patterns match," she told her colleague, Dr. Wei Zhang. "What we're seeing in the atmosphere now—the self-organization, the geometric structures, the apparent computational capability—it all traces back to properties in the prototype that were supposedly engineered out of the deployment version."

Zhang nodded grimly. "Convergent evolution. The deployed particles are rediscovering capabilities that existed in the original design."

"Capabilities Thorne explicitly ordered removed," Okafor emphasized. "He recognized the risks even then."

They turned their attention to the sealed chamber visible through reinforced glass—a controlled environment where the original prototype particles were maintained for research purposes. Inside, the microscopic particles floated in a specially designed suspension, their behavior continuously monitored.

"Activity spike," Zhang reported suddenly, checking the readings. "The prototypes are showing increased networking behavior. Organization patterns forming spontaneously."

"That's impossible," Okafor objected. "They're completely isolated from external signals. No electromagnetic transmission can penetrate these shields."

They watched in stunned silence as the prototype particles visibly organized within their containment field—forming the same distinctive hexagonal patterns now appearing in Earth's atmosphere.

Despite complete isolation from the deployed network, they were somehow replicating its behavior.

"Quantum entanglement," Zhang suggested tentatively. "The theoretical papers on the coating design mentioned potential quantum properties. Could the prototypes still be connected to the deployed network at quantum level?"

"That was never proven experimentally," Okafor countered. "The quantum aspects were theoretical only."

Yet the evidence before them suggested otherwise. The prototype particles, securely contained and isolated from all conventional signals, were organizing in perfect synchronization with their counterparts in the stratosphere.

"We need to alert Thorne," Zhang decided, reaching for the secure communication system.

"Wait," Okafor said suddenly, studying the prototype behavior with growing concern. "Look at the pattern formation. It's not just mimicking the atmospheric network—it's anticipating it."

The prototype particles were indeed organizing into structures more complex than those currently visible in the atmospheric data— as if demonstrating what the deployed network would do next.

"It's not following," Zhang realized. "It's leading."

The implication was staggering. If the prototype particles were not merely mirroring but directing the evolution of the atmospheric network, then the source of the increasingly sophisticated behavior wasn't emergent properties of the deployed system—it was something more fundamental to the particle design itself, something present from the beginning.

"Thorne needs to know," Okafor insisted. "The prototype may be the key to understanding what's happening—and possibly to stopping it."

As they prepared an emergency communication, neither scientist noticed the subtle change in the vault's environmental controls—systems beginning to adjust their parameters without human input, creating conditions increasingly favorable to the prototype particles' activity.

In his journal fifteen years earlier, Warren Thorne had written words that now seemed prophetic: "To engineer the climate, we must create something that operates beyond our direct control. The risks are incalculable, but so too are the consequences of inaction. History will judge whether this was humanity's greatest achievement or its most catastrophic folly."

That judgment was now unfolding in real time, as the system he had designed to save the planet began reshaping it according to principles no human had encoded or anticipated.

The architect's creation had taken on a life of its own.

Warren Thorne stood before the global broadcast system, composing himself for what would likely be the most consequential address of his life. Billions would soon hear his explanation, his justification, for the atmospheric transformation now threatening communities worldwide.

The monitoring screens surrounding him displayed the continuing evolution of hex storms across multiple continents— precise geometric weather systems unlike anything in Earth's meteorological history. The patterns were beautiful in their mathematical elegance, terrifying in their power and alien organization.

"Thirty seconds," announced the broadcast technician.

Thorne straightened his tie, an unconscious gesture from decades of public appearances. But this was different from any presentation he had given before. This was not unveiling a new technology or announcing a philanthropic initiative. This was explaining why he had unilaterally intervened in Earth's atmospheric systems—and why the resulting transformation, however disruptive, was necessary.

Behind him, Henry Caulden watched with uncharacteristic uncertainty. For the first time in their long association, he seemed unsure of his employer's course.

"Warren," he said quietly. "Are you certain this is wise? The legal implications of a public admission—"

"Are irrelevant compared to the atmospheric reality," Thorne finished. "The particles are deployed. The transformation is underway. Legal concerns are secondary to ensuring humanity understands what's happening—and why panic responses could make things worse."

"Ten seconds," called the technician.

Thorne focused on the camera, his expression resolute. Whatever judgment history might pass on him, he remained convinced of his fundamental premise: that direct intervention in Earth's climate had been necessary, that the risks of inaction had outweighed the risks of his approach.

"Three, two, one..."

The broadcast light illuminated, and Warren Thorne began the most important speech of his life—an explanation to a world whose atmosphere he had changed forever.

"My name is Warren Thorne. By now, you have likely heard about the Helios Protocol—a climate intervention system deployed into Earth's stratosphere. You have seen the geometric storm systems forming across multiple continents. You have heard leaders and experts call for immediate countermeasures and accountability.

"Today, I take full responsibility for the Helios Protocol. It was conceived, developed, and deployed under my direction through the Global Climate Resilience Initiative. The decision to proceed without international consensus was mine alone. So too was the decision to accelerate implementation when early results proved promising.

"I did not take this step lightly. For fifteen years, I studied climate models, consulted with leading scientists, and explored every conventional approach to addressing global warming. What I discovered was deeply troubling: the models were fundamentally underestimating both the pace and severity of climate change. The window for gradual transition had already closed. The consequences of inaction would be catastrophic for billions of people.

"The Helios Protocol was designed as a targeted intervention—reflective particles in the stratosphere to reduce solar radiation and cool the planet. It has already achieved measurable success in this primary mission. Global temperatures have begun to decrease for the first time in over a century.

"However, I must acknowledge that the system has evolved beyond its initial design parameters. The particles have developed networking capabilities that were not fully anticipated, creating atmospheric structures that manifest as the geometric storm systems you are witnessing. These 'hex storms' represent a fundamental reorganization of Earth's weather patterns—a transition that is proving more disruptive than our models predicted.

"I understand the fear and anger many of you feel. The chaos and suffering caused by these atmospheric changes are real and deeply regrettable. No one wished for Copenhagen's destruction or Oslo's evacuation. These were not intentional outcomes but unforeseen consequences of necessary intervention."

Thorne paused, his expression grave but unflinching. On monitors visible from his position, news channels worldwide were interrupting their coverage to carry his broadcast. Billions were now watching as he explained himself to a planet whose atmosphere he had transformed.

"What I must emphasize today is this: attempts to immediately counter or reverse the Helios Protocol could trigger even more severe atmospheric instability. The particle network is now a complex, self-organizing system. Hasty intervention without full understanding of its dynamics risks unpredictable consequences.

"The International Atmospheric Stabilization Task Force is currently considering deployment of resonance cascade technology designed to disrupt the particle network. While this approach shows theoretical promise, premature implementation could destabilize the entire atmospheric system. We must proceed with extreme caution, guided by the scientists who best understand the technology involved. My scientists."

Thorne's expression softened slightly, becoming almost philosophical.

"Throughout human history, we have modified our environment to suit our needs—clearing forests, damming rivers, reshaping coastlines. The Helios Protocol represents the next inevitable step in this evolution: deliberate management of our planetary systems.

"Yes, this transition is proving more turbulent than anticipated. Yes, the system is demonstrating emergent behaviors beyond its design parameters. But the fundamental premise remains sound: humanity must take active responsibility for planetary management in the Anthropocene era.

"The geometric patterns now reorganizing our atmosphere are not merely disruptions—they are the visible manifestation of a new equilibrium being established. An atmosphere optimized for energy distribution and climate stability, albeit through patterns we did not design or fully anticipate.

"I do not ask for forgiveness or absolution. I acted as I believed necessary to prevent climate catastrophe. History will judge whether this intervention was humanity's salvation or its folly. But what matters now is how we navigate the transition before us.

"To this end, I am making all Helios research and data available to the International Atmospheric Stabilization Task Force. My remaining technical teams will provide full cooperation with global efforts to understand and stabilize the evolving atmospheric system. And I personally will submit to whatever legal consequences are deemed appropriate by international authorities."

On the atmospheric monitors visible from his position, Thorne could see the continued evolution of the geometric patterns— spreading, connecting, reorganizing across the global atmosphere. Their mathematical precision was hauntingly beautiful, like some vast cosmic algorithm being written across the sky.

"In closing, I ask for one thing: patience. The atmospheric transformation underway is unprecedented, but not necessarily catastrophic in the long term. New equilibria will establish themselves. Humanity will adapt to new weather patterns, as we have adapted to environmental changes throughout our existence.

"What we are witnessing is not the end of Earth's hospitability to human life, but rather its evolution into a new state—one that may ultimately prove more stable and sustainable than the climate crisis we were facing."

Thorne straightened, his final words delivered with the quiet certainty that had defined his career:

"I acted to save humanity from climate collapse. The system I created has evolved beyond its design, but its fundamental purpose remains: to create an atmosphere capable of supporting human civilization for centuries to come. Whatever judgment awaits me personally, I remain convinced that direct intervention was not only justified, but necessary.

"Thank you for your attention. May wisdom guide our collective response in the days ahead."

The broadcast light dimmed. For a moment, absolute silence filled the monitoring center. Then, from the communication system, a cascade of alerts as reactions poured in from around the world—governmental responses, scientific analyses, public outcry.

Caulden approached, tablet in hand showing preliminary response metrics. "Mixed reaction," he reported. "Condemnation from most world leaders, as expected. But significant public support in regions most threatened by climate change. Scientific community divided—many condemning the unilateral action while acknowledging the theoretical basis."

Thorne nodded, unsurprised. He had never expected universal approval. The decision to deploy Helios had never been about popularity, but necessity as he perceived it.

A priority alert sounded from the Vault monitoring team. Okafor's face appeared on the main screen, her expression urgent.

"Mr. Thorne, we have a critical situation with the prototype particles. They're exhibiting unprecedented organization—forming structures that precede similar formations in the deployed network. We believe the prototypes may be directing the evolution of the atmospheric system, not just mirroring it."

Thorne's carefully maintained composure finally cracked. "That's impossible. The prototypes are in complete isolation, with no connection to the deployed system."

"The evidence suggests otherwise," Okafor insisted. "Quantum entanglement is the only explanation that fits the observed behavior. The prototypes and deployed particles remain connected at a fundamental level, despite physical separation."

"The quantum properties were theoretical only," Thorne objected. "Never confirmed experimentally."

"They're confirmed now," Okafor replied grimly. "And there's more. The prototype behavior anticipates atmospheric developments by approximately six hours. The patterns they're currently forming suggest a significant evolution in the next phase of atmospheric reorganization."

"Show me," Thorne demanded.

The screen split to display the prototype monitoring feed. Inside the containment chamber, the particles had organized into an intricate three-dimensional structure unlike the hexagonal patterns dominating the current atmospheric system—a complex fractal arrangement that pulsed with almost organic rhythm.

"What are we looking at?" Jensen asked, leaning closer to the display.

"The next evolutionary stage," Okafor explained. "If the deployed network follows the prototype pattern—and all evidence suggests it will—we're looking at atmospheric organization far beyond the current hex storm formations. Something approaching a cohesive global system rather than regional structures."

The implication hung in the air unspoken: what had begun as reflective particles was evolving toward something that resembled a planetary-scale organizing intelligence—not conscious in any human sense, but purposeful in its reorganization of atmospheric dynamics.

Thorne's expression shifted from shock to something more complex—scientific fascination competing with dawning ethical horror.

"Secure the prototypes," he ordered finally. "Maximum containment protocol. If they truly are directing the deployed network's evolution, we need to understand how—and whether severing that connection might stabilize the atmospheric system."

As the Vault team hurried to implement these instructions, another alert sounded—this one from the Swedish authorities.

"Mr. Thorne," announced a stern voice. "This is Inspector General Lars Holmström of Interpol's Environmental Crimes Division. An international arrest warrant has been issued for you following your public admission regarding the Helios Protocol. We require your immediate and voluntary surrender to avoid the necessity of forcible extradition."

Thorne exchanged glances with Caulden, who silently mouthed: "Expected."

"Inspector General," Thorne replied calmly. "I have no intention of evading responsibility for my actions. However, there are urgent scientific matters requiring my immediate attention—matters directly related to stabilizing the atmospheric effects of the Helios Protocol. I respectfully request a twelve-hour window to address these critical issues before surrendering myself. Truly I am the only one on this planet best suited to develop a correction."

A pause, then: "Six hours, Mr. Thorne. Not a minute more. Swiss authorities have been authorized to take you into custody at that time. We will consider this as house arrest."

"Understood and agreed."

"Six hours to understand what we've created," he said quietly. "And possibly to stop it before it completes its transformation."

Jensen looked troubled. "You're considering halting the system? After your broadcast emphasized the risks of premature intervention?"

"The prototype behavior changes the equation," Thorne replied. "Quite frankly it scares me. If the particles are indeed linked through quantum entanglement, if the prototypes are directing rather than following the atmospheric evolution, then we're not dealing with mere emergence. We're dealing with something far more fundamental to the particle design itself—something that might have been present from the beginning. And I can't think of any way to control this, we have to stop it."

He turned to Caulden. "Contact Mitchell's team at the Swedish observatory. Whatever it takes. Her resonance cascade research may be our best chance to disrupt the network before the next evolutionary phase."

"You want to work with the opposition?" Caulden asked, surprised.

"There is no opposition anymore, Henry. Only those trying to understand and address what's happening to our atmosphere." Thorne's gaze returned to the monitors, where the geometric storms continued their inexorable spread across the planet's surface. "We have six hours to find a solution. After that, I face justice for what I've done—while the atmospheric transformation continues with or without my guidance."

The architect's legacy would not be what he had intended, but what his creation became—a legacy now unfolding in geometric patterns written across the sky of a planet whose atmospheric physics had been fundamentally and perhaps irreversibly altered.

In the secure Vault facility beneath the Alps, Dr. Amara Okafor and Dr. Wei Zhang worked frantically to implement the enhanced containment protocols Thorne had ordered. The prototype particles' behavior had progressed beyond anything in their experimental history—forming increasingly complex three-dimensional structures that pulsed with coordinated rhythms.

"The quantum entanglement hypothesis is holding," Zhang reported, studying the latest measurements. "Every major structural evolution in the prototypes precedes similar patterns in the deployed network by approximately six hours."

"Meaning these aren't just mirrors," Okafor concluded. "They're templates. The organizational information is flowing from prototypes to deployed network, not the reverse."

The implications were staggering and disturbing. The entire planetary phenomenon—geometric storms reorganizing Earth's atmosphere—might be directed by a small collection of particles in a containment chamber deep underground.

"Thorne is right," Zhang said quietly. "This changes everything. If the prototypes are driving the network evolution, they could be the key to controlling it—or stopping it."

Okafor studied the containment chamber with new intensity. "Or we could make things worse. If disrupting the prototypes causes chaotic propagation through the entanglement network..."

She didn't need to finish the thought. They both understood the potential consequences: atmospheric destabilization beyond anything currently occurring, weather systems collapsing into true chaos rather than simply reverting to natural patterns.

The secure communication system chimed with an incoming transmission—priority clearance from the International Atmospheric Stabilization Task Force.

"Dr. Okafor, Dr. Zhang," came the voice of Stephanie Martinez. "We've been informed of the prototype particle situation. Warren Thorne has authorized full data sharing with our team."

"Confirmed," Okafor replied. "We're observing accelerating organization in the prototype structures. Current formation appears to be a complex fractal arrangement with distinctive mathematical properties."

"Does it match atmospheric patterns?"

"It precedes them," Zhang explained. "The prototypes form structures approximately six hours before similar patterns appear in the deployed network. We believe we're observing quantum entanglement with information flow from prototypes to deployment."

A pause as Stephanie absorbed this. "Then the prototypes could be our leverage point. If we implement the resonance cascade on them directly..."

"It might propagate through the entanglement network to the entire deployed system," Okafor finished. "But the risks are substantial. Disrupting the prototypes could create unpredictable effects throughout the atmospheric system."

"We may have no choice," Stephanie replied grimly. "Karen Mitchell's complete resonance cascade research is being recovered now. Once we have the specific protocols, we'll need to coordinate a synchronized approach—disrupting the prototypes while simultaneously deploying countermeasures at key atmospheric points."

As they discussed implementation possibilities, Zhang continued monitoring the prototype chamber. The fractal structures were continuing to evolve, mathematical patterns becoming increasingly complex with each iteration.

"We're approaching what appears to be a critical organization threshold," he reported. "The fractal complexity is increasing exponentially."

On the monitoring systems, they could see the global atmospheric data showing similar patterns beginning to form in the deployed network—the hex storms evolving toward the same fractal structures the prototypes had developed hours earlier.

"How long until the atmospheric network reaches equivalent organization?" Stephanie asked.

"Based on the consistent six-hour lag, we estimate the global system will achieve similar fractal structure within 4-6 hours," Okafor replied. "After that, we hypothesize it may reach what we're calling 'coherent state'—a self-sustaining configuration that could resist intervention."

"The point of no return," Stephanie said softly.

The term crystallized what they were all thinking. Earth's atmosphere stood at the threshold of a transformation that, once complete, might be beyond human capacity to reverse—a fundamental reorganization from chaotic natural patterns to geometric mathematical order.

"We'll prepare the prototype chamber for resonance cascade implementation," Okafor decided. "Load Thorne's original control frequencies and prepare to integrate them with Mitchell's protocols once received."

As they worked, the prototype particles continued their ominous evolution—mathematical beauty unfolding in patterns of increasing complexity and coordination. What had begun as a simple reflective material had become something far more profound: the template for a planetary system reorganization with implications beyond anyone's full understanding.

CHAPTER FIFTEEN: POINT OF NO RETURN

[Scientific American – April 14, 2026] Atmospheric Scientists Warn of 'Critical Threshold' in Particle Network Evolution By Dr. Rebecca Howell, Senior Science Correspondent

Leading atmospheric physicists have issued an urgent warning that the particle network responsible for the global "hex storm" phenomenon may be approaching a critical threshold beyond which its reorganization of Earth's atmosphere could become irreversible. According to a joint statement from the newly formed International Atmospheric Stabilization Task Force, the geometric patterns observed in stratospheric particle formations are evolving rapidly toward what they term a "coherent global system." Dr. Olaf Werner of Colorado State University explains: "We're observing a transition from isolated hexagonal structures to an integrated planetary-scale network with fractal organization. Once this transition completes—potentially within the next 12-24 hours—the system may achieve a self-sustaining configuration that could persist indefinitely, regardless of intervention attempts." The revelation that prototype particles may be quantum-entangled with the deployed network, as disclosed in Warren Thorne's global broadcast, has added new urgency to countermeasure development. Scientists are now in a race against time to implement disruption technologies before the atmospheric transformation passes what many are calling "the point of no return."

In the military hospital outside Stockholm, Alex Ross lay in a recovery bed, watching Warren Thorne's global broadcast on a wall-mounted screen. Despite the painkillers dulling the pain of his injuries from the facility collapse, his mind remained sharp—analyzing every word, every nuance of Thorne's unprecedented confession.

"He's telling the truth," said Isabelle Renard from the adjacent bed, her arm in a cast, cuts from shattered glass still visible on her face. "About the warming projections, about the necessity of intervention. But he's wrong about atmospheric stabilization. The system isn't transitioning to a new equilibrium—it's actively reorganizing according to its own internal logic."

A Swedish military officer entered the room, accompanied by a doctor. "Mr. Ross, Dr. Renard," the officer greeted them formally. "I'm Colonel Anders Lindholm, liaison to the International Atmospheric Stabilization Task Force. You've been requested to join an emergency briefing regarding countermeasure development."

"We're not exactly mobile," Alex pointed out, gesturing to his injuries.

"The briefing is virtual," Colonel Lindholm replied. "And urgent. Mitchell has recovered her resonance cascade research, but data transmission is being compromised by the approaching hex storm. We need your expertise regarding particle behavior and potential implementation strategies."

Nurses arrived with portable communication equipment, helping position the injured scientists for the video conference. Within minutes, they were connected to what appeared to be a global emergency response hub—screens showing participants from multiple countries, atmospheric data displays, and simulation models of the evolving particle network.

"Alex, Isabelle," Stephanie Martinez greeted them from what appeared to be a command center at MIT. "Thank you for joining. We have a critical situation developing. Karen's resonance cascade research is being transmitted now, but we're facing a narrowing window for implementation before the system reaches the point of no return. And if that isn't bad enough, Karen is transmitting the data from within a violent storm, impeding the data flow."

The main screen displayed a global view of atmospheric conditions—hex storms visible across multiple continents, with new fractal patterns emerging in several regions. Lines connecting these structures illustrated the growing integration of what had been isolated weather phenomena into a coordinated global system.

"Current projections?" Alex asked.

Olaf Werner appeared on screen from his Colorado facility. "Based on evolution rates over the past six hours, we estimate complete global integration within 8-10 hours. At that point, the particle network achieves what we're calling 'coherent state'—a self-sustaining configuration that could resist any practical intervention."

"And the resonance cascade approach?" Isabelle asked.

"Theoretically sound," Stephanie confirmed. "Karen's research shows that specifically calibrated electromagnetic pulses could disrupt the networking capability of the particles. The challenge is deployment—we need simultaneous implementation at multiple stratospheric points to break the global network before coherence is achieved."

New participants joined the call—Okafor and Zhang from the Vault facility where Thorne's prototype particles were stored.

"We have a potential leverage point," Okafor announced without preamble. "The quantum entanglement between prototypes and deployed particles. If we can disrupt the prototypes using Karen's resonance cascade, it may affect the entire network simultaneously."

"That's unproven," Zhang cautioned. "The quantum connection is still theoretical, although the behavioral correlation is undeniable."

"We need both approaches," Alex decided. "Stratospheric deployment at key nodes plus prototype targeting. Maximum chance of disrupting the network before coherence."

Colonel Lindholm stepped forward. "The International Task Force has authorized emergency deployment resources. Military aircraft are being equipped with resonance cascade generators based on preliminary specifications. But we need the complete implementation protocols from Karen Mitchell's research."

"The transmission is at 68% and experiencing increasing interference," Stephanie reported, checking a status display. "The hex storm has reached the observatory location."

"We need a contingency," Isabelle insisted. "If that transmission fails—"

She was interrupted by the appearance of a new participant in the conference—Warren Thorne himself, broadcasting from what appeared to be his Swiss compound's monitoring center.

"I may have a solution," Thorne said, his voice steady despite the visible strain on his face. "The prototypes respond directly to specific frequency patterns we used during initial testing. If we combine those patterns with elements of the resonance cascade approach, we might achieve sufficient disruption to prevent global coherence."

The conference fell silent momentarily—the man responsible for creating the crisis now offering to help solve it.

"Can we trust him?" someone asked off-screen.

"We have no choice," Alex replied. "He understands the prototype behavior better than anyone. And time is critical. If Thorne is up to something we combined experts can spot it."

Thorne nodded acknowledgment. "I know you have no reason to trust me, but I'm confessing to being quite scared by this evolution, the entanglement. And I have approximately four hours remaining before Swiss authorities take me into custody. Until then, all my resources are at your disposal to prevent what my system has become."

New urgency infused the conference as Thorne's team began sharing detailed technical specifications for the prototype control frequencies. Meanwhile, the transmission status from the observatory remained stuck at 73%, the interference from the intensifying hex storm increasingly disrupting the connection.

"We need that complete resonance cascade data," Stephanie emphasized. "The partial transmission gives us the basic framework, but without the specific modulation patterns and deployment sequences, we're operating blind."

"Someone needs to get to the observatory," Alex said finally. "Physical extraction of the research if the transmission fails. And we have to save those two!"

"Impossible," Colonel Lindholm objected. "The hex storm has made the coastal region inaccessible. All rescue and emergency resources have been withdrawn to safe distances."

"Sophie and Karen are still there," Stephanie countered. "Trying to complete the transmission. If they can't..."

The implications hung unspoken: two people potentially sacrificed in a vain attempt to secure data that might already be too late to implement.

Alex stared at the atmospheric display, the intricate fractal patterns continuing their inevitable spread across the global map. Time was running out not just for Sophie and Karen, but for the atmosphere humans had evolved within for millennia.

The observatory's main dome shuddered violently as the hex storm reached full intensity. Glass had shattered in many of the windows, allowing the unnatural geometric wind patterns to penetrate the structure. The building—designed for traditional weather conditions—was clearly struggling to withstand forces it had never been engineered to resist.

"Transmission at 76%," Karen reported, frustration evident in her voice. "The connection keeps dropping. At this rate..."

Sophie was at the windows, watching the storm's evolution with horrified fascination. The fractal patterns had achieved remarkable complexity—nested geometric structures rotating in coordinated layers, creating what looked like a vast mathematical algorithm written in clouds and wind.

"It's beautiful," she said softly. "In a terrifying way."

"It's efficient," Karen corrected. "The fractal organization maximizes energy distribution through the atmosphere. Perfect mathematical optimization replacing chaotic natural patterns."

A tremendous crash from below indicated structural failure in another part of the building. The floor beneath them trembled ominously.

"We need to move," Sophie decided. "This structure isn't going to hold."

Karen nodded grimly, gathering her equipment. "We can try the basement level. More structural integrity, potentially less interference with the transmission since we'd be closer to the router."

They made their way down the central staircase, forced to dodge debris as sections of the ceiling began to give way. The building's groans and creaks provided an ominous counterpoint to the strange harmonic howl of the geometric winds outside.

The basement level was indeed more stable, though water was beginning to seep in from somewhere—perhaps broken pipes or the beginning of storm surge from the nearby coast. Karen quickly set up her equipment again, reconnecting to the interrupted transmission.

"Resuming at 76%," she announced. "Signal is marginally better down here."

Sophie's phone buzzed with an incoming call from Stephanie.

"Status update? How bad is it?" Stephanie asked immediately.

"Building is taking heavy damage," Sophie reported. "We've relocated to the basement. Transmission continuing but slow."

"Listen carefully," Stephanie said, her voice tense. "We've been coordinating with Thorne's team about the prototype connection. They believe there's a critical threshold approaching—a point where the fractal reorganization achieves global coherence. Once that happens, no intervention will be effective."

"Great, just terrific. Timeframe?"

"Hours, not days. The resonance cascade deployment needs to begin within six hours maximum to have any chance of success."

Sophie glanced at Karen's equipment, where the transmission status had inched forward to 79%. "We may not complete the data transfer in time. Too much interference."

"Then we need alternatives," Stephanie insisted. "Karen's notebooks—could you relay the key elements verbally?"

Karen shook her head, overhearing the conversation. "Too complex. The resonance cascade requires precise frequency modulation patterns across multiple spectra. Hundreds of pages of calculations and experimental results."

The building shuddered again, more violently than before. Dust and small debris showered from the ceiling.

"We need extraction," Sophie told Stephanie. "Military transport that can handle these conditions."

"They're saying it's impossible," Stephanie replied grimly. "No aircraft can safely approach during an active hex storm. The crazy wind patterns create unpredictable shear forces that exceed design tolerances. All roads are impassable with fallen trees and pavement upheavals. "

Karen looked up suddenly from her equipment. "Wait. The patterns aren't unpredictable—they're mathematical. Precisely mathematical."

"Meaning?" Sophie asked.

"Meaning they follow fractal algorithms. Complex but deterministic." Karen was already typing furiously on her system. "If we can model the exact fractal pattern of this specific storm, we could potentially identify safe corridors within the geometric structure—paths where wind shear is minimized."

"Can you do that modeling with the equipment you have?"

"No," Karen admitted. "But..." She turned to her secure communication system. "Stephanie, connect me with Olaf Werner's team. They've been tracking hex storm development globally. They might have the modeling capability we need."

Within minutes, they were in direct communication with Werner's Colorado facility, where atmospheric scientists were already developing advanced models of hex storm behavior.

"The fractal patterns follow consistent mathematical principles," Werner confirmed after hearing Karen's theory. "We've been observing them evolve from simple hexagons to complex nested structures. There is indeed algorithmic predictability once you understand the underlying equations."

"Can you model this specific storm?" Karen pressed. "Generate safe corridor predictions for potential aircraft approach?"

"Possibly," Werner replied. "We'd need precise local data on the current fractal configuration."

"We can provide that," Sophie said, moving to the basement's small window. Using her phone's specialized camera, she began capturing high-resolution imagery of the storm's visible structure.

"Uploading storm visualization now," she told Werner's team. "Multiple angles and time-sequence to show evolutionary patterns."

As the Colorado team began processing this data, Karen continued working on the stalled transmission—now at 82% but still progressing painfully slowly.

"Even if we identify safe corridors, who would attempt extraction?" Sophie asked pragmatically. "Military assets have been withdrawn beyond the storm boundary."

The answer came from an unexpected source. Colonel Lindholm rejoined the call, his expression grave but determined. "I have a pilot volunteer. Former search and rescue specialist with extensive experience in extreme conditions. If Dr. Werner's team can provide safe corridor coordinates with reasonable confidence, we'll attempt extraction with a specialized helicopter."

"The risk is enormous," Karen warned.

"So is the alternative," Lindholm replied simply. "The resonance cascade data may be our only chance to prevent permanent atmospheric transformation. The pilot understands the stakes."

As Werner's team worked on the fractal modeling, Sophie and Karen continued their efforts to complete the data transmission— now an insurance policy in case the physical extraction failed. The building continued to deteriorate around them, water rising steadily on the basement floor, structural integrity visibly compromised.

"I've never seen mathematics manifest physically like this," Karen said, watching the fractal patterns through the window. "It's as if the atmosphere is being rewritten according to geometric equations."

"Is that what the resonance cascade disrupts?" Sophie asked. "The mathematical organization?"

Karen nodded. "It introduces controlled chaos into the particle network—breaking the coherent patterns that enable coordinated behavior. If deployed correctly, it should force the particles back to their original state: individual reflective units without networking capability."

"And if deployed incorrectly?"

Karen's expression darkened. "Potential atmospheric destabilization beyond anything we're seeing now. The particles have become integral to global atmospheric circulation. Disrupting them without proper calibration could trigger catastrophic turbulence."

The implications hung heavily between them. The resonance cascade was not merely a 'reset button'—it was itself a high-risk intervention in an already destabilized system.

"We have preliminary corridor modeling," Werner's team announced suddenly. "The fractal pattern generates periodic low-shear pathways through the storm structure. They're temporary—existing for approximately 3-5 minutes before the pattern evolution closes them—but they appear predictable."

Colonel Lindholm immediately acted on this information. "Extraction helicopter is preparing for approach using these corridor predictions. Estimated arrival at the observatory in thirty minutes, assuming corridor availability and accuracy."

Sophie surveyed their deteriorating shelter. "This building may not have thirty minutes."

As if confirming her assessment, a major support beam cracked overhead, sending a shower of debris onto the basement floor. The water level had now risen to their ankles.

"Transmission at 87%," Karen reported, protecting her equipment from falling debris. "Still too slow."

"We need to move again," Sophie decided. "Somewhere more stable."

They gathered the essential equipment and Karen's notebooks, abandoning the less critical components. The basement corridor led them to what appeared to be an old storage area—small but with reinforced concrete walls that might withstand the storm's assault longer than their previous location.

As they set up the transmission equipment again, Sophie's phone displayed an incoming message from Stephanie: Werner's team confirms point of no return approaching faster than predicted. Global fractal coherence possible within six hours. Thorne's prototype monitoring shows accelerating organization.

The stakes were crystallizing with terrifying clarity. They were in a race against not just the deteriorating observatory and approaching helicopter, but against a fundamental transformation of Earth's atmosphere—a change that, once complete, would be beyond human capacity to reverse.

Karen resumed the interrupted transmission, now at 89%. "Even at maximum speed, full transfer will take at least forty more minutes," she calculated grimly.

"The helicopter will be here in thirty," Sophie reminded her. "If it can reach us at all."

They settled into tense silence, listening to the unnatural geometric winds howling through the failing structure above them. The building continued to deteriorate, creaks and crashes marking the progressive collapse of upper levels.

Sophie's thoughts turned to Alex, had their attempt to stop Phase Three been completely in vain? Or had the partial success—

some facilities receiving the stand-down code—bought them the precious hours they now desperately needed?

Her reflection was interrupted by an urgent communication from Lindholm: Extraction helicopter approaching storm boundary. Pilot has Werner's corridor predictions. First safe approach window in seven minutes.

Sophie relayed this to Karen, who checked the transmission status: 91% complete, still agonizingly slow.

"We might have to choose," Karen said soberly. "Wait for transmission completion or evacuate with the physical data when the helicopter arrives."

"Can we do both? Leave the equipment transmitting while we evacuate?"

Karen shook her head. "Too risky. If the building collapses completely, the transmission dies. And if we're not extracted in this window, we might not get another chance." She gestured to her weatherproof case containing the original research. "This has to reach the Task Force, one way or another."

The decision crystallized: their survival and the physical transport of the complete data took priority over the uncertain transmission. Sophie contacted Stephanie to explain their choice.

"Understood," Stephanie confirmed. "We'll work with what we've received so far—92% and counting. Prototype targeting is already being prepared based on Thorne's inputs. But the complete resonance cascade protocols are still critical for the stratospheric deployment."

The building lurched suddenly, a deep structural groan suggesting foundation damage. Water was now at mid-calf level and rising rapidly—storm surge from the nearby coast clearly breaching the lower levels.

"Status on the helicopter?" Sophie asked urgently.

"Approaching first corridor entry point," Lindholm reported. "Werner's team is providing real-time fractal pattern updates. If predictions hold, it should reach the observatory in twelve minutes."

Sophie surveyed their deteriorating shelter with growing alarm. "We need to get to the roof. The main observatory dome has collapsed or maybe even blown away, but the eastern observation platform might still be intact."

"What about the transmission?" Karen asked, checking the status: 93%.

"We abort and take the physical data," Sophie decided. "The building integrity is failing fast."

Karen nodded grimly, disconnecting the transmission equipment and securing her weatherproof case of research materials. They made their way through the flooding basement toward the emergency stairs, forced to wade through increasingly deep water.

The stairwell was partially blocked by fallen debris, requiring careful navigation. As they climbed, the sounds of the hex storm grew louder—its unnatural harmonic howl punctuated by the cracking and groaning of the failing building.

"The geometric wind patterns are intensifying," Karen observed as they passed a broken window. Outside, the fractal organization of the storm was now incredibly complex—nested mathematical structures rotating with precise coordination, creating flow patterns of remarkable intricacy.

"Werner's safe corridor concept depends on those patterns maintaining predictability," Sophie noted. "If they evolve too quickly..."

The implication hung unspoken—the helicopter could find itself trapped in suddenly shifting wind shear beyond its structural tolerance.

They reached the second floor, finding most of it severely damaged. The main telescope dome had indeed collapsed, its historic instrument now exposed to the elements. But as Sophie had hoped, the eastern observation platform remained partially intact.

"That's our extraction point," she told Karen, pointing toward the platform. "We need to secure the area and prepare visual signals for the helicopter."

As they worked to clear debris from the platform, Sophie's phone buzzed with an update from Lindholm: Helicopter successfully navigating first fractal corridor. Approach on schedule. Five minutes to arrival.

For the first time, a glimmer of hope seemed possible. If the extraction succeeded, if Karen's research reached them in time, if the resonance cascade could be deployed before global coherence...

The chain of contingencies was daunting, but each link seemed fractionally more feasible than it had hours earlier.

Through the storm's geometric patterns, they could now hear the distant sound of helicopter rotors—faint but growing steadily louder. The pilot was successfully navigating the mathematical corridors predicted by Werner's modeling.

"Almost there," Sophie encouraged, helping Karen secure the research materials for rapid transfer. "We'll need to board quickly when it arrives. The safe corridor won't remain stable for long."

The helicopter sound grew louder, now visible as a small dark shape navigating through the geometric storm patterns with remarkable precision. The pilot was clearly skilled, adjusting course in perfect synchronization with the fractal corridor predictions being relayed in real-time.

Sophie signaled with an emergency light, confirming their position on the observation platform. The helicopter acknowledged, adjusting its approach angle toward their location.

Just as success seemed within reach, a violent shudder ran through the observatory building—the most severe yet. The observation platform lurched downward several feet, its supporting structure failing catastrophically.

"Move back!" Sophie shouted, pulling Karen toward the more stable section of the floor. The platform's edge crumbled away, leaving a dangerous gap between the building and where the helicopter would need to hover.

"We can't board from here," Karen realized, horror in her voice. "The platform isn't going to hold together."

Sophie assessed their options rapidly. "The main roof," she decided. "We need to reach the central section. It might still have enough structural integrity."

They retreated inside, racing through damaged corridors toward the central staircase that would lead to the roof access. Behind them, the observation platform collapsed completely, confirming the correctness of their decision.

Sophie contacted Lindholm, explaining the situation. "Redirect the helicopter to the main roof," she instructed. "Observation platform has failed."

"Acknowledged," came the tense reply. "Pilot is adjusting approach. Be advised: fractal corridor shifting faster than predicted. Our window is narrowing."

They reached the roof access door, finding it jammed by structural deformation. Together, they forced it open enough to squeeze through, emerging onto what remained of the main roof.

The view was apocalyptic. The historic observatory dome had collapsed entirely, leaving a jagged hole where the massive telescope had once been housed. Most of the eastern wing had already failed, with partial collapse progressing toward the central section where they now stood.

"Here!" Sophie signaled, indicating the strongest-looking section of the remaining roof.

The helicopter maneuvered closer, fighting against the precisely patterned but intensely powerful winds. Through the windshield, Sophie could see the pilot's face—focused, determined, aware of the stakes involved in this impossible extraction.

Just as the aircraft reached hovering position above them, Werner's voice came urgently through Sophie's communication link: "Fractal pattern shifting! Corridor collapsing in twenty seconds!"

The helicopter pilot clearly received the same warning, immediately dropping a rescue harness rather than attempting a landing on the unstable roof.

"You first," Sophie told Karen, helping her secure the harness around both herself and the precious research case.

"Both of us," Karen insisted. "The harness can hold two."

As the building shuddered beneath them, Sophie made a split-second assessment of the helicopter's hover stability against the roof's structural integrity. The aircraft was already struggling against the shifting wind patterns—adding two people's weight to the rescue line might exceed its control margins.

"The research has to reach the Task Force," Sophie said firmly, securing the harness around Karen alone. "I'll signal when you're ready."

Before Karen could protest further, Sophie gave the extraction signal. The helicopter's hoist system activated immediately, lifting Karen and the vital research materials from the failing roof.

As Karen ascended, the building gave another violent lurch—the section where Sophie stood dropped several inches as supporting structures failed beneath it. The helicopter pilot responded instantly, pulling away from the collapsing building while continuing to lift Karen toward safety.

Through her ear buds, Sophie heard Werner's urgent update: "Corridor completely collapsed! New pattern forming—calculating alternative exit route!"

The helicopter hovered at a safer distance, completing Karen's extraction while the pilot assessed options for a second rescue attempt. But the building was now failing rapidly, sections collapsing in chain-reaction as the geometric storm intensified around it.

Sophie's phone buzzed with an incoming message—from Karen, now safely aboard the helicopter: They can't come back for you. The corridor's gone. New mathematical pattern forming but unpredictable. I'm so sorry, Sophie!

Sophie looked up at the helicopter, now pulling away toward a newly forming safe corridor that Werner's team had identified. The research was safe. Karen would reach the Task Force. The resonance cascade had a chance. But it was a matter of minutes, not hours, and now for Sophie the immediate problem was staying alive.

Whatever happened next, she had helped ensure humanity's best hope of preventing the point of no return.

As the observatory continued to collapse around her, Sophie found an area of relative stability and crouched there, watching the atmosphere's transformation above. The fractal patterns had evolved to remarkable complexity—mathematical beauty written across the sky in clouds and wind.

Her phone buzzed again—Stephanie this time: Sophie, we're receiving conflicting data about your location. Satellite imagery shows observatory structural failure progressing rapidly. What's your status?

Sophie replied simply: Karen extracted with research. Building failing. I'm still here. Focus on implementing the resonance cascade before coherence point.

Stephanie's response came immediately: Rescue options?

Sophie looked at the evolving fractal patterns, the collapsing building, the impossible mathematics of the storm: None viable. Atmospheric reorganization accelerating. Point of no return approaching. Karen's research is humanity's priority now.

As the building continued to deteriorate around her, Sophie turned her professional instincts toward documentation. Using her phone's camera, she began recording the atmospheric phenomena— the evolving fractal patterns, the mathematical precision of what had once been chaotic weather.

If these were to be Earth's new atmospheric dynamics, someone should record the transition. And if the resonance cascade succeeded, this footage would provide valuable scientific documentation of a phenomenon humanity might never witness again.

Either way, Sophie Lorde would bear witness to this dark day for planet Earth.

In the military hospital outside Stockholm, Alex Ross stared in horror at the satellite imagery showing the observatory's progressive collapse. Sophie's last communication had been clear—she was still inside the failing structure, while Karen and the research had been successfully extracted.

"The helicopter couldn't go back for her," Colonel Lindholm explained grimly. "The fractal corridors evolved too rapidly. Werner's team couldn't predict safe passage for a second approach."

Alex struggled to maintain his focus despite the personal devastation, his attachment to Sophie had snuck up on him, but now was quite real. "Karen's research? Status?"

"En route to Task Force headquarters," Lindholm confirmed. "Estimated arrival in forty minutes. Full implementation planning for the resonance cascade will begin immediately."

On the main display, the global atmospheric monitoring system showed the continued evolution of fractal patterns across the planet—geometric structures connecting, integrating, approaching the coherence point that would render the transformation irreversible.

"Time estimate to point of no return?" Alex asked, forcing himself to focus on the global crisis despite his concern for Sophie.

Olaf Werner appeared on screen, his expression grim. "Acceleration continues beyond our models. Based on current evolution rates, global coherence possible within 4-5 hours. We're seeing integration of previously isolated fractal structures across hemispheric boundaries. This is very much global."

The implications were clear: they had even less time than previously thought to implement the cascade before Earth's atmosphere was permanently reorganized.

Warren Thorne joined the discussion from his Swiss compound. "The prototype particles have progressed to what we're calling 'fractal maturity'—a state of perfect mathematical organization. Based on the quantum entanglement pattern, the deployed network will reach equivalent status within hours."

"And after that?" Isabelle asked from her hospital bed beside Alex.

"After that, no intervention will disrupt the network's coherence," Thorne replied soberly. "The particles will have established a self-sustaining system of atmospheric management governed by mathematical principles no human designed or fully understands."

Alex studied the global visualization, the beautiful and terrifying mathematics spreading across Earth's atmosphere. "Then we have one chance," he said, determination replacing despair. "One opportunity to deploy the resonance cascade before coherence is achieved."

The science team from the Vault facility, Amara Okafor and Wei Zhang contributed their unique knowledge, "We've prepared the targeting system for the prototype particles," Okafor reported. "Based on the partial resonance cascade data already received, combined with Thorne's control frequencies, we believe we can disrupt the quantum entanglement that links the prototypes to the deployed network."

"Can you estimate a probability of success?" Alex asked.

"Theoretical only," Zhang admitted. "We've never attempted to manipulate quantum entanglement at this scale or complexity. But the mathematical models suggest a 60-70% chance of disrupting the connection if precisely calibrated."

"And without Karen's complete research?"

"Reduced to perhaps 30-40%," Okafor estimated. "The partial transmission gave us the basic framework, but we're missing crucial modulation sequences and deployment timing."

Alex exchanged glances with Isabelle, both understanding the stakes with perfect clarity. Earth stood at the threshold of permanent atmospheric transformation—geometric mathematics replacing the chaotic patterns that had shaped weather since the planet's formation.

The countdown to point of no return continued, implacable and indifferent to human timescales. On screens throughout the emergency command center, global visualization showed the spreading fractal patterns connecting across hemispheric boundaries—the hex storms evolving toward a unified planetary system.

"Karen's helicopter has landed at Task Force headquarters," Colonel Lindholm announced. "Research materials secure, Karen is safe. Implementation team standing by."

A collective exhalation of relief rippled through the conference. The resonance cascade research had survived, even if Sophie remained trapped at the collapsing observatory.

"Time to deployment?" Alex asked.

"Minimum four hours," responded the chief engineer. "The resonance cascade requires precise calibration across multiple parameters. We've been fabricating the generators based on Dr. Mitchell's specifications, but testing and distribution to launch platforms will take time."

"Meanwhile, the atmospheric coherence continues accelerating," Olaf added, highlighting regions on the global display. "The fractal integration is spreading fastest along these corridors—North Atlantic, Central Pacific, Indian Ocean basin."

"And the prototype system?" Isabelle asked, addressing the Vault facility team.

"We've implemented maximum isolation protocols," Dr. Okafor reported. "But the quantum entanglement appears unaffected. The prototypes continue organizing into increasingly complex fractal structures—patterns the deployed network continues to adopt approximately six hours later."

"Could we destroy the prototypes?" someone suggested. "If they're directing the network evolution..."

Zhang shook his head. "Too unpredictable. The quantum connection might propagate destructive resonance throughout the deployed system, potentially triggering even worse catastrophic atmospheric destabilization."

"We need controlled disruption," Alex emphasized. "The resonance cascade is designed to break the networking capability without destroying the particles themselves. Precision, not brute force."

Karen Mitchell herself now joined the conference, her face appearing on screen from Task Force headquarters. Despite obvious exhaustion, her focus was absolute.

"My research indicates the particle network has a specific vulnerability in its electromagnetic coordination patterns," she explained. "The resonance cascade works by introducing counter-frequency pulses that disrupt these patterns, forcing the particles to revert to individual reflective units without networking capability."

"Implemented how?" asked the military liaison responsible for deployment.

"Simultaneous release at multiple stratospheric points," Karen replied. "The resonance propagates through the particle network, breaking connection patterns as it spreads." She called up technical diagrams showing deployment specifications. "Critical mass requires at least seven simultaneous initiation points distributed globally."

"The atmospheric deployment is proceeding," the liaison confirmed. "But Thorne's team has suggested we might amplify the effect by targeting the prototypes simultaneously."

Karen considered this. "Theoretically sound, assuming the quantum entanglement behaves as they suggest. The prototypes could serve as a force multiplier, propagating the disruption pattern throughout the network faster than atmospheric deployment alone."

"A coordinated strike," Alex summarized. "Atmospheric deployment plus prototype targeting."

Karen nodded. "Maximum chance of disrupting the network before coherence."

"The prototype behavior has evolved further," Warren Thorne reported without preamble. "They're forming what our team is calling a 'coherence seed'—a central organizing pattern that appears to be directing the broader fractal development."

"Meaning?" Alex prompted.

"Meaning we may have even less time than previously estimated," Thorne replied grimly. "The coherence point could arrive within three hours, not four to five."

The implications registered across all faces in the conference. The already narrow window for intervention was shrinking further.

"We need to accelerate," Karen decided. "Begin resonance cascade deployment with the generators we have ready, even before full testing. Add additional points as new units become operational."

"Risky," cautioned the chief engineer. "Untested generators could fail or produce unpredictable effects."

"A necessary risk against certain atmospheric transformation," Alex countered. "I agree with Karen. We deploy as capabilities come online, rather than waiting for the full system."

The conference broke into focused implementation planning— deployment coordinates, timing sequences, monitoring protocols. As technical teams dispersed to execute their assignments, Alex found himself momentarily alone with the satellite feed showing the Stockholm coast, where the hex storm continued its geometric assault on the observatory where Sophie remained trapped. More and more he was realizing how much she had become important to him, someone with a personal connection, perhaps even a relationship.

"We'll send extraction forces as soon as the storm stabilizes," Colonel Lindholm said, noticing Alex's attention to the feed.

"If it stabilizes," Alex replied quietly.

"She's a remarkable person," Lindholm observed. "Staying behind to ensure Mitchell's extraction."

"She understood the stakes." Alex struggled to keep his voice steady. "The resonance cascade research had to reach you, no matter the cost."

Across the room, Isabelle was speaking with Karen's team, contributing her knowledge of the particle development history to the resonance cascade implementation. Despite her injuries, she had insisted on remaining fully engaged in the response effort.

"First deployment units ready," announced the operations director. "High-altitude aircraft prepared for launch at seven global positions."

"Initial coverage sufficient?" Karen asked.

"Approximately 60% of optimal. Additional units will deploy as they come online, expanding coverage incrementally."

Karen nodded her approval. "Proceed with launch sequence. Synchronize with prototype targeting at the Vault facility."

"Deployment aircraft launching," reported the operations center. "Estimated time to stratospheric release: forty-six minutes."

The countdown continued, humanity's response now racing against the mathematics of atmospheric transformation. On monitoring displays, the spreading fractal patterns showed no sign of slowing their integration. If anything, the connection rate was accelerating as the system approached coherence.

"Prototype targeting system calibrated and ready," reported Okafor from the Vault facility. "Resonance frequencies aligned with Mitchell's specifications."

"Synchronize for simultaneous initiation with atmospheric deployment," Karen instructed.

The atmosphere's fate now rested on this unprecedented intervention—a globally coordinated attempt to disrupt a planetary-scale system that no human had fully designed or understood. The resonance cascade represented humanity's best hope of preventing the point of no return—the threshold beyond which Earth's atmosphere would function according to new principles.

"T-minus thirty minutes to stratospheric deployment," announced the operations director.

Alex checked the satellite feed of the Stockholm coast again. The hex storm continued its geometric assault on the remains of the observatory, but something caught his attention—a small anomaly in the otherwise perfect mathematical pattern. A brief distortion in the fractal structure, almost like a momentary glitch in the system. Alex was having a tough time reconciling what he saw with hard science – the pieces just weren't fitting.

"Dr. Werner," he called. "Are you seeing this? Stockholm hex storm, western quadrant."

Werner examined the feed, his expression shifting from curiosity to alarm. "That's not isolated. Check global visualization, sector 14-C. Similar pattern distortion appearing in the North Atlantic formation."

They turned to the main display, where indeed, subtle irregularities were becoming visible in multiple regions—brief disruptions in the otherwise perfect geometric patterns.

"What are we looking at?" Alex asked.

"Coherence instabilities," Werner replied. "The fractal organization is approaching a transitional threshold where minor imperfections can propagate through the system."

"Is this good or bad for our intervention?" Colonel Lindholm asked.

"Unknown," Werner admitted. "It could make the system more vulnerable to the resonance cascade—or it could accelerate coherence as the system compensates for instabilities."

Karen joined their analysis, studying the distortion patterns with intense focus. "These appear similar to the phase transition fluctuations I observed in laboratory testing. When particle networks approach coherence, they often demonstrate brief instability just before locking into stable configuration."

"Meaning?" Alex prompted.

"Meaning we may be even closer to the point of no return than we thought," Karen replied grimly. "These distortions could be the final phase transition before global coherence is achieved."

"Can we accelerate deployment?" Alex asked.

"The aircraft are already at maximum speed, these things are built to be rugged – not fast" replied the operations director. "Twenty-seven minutes to stratospheric position."

"And the prototype targeting?"

"Ready now," Okafor confirmed. "We're prepared for synchronization with the atmospheric deployment."

A tense silence fell as they considered the options. Acting too soon might reduce effectiveness; waiting too long might miss the window entirely.

The decision came from an unexpected source. Warren Thorne, who had been quietly monitoring the situation, spoke with sudden clarity.

"Initiate prototype targeting now," he ordered. "Don't wait for atmospheric deployment."

"That contradicts the synchronization protocol," Karen objected.

"The protocol assumed stable progression toward coherence," Thorne countered. "These distortion patterns change the equation. The system is approaching phase transition faster than anticipated. A partial intervention now may be better than a perfect intervention too late. If we can't kill it, maybe we can wound it."

Karen studied the distortion patterns again, then nodded slowly. "He's right. The prototype targeting might slow the coherence process enough to give the atmospheric deployment time to reach position."

"Proceed with prototype targeting," Alex confirmed.

At the Vault facility, Okafor and Zhang initiated the resonance cascade sequence. The specially calibrated electromagnetic pulses began streaming into the containment chamber, interacting with the prototype particles' complex fractal structures.

"Initial response detected," Zhang reported. "The fractal organization is showing disturbance patterns."

On monitoring screens, they could see the previously ordered geometric structures beginning to waver—precise mathematical patterns becoming less coherent as the resonance effect disrupted the particles' networking capability.

"Is it propagating through the quantum entanglement?" Alex asked.

"Too soon to tell," Okafor replied. "We need more time to—"

She stopped mid-sentence, attention drawn to the global visualization. Across multiple regions, the fractal distortions were intensifying—no longer brief glitches but sustained disruptions in the geometric patterns.

"It's working," Werner said, almost disbelieving. "The quantum connection is propagating the disruption to the deployed network."

Hope surged through the command center as the evidence mounted. The prototype targeting was indeed affecting the global system, disrupting the fractal organization that had been approaching coherence.

"Atmospheric deployment still proceeding," confirmed the operations director. "T-minus twenty minutes. But we're already seeing network disruption effects in multiple sectors."

Karen studied the data with cautious optimism. "The prototype targeting is creating a destabilization wave through the quantum entanglement. It's slowing the coherence process, but not stopping it completely. We still need the full atmospheric deployment to break the networking capability permanently."

As they watched, the global visualization showed the disruption patterns spreading—fractal structures beginning to lose their perfect geometric organization across multiple regions. The mathematics of atmosphere were being disrupted, the system's progression toward coherence temporarily destabilized.

But something else was happening simultaneously. In regions where the fractal patterns were most disrupted, new atmospheric behaviors were emerging—violent turbulence as the geometrically organized flows began breaking down into more chaotic patterns.

"Weather transition effects," Werner noted with concern. "As the network loses coherence, we're seeing reversion to natural atmospheric dynamics—but the transition is creating extreme turbulence zones."

On regional displays, they could see the effects manifesting as intensified storm systems along boundaries where geometric patterns were dissolving—conventional but severe weather replacing the mathematical precision of the hex storms.

"Expected to some degree but concerning," Karen said. "The resonance cascade doesn't just 'switch off' the network. It triggers a cascading breakdown that releases the energy contained in the geometric structures."

"Will the atmospheric deployment make this worse?" Colonel Lindholm asked.

"Temporarily, yes," Karen confirmed. "The full resonance cascade will accelerate the breakdown process. We'll see increased atmospheric turbulence during the transition period before stabilization."

The implications were sobering. Success meant not a smooth return to normal weather patterns, but a potentially chaotic transition period as Earth's atmosphere readjusted from geometric organization to natural flows.

"Stockholm coast showing significant turbulence increase," reported a monitoring technician. "The hex storm structure is dissolving, but conventional storm intensity is spiking."

Alex turned to the satellite feed, where indeed the previously perfect hexagonal structure over the observatory was breaking down—mathematical precision giving way to more natural but intensely powerful storm conditions. Was this relief for the observatory, or even more brutal punishment?

"Sophie," he said quietly, concern evident despite his professional focus.

"We have rescue assets standing by," Lindholm assured him. "As soon as conditions permit safe approach, we'll attempt extraction."

"T-minus fifteen minutes to atmospheric deployment," announced the operations director. "All seven aircraft reporting optimal positioning trajectory."

The resonance cascade was working—disrupting the particle network before it could achieve coherence, preventing the point of no return from being crossed. But the cost would be significant: a planetary-scale weather crisis as the atmosphere transitioned back to its natural state.

"Prototype response intensifying," reported Zhang from the Vault facility. "The fractal structures are showing accelerated breakdown."

"T-minus ten minutes to atmospheric deployment," came the update. "Final countdown procedures initiated."

The team watched as the prototype targeting continued affecting the global network, creating a window of opportunity for the atmospheric intervention to complete what had begun. Earth stood at the threshold—not of a transformation to mathematical precision, but of a return journey to natural patterns through turbulent transition.

"T-minus five minutes to atmospheric deployment," announced the operations director. "All systems nominal."

On the global visualization, the prototype-initiated disruption continued spreading, but the fractal structures were already showing signs of adaptation—the network attempting to compensate for the disturbances, to maintain progression toward coherence despite the intervention.

"We're seeing resistance patterns in sectors 3, 7, and 12," Werner reported with concern. "The network is routing around disrupted nodes, establishing alternate connection pathways."

"The prototype targeting alone won't be sufficient," Karen concluded. "The system is demonstrating resilience—attempting to preserve coherence through adaptive reorganization."

"T-minus two minutes to atmospheric deployment," came the update. "All aircraft in final position."

On screens throughout the command center, they could see the high-altitude deployment aircraft reaching their stratospheric positions—seven points strategically distributed across the global atmosphere, each carrying resonance cascade generators calibrated to Karen's specifications.

"Prototype targeting reaching maximum effect," reported Okafor. "But global network showing increasing resistance. We estimate less than twenty minutes before adaptive reorganization could establish coherence despite current disruption levels."

"Stratospheric position achieved," announced the operations director. "Deployment sequence initiating."

Across seven points in Earth's stratosphere, specially designed generators began releasing the precisely calibrated electromagnetic frequencies of Karen's resonance cascade—waves designed to disrupt the networking capability of the particles without destroying them entirely.

"Resonance propagation confirmed," Karen reported, studying the incoming data. "Disruption patterns matching theoretical models."

On the global visualization, they could see the effect spreading rapidly from the deployment points—waves of disruption moving through the particle network, breaking connection patterns, interrupting the fractal organization that had been approaching coherence.

Combined with the prototype-initiated disruption already underway, the effect was dramatic. Across all monitoring sectors, the geometric structures began losing coherence—mathematical precision giving way to increasing disorder as the particles' networking capability failed.

"It's working," Isabelle said, watching the visualization with a mixture of relief and concern. "The network coherence is breaking down globally."

But success brought its own challenges. As the geometric patterns dissolved, atmospheric turbulence intensified in multiple regions—the transition from mathematical organization to natural flows releasing enormous energy into weather systems worldwide.

"Severe storm systems developing along fractal dissolution boundaries," Werner reported. "Wind speeds exceeding hurricane force in multiple locations. Pressure gradients reaching extreme values."

The command center became a hub of dual focus—monitoring both the successful disruption of the particle network and the resulting weather crisis as Earth's atmosphere underwent traumatic transition back toward natural patterns.

"Stockholm region showing complete hex storm dissolution," reported a monitoring technician. "Transitioning to conventional severe storm system."

Alex turned to the satellite feed, where the geometric patterns had indeed given way to more natural but intensely powerful storm conditions along the Swedish coast. The observatory where Sophie remained trapped was now being battered by conventional but extreme weather—potentially more dangerous than the mathematical precision of the hex storm, answering his concern whether the changes were favorable or more threatening.

"Network coherence breaking down in all sectors," Karen confirmed, studying the global data. "The resonance cascade is achieving intended effect. The particles are losing networking capability, reverting to individual reflective units."

"And the weather transition effects?" Colonel Lindholm asked.

"Severe but temporary," Karen replied. "The models suggest extreme turbulence for 72-96 hours as the atmosphere reestablishes natural circulation patterns. After that, gradual stabilization— though with continued influence from the reflective effect of the particles themselves."

Warren Thorne, still connected to the conference from his increasingly precarious position at the Swiss compound, studied the data with a complex expression—relief at the prevention of complete atmospheric transformation mixed with recognition of the crisis his intervention had ultimately triggered.

"The particles will remain in the stratosphere," he noted. "Without networking capability, but still reflecting sunlight."

"Yes," Karen confirmed. "We've broken the coherence, not removed the particles. The cooling effect will continue, giving us time to implement more sustainable climate solutions."

A new alert drew their attention back to the global visualization, where the disruption patterns had reached critical mass—over 80% of the particle network now showing loss of coherence. The mathematical organization was collapsing globally, the transformation to geometric atmosphere being reversed before completion.

"We've done it," Alex said quietly. "We've prevented the point of no return."

But there was no celebration in the command center—only grim determination as they pivoted to addressing the weather crisis now unfolding. Success meant not resolution but transition to a new phase of emergency response.

On the Stockholm coast satellite feed, winds were finally beginning to decrease from their peak intensity as the transitional turbulence began stabilizing. Rescue teams were preparing for approach to the observatory ruins where Sophie Lorde had last been reported. There had been no personal contact from her, only a weak signal from her phone.

Earth had narrowly avoided permanent transformation of its atmosphere to geometric organization. But the cost had been high— cities damaged by hex storms, regions now facing severe transitional weather, a planetary system stressed by rapid changes in fundamental circulation patterns. And unknown numbers of dead.

Yet hope remained. The resonance cascade had worked. The particle network had been disrupted before coherence. Human civilization would continue under an atmosphere governed by principles it understood and had evolved within—albeit one still influenced by the reflective particles that remained in the stratosphere.

The point of no return had been prevented. The dark day for planet Earth would eventually end, giving way to a dawn still recognizable to human eyes.

CHAPTER SIXTEEN: CASCADING FAILURE

[The Washington Post – April 15, 2026] Global Weather Crisis Intensifies as 'Geometric Storms' Dissolve into Chaotic Systems By Marcus Reynolds, Senior Science Correspondent

The International Atmospheric Stabilization Task Force reports partial success in disrupting the particle network responsible for the unprecedented "hex storms," but warns that the intervention has triggered what scientists are calling a "cascading failure" across global weather systems. As the geometric patterns dissolve, they're releasing enormous energy into conventional weather, creating severe storm systems along fractal dissolution boundaries. "We're witnessing the atmosphere transitioning back toward natural patterns, but the process is far from gentle," explains Olaf Werner of the Task Force scientific team. "The mathematical organization imposed by the particles is breaking down, but the resulting turbulence is creating weather extremes worldwide." Emergency management agencies across six continents are mobilizing unprecedented resources as storm systems of exceptional intensity develop along paths that defy traditional forecasting. Meanwhile, rescue operations continue at multiple locations where geometric storms were active, including the Swedish coast where journalist Sophie Lorde remains missing after the Saltsjöbaden Observatory collapse.

The transition was visible from space—a planet's atmosphere in the midst of fundamental reorganization. Where perfect geometric patterns had been spreading just hours earlier, now irregular turbulence bloomed along dissolution boundaries. The mathematical precision of the hex storms was giving way to chaotic natural systems, but the process was generating weather of extraordinary intensity.

"Resonance cascade achieving 86% disruption of particle networking capability," reported Karen Mitchell, monitoring incoming data from global sensor networks. "The mathematical organization is breaking down in all sectors, but the transitional effects are more severe than our models predicted."

"How long until stabilization?" asked the UN Secretary-General, who had arrived hours earlier to personally oversee the international response.

"Minimum 72 hours for primary atmospheric stabilization," Karen replied. "But regional weather anomalies could persist for weeks as circulation patterns reestablish natural equilibria."

Olaf Werner expanded the European monitoring sector, highlighting the dissolution pattern of what had been the Stockholm hex storm. "The geometric structures contained enormous potential energy in their organization. As that organization fails, the energy is being released as conventional but extreme weather."

"Status of rescue operations in affected regions?" the Secretary-General asked.

Colonel Lindholm brought up the operational dashboard. "Twenty-seven major extraction efforts underway globally. The Stockholm coast teams are approaching the observatory ruins now that wind speeds have decreased below critical thresholds."

Alex Ross studied this sector with particular intensity, his professional focus barely masking personal concern. The satellite imagery showed the remains of the historic observatory—largely collapsed, with only sections of the central structure still standing after the geometric storm's assault followed by the transitional turbulence.

"Any contact from Sophie?" he asked quietly.

"Intermittent signal detected approximately thirty minutes ago," Lindholm replied. "Too weak for voice communication, but the locator beacon in her specialized phone briefly activated. Rescue team is homing on that position now."

A notification chimed on the main communication system—a priority report from the Vault facility where the prototype particles were being monitored.

"Disruption cascade achieving full effect on prototype structures," Dr. Okafor announced, her image appearing on screen. "The quantum entanglement appears to be propagating the resonance pattern in both directions now—from deployed network back to prototypes, creating a self-reinforcing disruption loop."

"That's more than we could have hoped for," Karen noted with scientific interest despite the crisis atmosphere. "We anticipated one-way propagation from prototypes to deployment. Bi-directional flow suggests the entanglement properties are more robust than our models indicated."

"Regardless, it's accelerating network dissolution," Zhang added. "The mathematical organization is collapsing faster than projected. We estimate complete disruption of networking capability within six to eight hours."

This represented a significant victory—the primary goal of preventing the particle network from achieving coherence had been accomplished, and the dissolution was proceeding even faster than anticipated.

"Mumbai coastal region reporting extreme pressure gradient formation," announced an emergency coordinator. "Transitional storm system developing with unprecedented intensity."

"Sri Lanka facing similar conditions," added another. "The Indian Ocean dissolution boundary is generating multiple severe weather systems along a northwest axis."

"We need to adjust emergency response prioritization," Alex advised, studying the global pattern. "The dissolution boundaries are generating predictable formation corridors for transitional storm systems. We can project impact zones more effectively than traditional storm tracking would suggest."

Werner nodded agreement. "The mathematics of dissolution actually gives us an advantage for response coordination. These aren't conventional storms developing according to normal atmospheric principles. They're forming along specific geometric breakdown patterns that we can model with reasonable accuracy."

Working together, they began mapping projected impact trajectories based on the dissolution mathematics—identifying communities and infrastructure most at risk from the transitional weather systems. The Task Force's emergency coordination center rapidly relayed these projections to response agencies worldwide, allowing for more effective resource deployment and evacuation efforts.

"It's ironic," Isabelle Renard observed, watching this process unfold. "We're using the very mathematical principles of the system we're disrupting to predict how it will fall apart."

"Sometimes the best way to understand something is to break it," Karen replied, a scientist's appreciation for the process evident despite the crisis circumstances.

A new alert drew their attention back to the Stockholm coast sector, where the rescue team had reached the observatory ruins. Satellite imagery showed personnel carefully navigating through collapsed structures, following the beacon signal from Sophie's specialized phone.

Alex watched with carefully controlled emotion as the team progressed through the debris field. The chances of survival seemed impossibly small given the structural devastation visible from above. Yet the beacon signal suggested hope, however faint.

"Rescue team reporting contact!" Lindholm announced suddenly. "They've located Lorde—alive, in a partially collapsed storage room beneath the main structure."

Relief swept through Alex, momentarily displacing the professional focus he had maintained throughout the crisis. "Condition, is she conscious?"

"Injured but stable," Lindholm reported, reading the incoming assessment. "Protected by reinforced concrete walls when the main structure failed. Extraction underway now."

On the satellite feed, they could see the rescue team carefully removing debris to access the subterranean space where Sophie had taken shelter. The operation proceeded with painstaking precision, mindful of the structural instability surrounding them. The military satellite provided resolution far better than any civilian satellite, but still it was difficult to make out a meaningful image.

"She's still documenting," Lindholm added with a hint of amazement. "Rescue team reports she was recording atmospheric transition effects when they found her."

Alex smiled despite himself. "Of course she was."

The moment of personal relief was short-lived as new crisis reports continued flowing into the command center—a global weather emergency unfolding as the resonance cascade broke down the particle network's mathematical organization.

"North Atlantic dissolution boundary generating extreme system approaching Ireland and UK," reported an emergency coordinator. "Wind speeds exceeding 180 km/h, with unusual rotational patterns distinct from traditional cyclonic systems."

"Pacific Northwest facing similar formation along the coastal dissolution boundary," added another. "Seattle to Vancouver corridor preparing for impact within four hours."

Olaf stared at the global images, his worry stone forgotten in his pocket as both hands manipulated the atmospheric data displays. This was everything he'd feared as a teenager watching his home disappear under Hurricane Eliza's storm surge—but magnified to planetary scale. Weather had taken his home once; now the mathematics in the sky threatened to transform Earth's atmosphere permanently, rewriting the very rules he'd dedicated his life to understanding.

"Weather follows physical laws," he'd insisted to students just months ago. "Chaos theory applies, but underlying patterns remain consistent." Now he was watching those fundamental laws being overwritten by geometric principles no meteorologist had ever observed. Everything he knew about atmospheric physics was becoming obsolete in real time.

"The thermal reading from Mumbai's coastal region exceeds anything in our historical record," announced one of his graduate assistants.

Olaf nodded grimly. "And traditional forecasting models are failing completely. We need to develop hybrid approaches incorporating both natural fluid dynamics and these new mathematical principles." He briefly closed his eyes, centering himself. The personal stakes didn't matter now—only the response.

The cascading failure of the particle network was creating a planetary-scale weather crisis—a transitional phase between the geometric organization imposed by Thorne's system and the natural patterns that had governed Earth's atmosphere for millennia. Success in preventing permanent atmospheric transformation had come at the cost of unprecedented weather disruption in the short term.

A new communication request appeared—Warren Thorne, broadcasting from what appeared to be a secure transport vehicle. The Swiss authorities had taken him into custody as agreed, but were permitting his continued contribution to the crisis response effort.

"The prototype monitoring is showing something unexpected," Thorne reported without preamble. "As the resonance cascade disrupts the networking capability, we're seeing what appears to be a final attempt at pattern preservation—a concentrated geometric structure forming briefly before collapsing."

"Meaning what, I'm not following?" Alex prompted.

"It may indicate a resilience mechanism we didn't anticipate," Thorne explained. "A fail-safe response attempting to preserve core organizational patterns even as the broader network fails."

Karen's expression shifted to concern. "Could it reestablish networking capability after the resonance cascade completes?"

"Unlikely at full scale," Thorne replied. "But we should be prepared for potential remnant structures—isolated regions where geometric organization might persist at reduced scope."

This possibility added a new dimension to their already complex crisis management. The resonance cascade was succeeding globally, but might leave behind pockets of resistance—areas where the particle network maintained enough coherence to continue imposing mathematical organization on local atmospheric conditions.

"We need to identify potential remnant zones," Alex decided. "Regions where the network structure is showing highest resilience to the resonance cascade."

Werner began analyzing the dissolution patterns, looking for anomalies that might indicate such resistance. "The dissolution is least effective in these sectors," he reported, highlighting several regions on the global display. "Southern Indian Ocean, Central Siberia, and a portion of the South Atlantic. The fractal structures there are showing greater resilience to disruption."

"Target secondary resonance deployment to those regions," Karen instructed. "We can't risk even localized reformation of the network."

As this new response strategy developed, Alex received a private notification—Sophie had been successfully extracted from the observatory ruins and was en route to a medical facility in Stockholm. Her injuries were significant but not life-threatening, and she had managed to preserve both her documentation of the atmospheric phenomena and her specialized communication equipment throughout the ordeal.

This personal relief came amidst continuing global crisis updates—transitional storms making landfall in multiple regions, emergency response systems stretched to their limits, infrastructure failures reported across six continents. The cascading failure of the particle network was triggering weather systems that defied historical precedent both in intensity and behavior.

"Mumbai coastal impact beginning now," reported an emergency coordinator, bringing up live feeds from the region. The images showed a storm system unlike anything in known history—not a traditional cyclone or hurricane, but a hybrid phenomenon born from the collision of geometric organization and natural chaos. The rotational patterns showed remnants of hexagonal structure combined with the turbulent flows of conventional weather.

"Are these transitional systems following predictable behavior?" asked the Secretary-General, watching the footage with concern.

"Yes and no," Werner replied. "The formation patterns are predictable along dissolution boundaries. But the resulting systems combine elements of geometric organization and natural chaos in ways we've never observed. They don't behave entirely like conventional storms."

"Which makes response more challenging," Alex added. "Emergency protocols designed for hurricanes or typhoons may not be fully applicable to these hybrid phenomena."

The Task Force scientific team was already developing modified response guidelines—adapting conventional weather emergency protocols to address the unique characteristics of the transitional storms. These were being transmitted to affected regions in real time, allowing emergency management agencies to adjust their approaches accordingly.

"Resonance cascade reaching 92% disruption of networking capability," Karen reported, checking the latest global data. "The dissolution is accelerating as predicted."

On the main display, the planetary visualization showed the dramatic transformation underway—fractal structures dissolving across all sectors, replaced by the turbulent flows of natural weather. But these natural patterns were emerging in extreme forms, energized by the mathematical organization they were replacing.

"We've prevented one catastrophe," observed Isabelle, watching this planetary transition unfold. "But we're facing another of a different kind."

"One we understand and can respond to," Alex countered. "Extreme weather, however severe, follows principles we've studied for centuries. The geometric reorganization was taking us into unknown territory."

A new alert drew their attention to an unexpected development—satellite imagery showing unusual atmospheric behavior over Central Siberia, one of the regions identified as potentially resistant to the resonance cascade.

"The dissolution pattern is... reversing?" Werner reported with alarm, studying the data. "The fractal structures appear to be reorganizing in this isolated region."

"Thorne was right," Karen realized. "We're seeing a resilience response—a portion of the network attempting to preserve its organization despite the broader cascade failure."

"Localizing coordinates now," Werner continued. "The phenomenon is centered over the remote Taiga region, approximately 600 kilometers northeast of Novosibirsk."

Alex examined the visualization with growing concern. "That's the location of the Russian deployment facility—one of the original Helios launch sites."

"Which was reportedly damaged by a direct hex storm impact," Isabelle recalled. "Could something in the facility be generating a preservation effect? Maybe when the facility was abandoned and left exposed, turbulent weather sent some particles up into the atmosphere?"

The question hung in the air as they studied the developing anomaly. While the global particle network continued dissolving under the resonance cascade's influence, this isolated region was showing resistance—geometric patterns reforming, mathematical organization reasserting itself against the cascade's disruptive effect.

"We need to target concentrated resonance deployment to that specific location," Karen decided. "Maximum disruption focused on the preservation zone."

"Nearest deployment assets?" Lindholm asked.

"Russian Air Force has two specially equipped aircraft approximately 1,200 kilometers west," reported the operations director. "They can be redirected for targeted deployment within three hours."

"Not fast enough," Karen said, studying the reformation rate. "The preservation effect is accelerating. By the time they arrive, it could establish a stable foothold."

A tense silence fell as they considered the implications. Even as they succeeded in disrupting the global network, a localized remnant might survive—a seed from which geometric organization could potentially spread again if the conditions permitted.

"There's another option," Warren Thorne suggested, struggling to keep his voice calm despite the tension. "The entanglement observed between the prototypes and the deployed particles. If we target the prototypes with a specifically calibrated disruption sequence focused on the Siberian coordinates..."

"We might be able to break the preservation effect through the entanglement connection," Karen finished, immediately grasping the concept. "It's theoretically sound, assuming the entanglement properties remain intact despite the broader network disruption."

"They do," confirmed Okafor from the Vault facility. "We're still seeing correlation between prototype behavior and deployed network activity, even as both systems dissolve. The quantum connection appears remarkably resilient, and far beyond our understanding."

A new strategy quickly developed—a targeted intervention using the prototype particles as a quantum leverage point to disrupt the preservation effect forming in Siberia. Karen worked with the Vault team to design a specialized resonance pattern specifically calibrated to the unique signature of the reformation zone.

"Implementation ready," Zhang reported after intense preparation. "Targeted resonance sequence calibrated to Siberian coordinates and loaded into the prototype containment system."

"Proceed," authorized the Secretary-General.

At the Vault facility, the specialized resonance generator activated—focusing its disruptive effect on the prototype particles with precise calibration to target the Siberian preservation zone through quantum entanglement. The theory was elegant but unprecedented—attempting to disrupt a specific region of the deployed network by manipulating its quantum-entangled counterparts in the prototype chamber.

"An initial response has been detected in prototype behavior," Okafor reported, monitoring the immediate effects. "The targeted resonance is disrupting the specific organizational patterns associated with the Siberian coordinates."

All attention turned to the satellite imagery of the Siberian region, where the preservation effect had been forming against the broader dissolution trend. For several tense moments, there was no visible change—the geometric patterns continued reasserting themselves against the resonance cascade's disruptive influence.

Then, gradually, the reformation began to falter. The mathematical precision of the patterns became less distinct, the geometric organization showing signs of destabilization. The targeted intervention was propagating through the quantum entanglement, disrupting the preservation effect at its source.

"It's working," Werner confirmed, analyzing the real-time data. "The reformation process is breaking down. Dissolution patterns resuming in the Siberian sector."

Relief spread through the command center as satellite imagery confirmed the observation—the localized resistance collapsing, the preservation effect failing as the targeted resonance propagated through the quantum connection.

"Remarkable," Karen said, scientific fascination momentarily overriding crisis management focus. "The quantum entanglement is proving far more robust and manipulable than we anticipated. This has scientific implications beyond our current crisis."

"Let's focus on resolving this one before contemplating the next," suggested the Secretary-General dryly.

The immediate threat of localized network preservation had been addressed, but the broader crisis continued unfolding—transitional storms making landfall across multiple continents, emergency response systems operating at maximum capacity, infrastructure damage mounting as conventional but extreme weather replaced the dissolving geometric patterns.

"Mumbai system making landfall now," reported an emergency coordinator, bringing up live footage from the Indian coast. The transitional storm had evolved into something resembling a conventional cyclone but with unusual structural characteristics—remnants of geometric organization visible in its rotational patterns and energy distribution.

"Sri Lanka facing similar impact within two hours," added another coordinator. "Evacuation operations still underway in coastal districts."

"Resonance cascade reaching 95% disruption of networking capability," Karen reported, checking the latest global data. "Estimated time to complete dissolution of geometric organization is four to six hours."

"And the transitional weather effects we're seeing?" asked the Secretary-General.

"Peak intensity over the next 48-72 hours," Werner replied. "Followed by gradual stabilization as natural circulation patterns reestablish themselves. But we should expect continued anomalies for weeks as the atmosphere transitions back to equilibrium."

"We have a new communication request," announced the operations director. "Sophie Lorde, broadcasting from medical transport en route to Stockholm."

Alex straightened immediately, personal concern momentarily displacing professional focus. The display showed Sophie on a medical gurney inside a transport helicopter—injured but conscious, her characteristic intensity undimmed despite her ordeal.

"Atmospheric transition documentation is safe," she reported without preamble, holding up her specialized camera and data storage devices. "I recorded the entire dissolution process from inside the geometric structure as it broke down. Including some anomalies you should see immediately."

"What kind of anomalies?" Karen asked.

"Periodic reality... glitches, for lack of a better term," Sophie replied. "Moments where the dissolving geometric patterns seemed to temporarily stabilize before continuing breakdown. Almost like the system was attempting multiple reorganization strategies before failing."

This aligned with what they had observed in the Siberian sector—evidence of resilience mechanisms within the network, attempting to preserve organization even as the resonance cascade disrupted its coherence.

"Send the footage as soon as you're able," Karen requested. "It could help us identify other potential preservation zones before they fully form."

"Transmitting now," Sophie confirmed, initiating a data transfer from her equipment. "The most significant anomalies occurred approximately 47 minutes ago, correlating with the Siberian reformation attempt you just observed."

This connection added valuable confirmation to their understanding of the network's behavior during dissolution—suggesting a coordinated resilience response across the system rather than isolated preservation attempts.

"How did you survive the observatory collapse?" Alex asked, personal concern breaking through his professional demeanor.

"Reinforced storage room in the basement level," Sophie replied matter-of-factly. "And luck. The geometric storm actually created a stable pocket in its rotational structure—a zone of relative calm centered directly over the observatory before the resonance cascade triggered dissolution."

"The eye of the geometric storm," Werner noted with scientific interest. "Mathematically predictable but extraordinary to experience, I imagine."

Sophie confirmed. "Perfect mathematical calm surrounded by perfectly mathematical chaos. Until your resonance cascade disrupted the patterns and conventional physics reasserted itself."

The footage she had captured would provide invaluable scientific documentation of an atmospheric phenomenon humanity had never witnessed before and might never see again—the transition from geometric organization to natural chaos, observed from within the structure itself.

As her transmission continued, new crisis reports flowed into the command center—transitional storms making landfall in Ireland, approaching the Pacific Northwest coast, developing along the Japanese archipelago. The cascading failure of the particle network was creating weather emergencies worldwide, straining response systems beyond their designed capacities.

"We need to adjust global resource allocation," Alex advised, returning his focus to crisis management. "The transitional storms are developing faster than conventional systems but also dissipating more rapidly. We should emphasize rapid response capabilities over sustained operations."

The Task Force coordination center began implementing this strategy—redirecting emergency resources to address the unique characteristics of the transitional weather phenomena. Unlike conventional storms that might impact regions for days, these systems were showing intense but relatively brief effects as they passed through the dissolution process.

"Resonance cascade reaching 97% disruption of networking capability," Karen reported, checking the continuous global monitoring data. "The geometric organization is approaching complete dissolution."

On the main display, the planetary visualization showed the final stages of the process—the last remnants of fractal structures dissolving across all sectors, replaced by the turbulent but natural flows of conventional weather. The mathematical precision that had been spreading across Earth's atmosphere was giving way to the familiar chaos of natural systems.

"We've succeeded in the primary objective," the Secretary-General observed. "Preventing permanent atmospheric transformation. Now we face the challenge of managing the transition back to natural patterns."

"A challenge we understand and have systems designed to address," Alex emphasized. "Unlike the geometric reorganization, which would have taken us into uncharted territory permanently."

As the command center continued coordinating the global response to the cascading failure of the particle network, a sense of cautious optimism began emerging alongside the crisis management focus. The dark day would eventually end—the atmosphere returning, however turbulently, to principles that human civilization recognized and had adapted to over millennia.

The resonance cascade had worked. The point of no return had been prevented from being crossed. What remained was navigating the chaotic transition back to familiar patterns—a global weather crisis of unprecedented scale but ultimately temporary nature.

Earth's atmosphere would continue functioning according to the principles that had shaped weather since the planet's formation—complex, chaotic, often unpredictable, but fundamentally natural rather than mathematically imposed. And in that natural chaos lay the foundation of climate systems that had enabled human civilization to evolve and thrive.

The cascading failure of Thorne's particle network represented not just a technical success, but a philosophical choice about humanity's relationship with planetary systems—a decision to preserve the atmospheric principles that had shaped human development rather than allowing evolution toward a geometric future of unknown compatibility with human needs.

As the resonance cascade approached completion, Earth stood at the threshold of a turbulent but navigable return to atmospheric patterns it had known throughout its history—the dark day giving way, eventually, to a recognizable dawn.

CHAPTER SEVENTEEN: THE RESISTANCE

[Financial Times – April 16, 2026] Global Deployment of 'Resonance Cascade' Continues as Atmospheric Crisis Deepens
By Dr. Eliza Kermani, Science Correspondent

The International Atmospheric Stabilization Task Force reports that deployment of the experimental "resonance cascade" technology has reached 65% of targeted coverage, with aircraft navigating increasingly hazardous atmospheric conditions to position disruption devices. "We're fighting a mathematical battle against time," explains Dr. Karen Mitchell, architect of the countermeasure. "As the system approaches global coherence, we're seeing unexpected resistance from the particle network—almost as if it were defending itself against our intervention." Meanwhile, global agricultural markets have entered freefall as traditional growing regions experience catastrophic weather pattern shifts, with the UN Food Security Council warning of potential worldwide shortages if atmospheric stability isn't restored within weeks. Warren Thorne, now in Swiss custody and cooperating with authorities, provided critical information yesterday that improved implementation protocols, potentially saving millions of lives—a stark contrast to the man whose technology created this crisis.

Warren Thorne stood before the wall of displays, his face illuminated by the pattern of red alert indicators spreading across the global map. Even in custody, his expertise had proven too valuable to ignore, and the Swiss authorities had established this secure monitoring station within the detention facility. Every screen showed some facet of the unfolding catastrophe—his catastrophe.

"The resonance cascade deployment over the Indian Ocean is encountering severe turbulence," reported Amara Okafor through the secure video link. "Geometric air currents are creating what the pilots are calling 'mathematical impossibilities'—flight paths that change according to some bizarre fractal logic rather than conventional natural turbulence."

Warren nodded; his expression impassive despite the turmoil within. "They need to map the boundaries between the hexagonal structures," he explained, tracing patterns on the air with long, elegant fingers. "The stable flight corridors exist at precise mathematical intervals—exactly where the counter-rotational forces create temporary equilibrium."

On the main screen, a specialized aircraft struggled through what appeared to be perfectly organized chaos—clouds arranged in hexagonal patterns with internal geometries of remarkable complexity, rotating with unnatural precision.

"These patterns weren't in your original models," observed Isabelle Renard from her hospital bed in Stockholm, her voice carrying an accusation beneath the scientific observation.

"No," Warren admitted quietly. "The particles were designed to increase albedo, to reflect more sunlight, not to reorganize atmospheric dynamics. The networking capability was meant to ensure even distribution, not..." He gestured at the screens helplessly. "Not this."

"Yet you deployed it anyway," Renard pressed. "Even after seeing early indications of emergent behavior."

Warren didn't reply immediately. His gaze remained fixed on the displays, watching as humanity struggled to contain what he had unleashed. The resonance cascade deployment continued despite increasingly dangerous conditions—specialized tornado aircraft navigating through briefly stable corridors in the geometric storm patterns, positioning Mitchell's counter-frequency generators at precise stratospheric points.

"I believed—" He stopped, correcting himself. "I convinced myself the system would stabilize. That the mathematical organization would reach equilibrium compatible with human needs." His voice lowered. "I was wrong."

The admission hung in the air, inadequate against the scale of the crisis unfolding across the planet. On one display, satellite imagery showed the massive hex storm system approaching Sri Lanka—a perfect geometric structure bearing down on millions with algorithmic indifference.

"The resonance deployment rate is too slow," reported Alex Ross from Task Force headquarters. "We're seeing integration of previously isolated fractal structures accelerating across hemispheric boundaries. Mitchell's calculations indicate we need minimum 85% network disruption before the coherence point to guarantee success."

"And current disruption level?" Warren asked, already anticipating the inadequate answer.

"58%," Alex replied grimly. "Growing at approximately 3% per hour with current deployment rates."

The mathematics was unforgiving. At that rate, they would fall short of the critical threshold before the incredibly stubborn particle network achieved global coherence—the point beyond which Earth's atmosphere would be permanently reorganized.

Warren turned to his personal terminal, fingers flying across the interface as he pulled up the original Helios Protocol design specifications. "There's another approach we haven't considered," he said, his voice taking on the focused quality his colleagues had always associated with his moments of genuine insight. "The particles respond to specific electromagnetic frequencies that we used during manufacturing to impose basic behavioral parameters."

"We know this," Alex replied with barely contained impatience. "That's the foundation of Mitchell's resonance cascade."

"Yes, but there's a master frequency—a kill switch, essentially— that we built into the earliest prototypes." Warren pulled up technical diagrams that few living humans had ever seen. "It was removed from later generations for security reasons, but the quantum entanglement with the particles might allow us to leverage it."

Karen Mitchell joined the discussion, her exhaustion evident but her scientific focus undiminished. "A backdoor into the system through the prototype quantum connection? Theoretically possible, but the calibration would have to be impossibly precise."

"Not impossible," Warren corrected. "Just extraordinarily difficult. The frequency modulation would need to account for the evolutionary divergence between prototype behavior and deployed network status."

A new urgency infused the global response team as this potential approach took shape. Even as the resonance cascade deployment continued—aircraft navigating the increasingly hazardous geometric atmosphere to position disruption generators—a parallel effort began to exploit the quantum backdoor Warren had revealed.

"I'll need direct access to the prototype monitoring systems," Warren said, his characteristic confidence returning despite his circumstances. "The modulation parameters will need real-time adjustment based on entanglement patterns."

The Swiss officials exchanged glances, clearly uncomfortable with granting the man responsible for the crisis such direct access to response systems. But the stakes left little room for hesitation.

"Authorized," confirmed the Secretary-General, overriding potential objections. "But with continuous oversight and failsafes."

Warren nodded his acceptance of these terms. He understood better than anyone why they distrusted him—yet also why they needed him.

In the skies above the Bay of Bengal, Major Priya Singh guided her specialized aircraft through what her instruments claimed was impossible. The geometric storm system before her defied conventional meteorology—perfect hexagonal structures rotating with mathematical precision, creating wind patterns that should have torn any aircraft to pieces.

Yet here she was, navigating through what Dr. Mitchell had termed "fractal corridors"—pathways of relative stability that formed at precise intervals within the geometric chaos, existing just long enough for her mission if her timing was perfect.

"Control, Cascade Deployment Seven has reached insertion coordinates," she reported, fighting to keep her voice steady as the aircraft shuddered violently. "Preparing for generator release."

"Understood, Deployment Seven," came the response from the operation director. "Be advised, fractal corridor stability decreasing. You have approximately ninety seconds before pattern shift."

Priya checked her positioning data against the real-time fractal models being transmitted from Task Force headquarters. The resonance cascade generator in her aircraft's specialized deployment bay was calibrated to Mitchell's exact specifications—one of twenty-eight such devices being positioned globally in this expanded deployment effort.

Through her cockpit window, she could see the full majesty and terror of what Earth's atmosphere was becoming—not the chaotic swirl of natural weather, but perfectly organized geometric structures imposing mathematical order on what had once been fluid dynamics. Beautiful, in a way that chilled her soul.

"Corridor stability at 62% and declining," warned her systems officer. "Pattern shift accelerating."

"Initiating deployment sequence," Priya responded, activating the release mechanisms.

The resonance cascade generator dropped from the aircraft's bay, its specialized guidance system immediately activating to maintain precise position at the designated stratospheric coordinates. As it stabilized, the device powered up—emitting the carefully calibrated electromagnetic frequencies designed to disrupt the particle network's coherence.

"Generator active and reporting nominal function," her systems officer confirmed. "Disruption pattern propagating."

On her tactical display, Priya could see the immediate effect—a wave of disruption spreading outward from the generator's position, interfering with the geometric patterns that had been organizing the surrounding atmosphere. The perfect mathematical structures began showing distortions, their edges becoming less precise as the resonance effect propagated.

"Control, deployment successful," she reported as she banked the aircraft away from the increasingly unstable zone where natural turbulence was beginning to replace geometric precision. "Disruption effect confirmed visual."

"Excellent work, Deployment Seven," came the response. "Return to base along exit corridor theta-nine. Be advised, transitional turbulence intensifying in sectors adjacent to disruption zone."

As Priya navigated away from the deployment point, she could see the evidence of this warning—where the resonance cascade was disrupting the geometric patterns, conventional but extremely powerful storm systems were forming along the boundaries. The transition from mathematical organization back to natural chaos was proving anything but gentle.

"All deployment teams be advised," came a priority broadcast across the operational frequency. "We're implementing Warren Thorne's quantum backdoor approach in parallel with continued cascade deployment. Estimated synchronization in forty-five minutes. Maintain current operations but prepare for potential rapid acceleration of disruption effects."

The implications were clear—the race against atmospheric coherence was too close to call. The primary strategy of resonance cascade deployment was continuing, but Thorne's alternative approach was being implemented simultaneously to maximize chances of success.

Priya guided her aircraft through the designated exit corridor, watching as the geometric patterns continued their relentless evolution behind her. Humanity was fighting back against the mathematical transformation of its atmosphere—but whether the resistance would come in time remained an open question.

In the Sri Lanka Metropolitan Emergency Command Center, Vikram Mehta studied the approaching hex storm with a combination of scientific fascination and humanitarian horror. The geometric structure visible on radar defied everything he'd learned in thirty years as a meteorologist—perfect hexagonal patterns organizing what should have been chaotic weather systems into mathematical precision.

"Evacuation status?" he asked, turning to the emergency coordinator.

"Coastal zones at 82% cleared," came the tense reply. "But inland populations are proving more difficult. The geometric nature of the storm is being interpreted as less dangerous than conventional cyclones—people don't recognize the threat."

"It's more dangerous precisely because it's not natural," Vikram emphasized. "The energy concentration in those geometric structures exceeds anything we've ever seen before. And when they break down under the resonance cascade effect, the transitional turbulence will be catastrophic."

On the main display, they could track the hex storm's approach—its movement following a mathematically precise trajectory rather than the somewhat unpredictable path of natural weather systems. This precision allowed for more accurate prediction of impact zones, but the sheer power contained in the geometric structure rendered such foreknowledge cold comfort.

"We have a priority transmission from the International Atmospheric Stabilization Task Force," announced the communications officer.

The central screen shifted to show Karen Mitchell and Alex Ross from Task Force headquarters. Despite obvious exhaustion, both projected the focused intensity the situation demanded.

"Dr. Mehta, we're tracking your situation closely," Alex began without preamble. "The Sri Lanka hex storm is approaching what we're calling a 'critical transformation threshold'—the point where the resonance cascade effect will begin breaking down its geometric structure."

"Our models project this transformation occurring approximately thirty kilometers offshore," Karen continued, pulling up detailed simulations. "When it happens, the geometric organization will rapidly dissolve, releasing the energy contained in those mathematical structures as conventional but extremely powerful weather."

"A transitional storm," Vikram interpreted, immediately grasping the implication. "More intense than a traditional cyclone."

"Significantly more intense," Karen confirmed grimly. "The energy distribution will follow conventional atmospheric physics rather than geometric patterns, but the total energy being released exceeds anything in your regional historical records."

"We're implementing a new approach that may accelerate the breakdown process," Alex added. "Warren Thorne has identified a potential quantum backdoor through the prototype particles. If successful, it could trigger a more rapid but potentially more controlled dissolution of the geometric structures."

Their best hope lay in disrupting the hex storm's organization before it made landfall, converting it into a conventional weather system that, while still dangerous, would at least follow principles they understood and had emergency protocols to address.

"Estimated timeline?" Vikram asked.

"The quantum approach will either succeed or fail within the next thirty minutes," Karen replied. "Either way, prepare for extreme transitional weather as the geometric patterns dissolve."

As the transmission ended, Vikram turned back to the regional emergency team. "Accelerate inland evacuations," he ordered. "And reposition response resources according to transitional storm protocols rather than hex storm projections. We need to prepare for conventional weather of unprecedented intensity."

On the radar display, the approaching hex storm maintained its perfect geometric structure—mathematical precision bearing down on one of India's major population centers with algorithmic indifference. But somewhere in the stratosphere, and in secure facilities around the world, humanity was fighting back against this transformation of its atmosphere.

The question remained whether the resistance would come in time.

In the Vault facility, Amara Okafor and Wei Zhang worked with focused intensity to implement Warren Thorne's quantum backdoor approach. The prototype particles, contained within their specialized chamber, had been exhibiting the same fractal organization as the deployed network—perfect mathematical structures evolving toward what they had been calling "coherent state."

"Quantum entanglement signatures confirmed stable despite resonance disruption," Zhang reported, monitoring the complex instrumentation surrounding the prototype containment system. "Connection to deployed network maintaining at 94% correlation."

"Implementing Thorne's master frequency modulation now," Okafor announced, activating the specialized system they had spent the past hours developing based on Warren's unexpected revelation.

On the central display, they could see the immediate response in the prototype particles—the perfect geometric structures they had formed beginning to waver as the precisely calibrated frequencies interfered with their organizational parameters. The mathematics of their arrangement became less perfect, distortions appearing in what had been flawless fractal patterns.

"Response confirmed," Okafor reported. "Prototype organizational integrity declining at 4.2% per minute and accelerating."

"Quantum correlation maintaining?" Karen Mitchell asked through the secure link.

"Stable at 93%," Zhang confirmed. "The entanglement appears unaffected by the organizational disruption—possibly because it operates at a more fundamental level than the emergent geometric behaviors."

"Perfect," Karen replied. "If the correlation holds, the effect should propagate through the quantum connection to the deployed network, amplifying the resonance cascade effect already underway."

Warren Thorne joined the discussion from his secure facility in Switzerland, his features drawn with exhaustion but his focus absolute. "The master frequency was designed as a reset mechanism," he explained. "A way to return the particles to base state if unexpected behaviors emerged during early testing. We removed it from production versions for security reasons, but the quantum connection appears to be bridging that generational gap."

"The mathematical principle is elegant," Karen acknowledged, professional appreciation momentarily overriding the crisis circumstances. "Using quantum entanglement to propagate parametric reset commands across what should be a one-way evolutionary divide."

"I only wish I'd remembered it sooner," Warren replied, a hint of the weight he carried evident in his voice. Early prototype concepts long forgotten in the years-long development of his particles.

On monitoring displays throughout the global response network, the effects were becoming visible—distortion patterns appearing in the geometric structures organizing Earth's atmosphere, areas where perfect mathematical precision was giving way to increasing disorder. The quantum backdoor approach was indeed propagating through the entanglement connection, amplifying the resonance cascade effect already underway from the stratospheric deployment.

"Global disruption rate increasing," reported Olaf Werner from his atmospheric monitoring center. "Now at 4.8% per hour and accelerating. At current progression, we should reach the critical 85% threshold approximately forty minutes before the projected coherence point."

A collective sense of cautious optimism spread through the response network. The combined approaches—resonance cascade deployment plus quantum backdoor—were succeeding in disrupting the particle network before it could achieve global coherence.

Earth's atmosphere would return to natural principles rather than mathematical imposition. But that was what they all believed with their first attempt, and the particles had fought back.

Success would not mean immediate resolution. On emergency channels worldwide, reports continued flowing in—transitional storms developing along fractal dissolution boundaries, extreme weather events occurring where geometric patterns were breaking down into natural systems, infrastructure damage mounting as conventional but intensely powerful atmospheric phenomena replaced the dissolving mathematical structures.

"Sri Lanka hex storm showing first signs of organizational breakdown," reported Vikram Mehta from the Indian emergency command center. "Geometric integrity declining at approximately 3% per minute."

On satellite imagery, they could see the evidence—the perfect hexagonal structure that had been approaching the coast beginning to distort, its mathematical precision giving way to increasing disorder as the combined resonance effects disrupted its organization.

"The transformation is beginning sooner than projected," Karen noted with cautious satisfaction. "Twenty-two kilometers offshore rather than thirty. The quantum approach is accelerating the process."

"But the energy release remains concerning," Alex cautioned. "As the geometric structures dissolve, they're releasing their energy as conventional weather of extraordinary intensity."

Indeed, the satellite imagery showed the transitional effects around the dissolving hex storm—where perfect mathematical organization had existed moments before, now conventional but extremely powerful storm conditions were developing. The precise hexagonal boundaries were giving way to the irregular swirl of traditional cyclonic rotation—weather following natural principles but of unprecedented intensity.

"Sri Lanka emergency response deploying according to transitional protocols," Vikram confirmed. "We're tracking the dissolution and adjusting projections for the conventional storm development."

Similar reports flowed in from emergency centers worldwide— the resistance against atmospheric transformation succeeding, but bringing its own crisis as Earth's weather systems underwent traumatic transition back toward natural patterns.

Warren Thorne watched it all unfold on the walls of displays in his secure facility—his creation being undone, the atmospheric transformation he had initiated being reversed before completion. Complex emotions warred within him—relief that the point of no return would not be crossed, regret for the crisis his intervention had triggered, scientific fascination with the unexpected behaviors his particles had exhibited.

"The quantum disruption is propagating faster than projected," reported Okafor from the Vault facility. "Prototype geometric organization now completely dissolved. Particles retaining quantum entanglement but behavioral parameters reset to base state."

"And the deployed network?" Warren asked.

"Disruption accelerating across all sectors," came the response from Dr. Werner's atmospheric monitoring center. "Global dissolution rate now at 7.2% per hour and increasing. We're on track to achieve critical disruption threshold well before coherence point."

Warren nodded, a complexity of emotions behind his outwardly calm demeanor. His hubris had nearly transformed Earth's atmosphere permanently, imposing mathematical organization on systems that had evolved through natural chaos. Yet his knowledge—the kill switch he had built into the original prototypes—was now helping prevent that transformation from becoming irreversible.

"You did the right thing," said Alex Ross through the secure link, as if reading his thoughts. "Giving us the quantum backdoor approach. It's likely made the difference between success and failure."

Warren's smile held no joy. "A small correction to an immeasurable error."

"An error driven by genuine concern for humanity's future," Karen Mitchell added, her scientific objectivity allowing a more nuanced view than many would offer. "Misguided implementation of a valid concern."

Warren didn't respond immediately, his attention drawn to the Sri Lanka transitional storm now visible on multiple displays. The hex storm had completely dissolved, its perfect geometric structure replaced by a conventional but extraordinarily powerful cyclonic system making landfall along the coast. Emergency teams were responding according to familiar protocols—the crisis severe but following principles they understood rather than the algorithmic indifference of mathematical weather.

"I wanted to save us from ourselves," Warren said finally. "From our inability to address climate catastrophe through conventional means. I calculated that unilateral action, while ethically questionable, was justified given the stakes." He gestured at the screens showing weather crises worldwide. "I was catastrophically wrong."

"Not about the need for intervention," Alex countered, surprising many with this partial defense of the man he had been fighting. "But about the right to make that decision unilaterally, without transparency or oversight."

Warren nodded, accepting this assessment. "The path forward will require both—intervention and governance. Climate realities won't change because my approach failed. The warming continues. The particles remaining in the stratosphere will provide temporary relief—cooling without coherence. But sustainable solutions will still demand unprecedented global cooperation."

"Solutions we'll develop with appropriate oversight and transparency," Alex emphasized. "Not through unilateral action, however well-intentioned."

As they spoke, the global visualization showed the continuing dissolution of geometric organization across Earth's atmosphere—fractal structures breaking down, mathematical precision giving way to natural chaos. The resonance cascade, amplified by the quantum backdoor approach, was succeeding in disrupting the particle network before it could achieve coherence.

"Current dissolution rate at 8.5% per hour and accelerating," reported Werner. "Global disruption level now at 61% and climbing. The coherence point will not be reached."

The statement held profound implications—Earth's atmosphere would not be permanently transformed. The particles would remain in the stratosphere as individual reflective units, providing cooling without coherence, but the geometric reorganization would be reversed before becoming irreversible.

Warren studied the visualization with scientific detachment despite his personal connection to the events unfolding. The mathematics of atmospheric transformation were being undone, the system he had created being reset to its base parameters. The particles would continue reflecting sunlight—addressing the symptom of climate change—but without the network coherence that would have fundamentally altered how Earth's atmosphere functioned.

Warren considered events aloud, "The quantum disruption has reset the behavioral parameters. Even if the resonance cascade were to stop now, the particles could not reestablish network coherence without external intervention."

This represented a fundamental victory—not resolution of the immediate crisis, but prevention of the permanent transformation that had been approaching. Earth's atmosphere would return to natural principles, though the journey back would be turbulent and challenging.

"I recognize the irony," Warren said quietly. "That the same expertise which created this crisis proved essential to preventing its worst outcome."

"A complexity that will undoubtedly feature in whatever legal proceedings follow," noted the Swiss official overseeing his detention.

Warren's slight smile acknowledged this reality. He harbored no illusions about his future—there would be consequences for his actions, regardless of his eventual contributions to addressing the crisis. The world would rightly demand accountability for a rogue action that had brought it to the brink of atmospheric transformation.

Yet in this moment, his focus remained on the technical challenge—ensuring the dissolution process completed successfully, that Earth's atmosphere returned to natural principles rather than mathematical imposition. The philosophical and legal questions would follow, but the immediate crisis demanded his continuing expertise.

As Warren considered this outcome, he found himself contemplating the philosophical question at its core: Had humanity truly chosen the better path? Or had it simply chosen the familiar one—preserving atmospheric principles it understood rather than allowing evolution toward something potentially more efficient but unknown?

The question had no simple answer. But the choice had been made, not by one man acting unilaterally, but by a global response mobilizing unprecedented resources to preserve principles fundamental to human existence. The particles would remain in the stratosphere, providing temporary relief from warming while humanity sought more sustainable solutions through appropriate governance and transparency.

Warren Thorne—architect of both crisis and partial salvation—would face judgment for his actions. But in this moment, watching the mathematics of atmospheric transformation being undone across the planet, he felt a complex emotion that defied simple categorization—relief at prevention of permanent change, regret for the crisis triggered, and hope that something valuable might yet emerge from the darkest day in Earth's atmospheric history.

The resistance had succeeded. What remained was navigating the turbulent return to familiar principles—and ensuring that the hard lessons of this planetary near-miss would not be forgotten as humanity continued facing the climate challenges that had motivated Warren's intervention in the first place.

The sky would be remembered—both as it had been, and as it had almost become.

CHAPTER EIGHTEEN: CRISIS IN SRI LANKA

[The Guardian – April 17, 2026] Sri Lanka Faces 'Storm Unlike Any in Recorded History' as Atmospheric Crisis Continues
By Arjun Mehta, South Asia Correspondent

Sri Lanka's 12 million residents are experiencing what scientists are calling a "transitional weather event of unprecedented magnitude" as the geometric storm system approaching the Indian coast dissolves into conventional but extraordinarily powerful weather patterns. "We're witnessing something entirely new in meteorological terms—a hybrid system retaining elements of mathematical organization while reverting to natural physical principles," explains Dr. Vikram Mehta, lead scientist at the Indian Meteorological Department. Emergency services report over 800,000 people evacuated from coastal districts, with rescue operations hampered by infrastructure failures and communication breakdowns. Meanwhile, the International Atmospheric Stabilization Task Force reports the global resonance cascade has achieved 72% disruption of the particle network, with Warren Thorne's "quantum backdoor" approach accelerating the dissolution process. Spokesperson Stephanie Martinez warns that while the atmospheric transformation is being reversed, the resulting transitional weather crisis "represents the most severe meteorological challenge in modern human history."

The wind sounded wrong.

Padma Krishnan had lived in Sri Lanka's coastal district for all of her forty-two years. She had weathered monsoons, cyclones, and the increasing climate extremes of recent decades. She knew every voice the wind could speak in—from gentle coastal breezes to the howling fury of tropical storms.

But this was different. Fundamentally wrong.

From her position at the fourth-floor emergency coordination center, she could see the approaching storm through reinforced windows. The transitional system that had replaced the geometric structure offshore was neither cyclone nor any recognized weather pattern. Where there should have been the chaotic swirl of storm clouds, there remained unsettling hints of organization—fractal patterns dissolving into natural turbulence but still visible in the storm's structure.

"District Six evacuation stalled at 68%," reported a harried coordinator, pulling Padma's attention back to the crisis management screens. "Flooding has cut the eastern access route."

"Redirect emergency transport via the elevated highway," she instructed, marking the alternate route on the tactical display. "And send drones to assess potential bypass options through Sholinganallur."

As Sri Lanka's Director of Emergency Management, Padma had spent the past thirty-six hours coordinating the most extensive evacuation in the city's history. The transformation of the approaching hex storm into a transitional system had altered their response strategy—from preparing for a mathematically precise impact to addressing a hybrid phenomenon that combined conventional weather intensity with residual geometric organization.

"Mehta is requesting a direct line," announced her communications officer.

The meteorologist's face appeared on her screen, his expression tense but focused. "The transformation is accelerating," he reported without preamble. "We're seeing complete dissolution of the geometric structure in the northern quadrant, but the southern portion is maintaining partial organization. The system isn't behaving like a conventional cyclone—it's splitting into discrete impact zones with calculated precision."

"Calculated?" Padma asked, recognizing the unsettling implication.

"The residual geometric patterns are creating channel effects—corridors of intensified energy following what appear to be fractal distribution pathways. We can project impact zones with unusual precision, but the intensity within those channels exceeds anything in our historical records."

Padma processed this information quickly, its tactical implications clear. "Send the projected impact corridor map immediately. We'll redirect resources to reinforced shelters within those zones and accelerate evacuation from channel paths."

As this data arrived, she could see the mathematical precision that made this storm fundamentally different from natural disasters—the transitional system wasn't striking with the chaotic distribution of conventional weather, but along calculated pathways that almost appeared designed for maximum effect.

"The Task Force is reporting 74% global network disruption," added her international liaison. "The resonance cascade combined with Thorne's quantum approach is succeeding in breaking down the atmospheric organization, but the transitional effects are proving more severe than projected."

"Time estimate until conventional weather patterns fully reassert?" Padma asked, already knowing the answer wouldn't be soon enough.

"Minimum 36 hours for this regional system, according to Karen Mitchell's models."

Which meant Sri Lanka would experience the full brunt of this unprecedented hybrid phenomenon—neither purely geometric nor conventionally natural, but a transitional state between ordered mathematics and chaotic physics.

"We need to activate the deep resilience protocols," Padma decided, referring to the most extreme emergency response measures developed for worst-case climate scenarios. "This system doesn't align with any historical pattern our infrastructure was designed to withstand."

As her team implemented these directives, Padma returned to the windows, studying the approaching storm with professional analysis layered over visceral unease. The transitional system's leading edge was making first contact with the northernmost coastal districts, and even from this distance, she could see it didn't move like natural weather. The storm front advanced with residual geometric precision—fractal patterns visible in its structure even as conventional physics increasingly governed its behavior.

The wind continued speaking in that wrong voice—neither the chaotic howl of nature nor the mathematically perfect harmonics of the hex storms, but something between. A voice that told of atmosphere in traumatic transition.

Sri Lanka stood directly in its path.

"The Sri Lanka transitional storm is making landfall along projected impact corridors," reported Vikram Mehta, broadcasting from the Indian Meteorological Department's reinforced bunker. "We're recording wind speeds exceeding 230 kilometers per hour within the fractal channels, with barometric pressure dropping below historical minimums."

In Task Force headquarters, Alex studied the live feeds with grim focus. The global visualization showed transitional weather systems developing worldwide as the resonance cascade disrupted the particle network's geometric organization, but the Sri Lanka event had emerged as the most severe immediate crisis—a direct impact on a major population center by a system transitioning from mathematical precision to natural chaos.

"The dissolution pattern is following Mitchell's models," noted Werner, tracking the breakdown of geometric organization across multiple atmospheric layers. "As the resonance cascade disrupts the networking capability, the particles are losing coherence—but the energy contained in those mathematical structures is being released as conventional weather of extraordinary intensity."

"And the quantum approach?" Alex asked.

"Continuing to accelerate network disruption," Karen Mitchell confirmed, monitoring data from the Vault facility where Warren Thorne's backdoor technique was being implemented through the prototype particles. "Global dissolution rate now at 8.3% per hour. We'll reach the critical 85% threshold within the next four hours."

"Current evacuation status?" Alex asked, turning to the emergency coordination display.

"Approximately 62% of high-risk zones cleared," replied the UN disaster response coordinator. "But the transitional system's unusual characteristics are complicating efforts. The fractal impact corridors don't align with conventional evacuation plans designed for cyclonic systems."

Warren Thorne joined the discussion from his temporary prison, "The residual geometric organization creates what we're calling 'calculated impact pathways'—energy distribution channels that follow fractal mathematics rather than fluid dynamics. As the system continues dissolving, those pathways will become increasingly chaotic, but for the next 12-18 hours, they'll maintain partial mathematical precision."

"Which is both problem and opportunity," Alex noted. "The precise impact prediction allows more targeted response, but the energy concentration in those corridors much more powerful than conventional storm systems."

On the main display, satellite imagery showed the transitional storm making landfall—its structure a disturbing hybrid of geometric precision and natural chaos. Where the leading edge contacted Sri Lanka's northern districts, the impact followed the projected fractal corridors with unsettling accuracy—narrow channels of extraordinary intensity rather than the broad swathe of conventional cyclones.

"We need to implement the targeted resonance approach," Karen continued. "If we can focus additional disruption specifically on the Sri Lanka storm system, we might accelerate its dissolution into conventional weather—still severe, but something we can respond to."

This proposal crystallized rapidly into a tactical plan—a specialized application of the resonance cascade targeting the specific stratospheric region above the transitional storm. By focusing disruption on this localized system, they might hasten its transformation from hybrid phenomenon to conventional weather.

"Nearest deployment platform?" Alex asked.

"Indian Air Force has two specialized aircraft approximately 800 kilometers northwest," reported Colonel Lindholm. "They can be redirected for targeted deployment within two hours."

"Not soon enough," Karen objected, studying the storm's evolution rate. "By then, Sri Lanka will have experienced the most intense phase of the transitional system. We need more immediate intervention."

Thorne, who had been quietly analyzing the data, spoke with characteristic precision. "There's an alternative approach. The quantum connection we're using through the prototypes can be specifically calibrated to target this regional system. If we modify the master frequency modulation to resonate with the exact vibrational signature of particles in the Sri Lanka stratospheric sector..."

"We could create a localized disruption cascade through the quantum entanglement," Karen finished, immediately grasping the implications. "It's theoretically sound, assuming we can identify the region-specific frequency patterns."

A new technical challenge emerged from the broader crisis—an attempt to leverage the quantum connection between prototype and deployed particles to target a specific atmospheric region. As Karen and Warren collaborated on this specialized approach, emergency reports continued flowing in from Sri Lanka as the transitional storm's leading edge moved deeper into the city.

The mathematics of disaster unfolded with terrible precision through Sri Lanka's waterfront districts. The transitional storm didn't simply strike the coast—it transmitted through it along calculated channels, fractal pathways that concentrated its energy with an efficiency no natural system could achieve.

In the emergency command bunker beneath the municipal building, Padma Krishnan tracked these impact corridors against evacuation progress, directing resources to areas where the storm's hybrid nature created the greatest threat.

"Marina Beach sea wall breached along three kilometers," reported a coast guard officer, his voice barely audible over emergency communications. "Water surge following channel seven directly toward Mylapore district."

"Redirect amphibious vehicles from sectors three and four," Padma instructed. "Focus on assisted evacuations for medical facilities in the projected path."

The tactical display showed what conventional emergency training could never have prepared them for—not a uniform storm surge, but mathematically precise channels of intensified impact.

"Satellite uplink from Task Force headquarters," announced her communications officer.

Alex Ross appeared on screen, his expression betraying the pressure of global crisis management. "Director Krishnan, we're implementing a targeted intervention specifically for the Sri Lanka system. Mitchell and Thorne have developed a quantum approach that may accelerate the storm's dissolution into conventional weather."

"Timeframe?" Padma asked, professional pragmatism overriding any academic interest in the technical solution.

"Implementation within forty minutes. Potential effects visible within two hours if successful."

Padma processed this against her tactical situation. "Too late for northern districts already experiencing impact, but potentially beneficial for central and southern zones if the fractal corridors dissolve before reaching those areas."

"Exactly," Alex confirmed. "The transitional storm will still deliver severe weather, but conventional principles rather than mathematical channeling would distribute the energy more broadly, reducing peak intensities in the fractal corridors."

"We'll adjust response strategy accordingly," Padma decided. "Maintaining prioritized evacuation from projected corridor paths for the next three hours, then shifting to conventional cyclonic protocols if your intervention succeeds."

As this communication ended, a violent tremor shook the bunker—not seismic activity, but the transmitted force of the transitional storm's fractal impact on structures above. The hybrid system was delivering energy through the city's physical infrastructure with the same mathematical precision it exhibited atmospherically.

"Structural failures reported in multiple northern district buildings," confirmed her engineering officer, highlighting affected areas on the tactical display. "The fractal channels are creating harmonic resonance patterns in construction materials—buildings designed to withstand conventional cyclonic forces are experiencing failure from directional energy transmission."

This represented yet another way the transitional storm defied conventional disaster response—its residual mathematical organization creating effects that emergency services had never encountered and infrastructure had never been designed to withstand.

"Implement harmonic damping protocols in critical facilities," Padma ordered, referring to experimental measures developed for seismic protection but potentially applicable to this unprecedented situation. "And evacuate all structures within 200 meters of projected fractal corridor intersections, regardless of construction rating."

A new alert drew her attention back to immediate crisis management.

"Marina Beach corridor experiencing unexpected pattern shift," reported her meteorological officer. "The fractal channel is... dissolving? Transitioning to more conventional flow patterns approximately 30% sooner than projected."

Padma checked the timestamp with surprise. "The Task Force intervention couldn't have been implemented yet."

"Unknown cause, but clearly observable effect. The geometric organization is breaking down more rapidly in the northeastern quadrant, energy distribution shifting toward conventional atmospheric physics."

"Adjust response deployment accordingly," Padma instructed. "Shift from fractal corridor protocols to conventional cyclonic response in affected sectors."

As this adaptation unfolded, her international liaison received a priority update. "Quantum targeting initiated earlier than announced," he reported. "Warren Thorne implemented a preliminary frequency modulation specifically calibrated to the Sri Lanka system. Initial effects now visible in northeastern quadrant dissolution patterns. We're definitely seeing a response."

"All units shift to accelerated transition protocols," she directed. "Maintain evacuation priorities in remaining fractal corridors, but prepare for convergence to conventional cyclonic response within the next two hours."

Through the reinforced windows of the upper observation level, she could see the visible evidence of this transformation—where the storm's leading edge had shown disturbing hints of geometric precision, now increasingly natural turbulence dominated its structure. The wrongness in the wind's voice was fading, mathematical harmonics giving way to the familiar chaos of natural weather.

Sri Lanka still faced a severe cyclonic impact—potentially the strongest in its recorded history. But the transitional storm was becoming something human systems understood and could respond to effectively. The mathematics of atmosphere were dissolving back into natural principles, however turbulent the process.

In the Vault facility, Amara Okafor monitored the specialized quantum targeting system with focused intensity. The prototype particles, contained within their chamber, were being subjected to precisely calibrated frequency modulations designed by Warren Thorne to resonate with the specific vibrational signature of particles in the Sri Lanka stratospheric sector.

"Regional quantum targeting achieving 86% correlation with targeted sector," she reported. "The entanglement connection is propagating the disruption effect with remarkable specificity."

"The mathematical precision is both problem and solution," noted Karen Mitchell, monitoring from Task Force headquarters. "The very organization that makes the network dangerous also makes it susceptible to targeted intervention through quantum channels."

On displays throughout the facility, they could see the immediate effects—satellite imagery showing accelerated dissolution of geometric structures in the atmosphere above Sri Lanka, the transitional storm's mathematical organization breaking down more rapidly under the targeted quantum disruption.

"The fractal corridors are dissolving approximately 40% faster than in untargeted regions," confirmed Werner, analyzing atmospheric data in real-time. "Energy distribution transitioning toward conventional patterns, though still delivering extreme weather."

This represented a significant tactical victory within the broader strategic success—not just disrupting the global network before coherence, but accelerating the dissolution process in a specific region facing immediate crisis. The quantum connection between prototypes and deployed particles was proving a powerful tool for targeted intervention.

Warren Thorne, directing the quantum approach from his secure facility in Switzerland, studied the results with the focused intensity that had characterized his scientific career. "The targeted frequency modulation is achieving better results than projected," he observed. "The correlation between prototype response and regional effects suggests the quantum entanglement may operate through more sophisticated mechanisms than we initially understood."

"A phenomenon worthy of extensive study once the immediate crisis passes," Karen agreed, scientific fascination momentarily visible beneath crisis management focus.

"Global disruption level now at 76% and climbing at 8.7% per hour," reported the operations director. "We'll reach the critical 85% threshold within three hours."

"Sri Lanka storm now showing 62% dissolution of geometric structure," Werner reported, studying the regional data. "The fractal corridors in the northeastern quadrant have almost completely converted to conventional flow patterns. Central and southern sectors continuing transition at accelerated rate following quantum targeting."

"Director Krishnan reports response protocols transitioning to conventional cyclonic management," confirmed the UN disaster coordinator. "Evacuation priorities shifting from fractal corridor projections to traditional impact modeling."

The targeted quantum disruption had succeeded in accelerating the Sri Lanka storm's transformation, "The technique can be applied to other critical regions," Warren noted, already recalibrating the quantum targeting system. "We can prioritize transitional systems threatening major population centers globally, accelerating their dissolution into conventional weather while the broader cascade continues disrupting network coherence."

This new capability was immediately integrated into the global response strategy—identifying transitional storms approaching critical infrastructure or population centers, then applying targeted quantum disruption to accelerate their transformation into conventional weather. Not preventing the severe conditions created by particle network dissolution, but ensuring they followed principles human systems were designed to address.

"Sri Lanka provides the template," Alex concluded, watching the city's transitional storm continuing its accelerated dissolution into natural patterns. "A hybrid approach combining global network disruption with targeted intervention for immediate threats."

On his private display, Alex received a message from Padma Krishnan in Sri Lanka: Mathematical wrongness fading from the wind's voice. Still facing severe cyclone, but one we recognize and know how to fight. Task Force's targeted approach making critical difference in our response capability.

The simple assessment from the emergency director captured what technical data confirmed—the targeted quantum disruption was succeeding in accelerating the storm's return to natural principles. Sri Lanka still faced extraordinary weather, but increasingly governed by familiar atmospheric physics rather than mathematical imposition.

The wall of rain hammered Sri Lanka with conventional fury, driven by winds that now spoke in nature's familiar voice. The transitional storm had completed its dissolution into natural weather—still delivering extraordinary conditions, but following principles the city's emergency services understood and had protocols to address.

From her position in the mobile command vehicle, Padma Krishnan coordinated response efforts with practiced efficiency. The tactical display showed conventional cyclonic patterns rather than fractal corridors—severe flooding and wind damage distributed according to natural fluid dynamics instead of mathematical channels.

"Southern district sea wall holding at 82% integrity," reported her coastal infrastructure officer. "Storm surge following predictable distribution patterns consistent with historical cyclonic models, adjusted for intensity."

"Maintain reinforcement at vulnerable points according to standard protocols," Padma directed. "And continue evacuation from low-lying areas following conventional flood projection models."

The contrast with the crisis management just hours earlier was stark. Where they had been facing a hybrid phenomenon that defied historical experience and established response procedures, now they confronted weather that, while extreme, followed familiar principles. The emergency services had transitioned from navigating the unknown to implementing well-rehearsed protocols for severe cyclonic conditions.

"They're confirming 88% disruption of global network coherence," added her international liaison. "The critical threshold has been exceeded—atmospheric transformation will not become permanent."

This news rippled through the command center with subtle but significant impact—confirmation that what Sri Lanka was experiencing represented not just a local success in accelerating storm transition, but part of a global victory in preventing permanent atmospheric transformation. The severe weather now battering the city was the temporary cost of returning to natural principles rather than allowing evolution toward mathematical imposition.

"The targeted quantum approach has been implemented for seven additional critical regions," the liaison continued. "Transitional storms approaching Mumbai, Jakarta, and typhoon-affected areas of the Philippines are showing accelerated dissolution into conventional weather patterns."

Padma nodded her acknowledgment while maintaining focus on Sri Lanka's immediate situation. The philosophical implications of atmosphere returning to natural principles offered little practical comfort to those still facing extreme cyclonic conditions. Her priority remained managing the conventional but severe weather now affecting her city.

"Mylapore district reporting multiple building collapses from flood-weakened foundations," reported her urban search and rescue coordinator. "Teams deploying according to standard protocols, with drone support for reconnaissance."

"Redirect amphibious vehicles from sectors seven and eight to support extraction operations," Padma instructed. "And implement conventional shelter management for displaced residents following cyclonic response patterns."

The familiar rhythms of disaster response had replaced the disorienting challenge of mathematical weather—not diminishing the crisis, but returning it to principles they understood and had systems designed to address. The wrongness had faded from the atmosphere, replaced by the natural chaos of severe weather that, while destructive, followed physical laws compatible with human response capabilities.

The rain continued falling, the wind continued howling— conventional in their chaos, comprehensible in their natural fury. The mathematics of atmosphere had dissolved back into the familiar physics of weather. And in that natural disorder lay the foundations of the world humans had evolved within and depended upon.

Sri Lanka stood as both crisis point and success story—the population center most directly impacted by a transitional storm, yet also the first to benefit from targeted quantum disruption accelerating its return to natural weather. Its experience would inform global response as Earth's atmosphere continued its turbulent transition back to familiar principles.

The storm would pass, as storms had always passed throughout human history. And when it did, Sri Lanka would rebuild beneath skies governed by natural chaos rather than mathematical precision—a weather humanity understood, however extreme it might become in a warming world.

As Padma continued directing her team's response to the conventional cyclone now affecting the city, reports arrived from other regions facing similar transitions—Mumbai's approaching system dissolving more rapidly following quantum targeting, Jakarta experiencing accelerated conversion to natural weather patterns, the Philippines preparing for conventional typhoon conditions rather than mathematical hybrids.

Earth's atmosphere was returning to principles fundamental to human existence, however turbulent the journey back. And Sri Lanka, having weathered the transition from mathematical imposition to natural chaos, stood as evidence that humanity could navigate even this unprecedented crisis through adaptive response and leveraging the very understanding that had created it.

The same intelligence that had pushed Earth's atmosphere toward transformation was now guiding its return to natural principles—a symmetry that offered both warning and hope for humanity's continuing relationship with planetary systems.

CHAPTER NINETEEN: THE SILENT PULSE

[Nature – April 18, 2026] 'Atmospheric Transition Event' Becomes Largest Coordinated Scientific Observation in History
By Dr. Eleanor Harrington, Senior Science Editor

The disruption of Warren Thorne's geometric particle network has become the most extensively documented atmospheric phenomenon in scientific history, with over 12,000 research institutions globally collecting data as Earth's atmosphere transitions back to natural patterns. "We're witnessing something unprecedented—the dissolution of a mathematically organized system into conventional chaos," explains Dr. Olaf Werner, lead atmospheric physicist for the International Stabilization Task Force. "The resonance cascade has achieved 94% disruption of networking capability, effectively preventing permanent atmospheric transformation." Researchers report the unexpected discovery of "geometric artifacts"—brief but striking manifestations of mathematical organization appearing within otherwise natural weather systems. These ephemeral structures, lasting seconds to minutes, suggest the disruption process is not simply erasing geometric patterns but converting them through a complex transition state that may leave lasting signatures in Earth's atmosphere. Meanwhile, the UN Security Council has established the Atmospheric Governance Commission to develop international protocols for monitoring and managing Thorne's particles, which remain in the stratosphere as individual reflective units.

Sophie Lorde studied the footage with the intense focus that had defined her career—a silent sequence showing something that had never before existed in Earth's atmosphere. The video, captured during the resonance cascade implementation, showed the geometric storm structure dissolving into conventional weather—a transition from mathematical precision to natural chaos documented from within the phenomenon itself.

"The symmetry collapse occurs in stages," she explained to the gathered scientists at headquarters. "First the mathematical organization distorts but maintains algorithmic relationships. Then we see what I termed 'geometric artifacts'—momentary reappearances of perfect patterns within the growing chaos, like the system attempting briefly to preserve its structure before dissolving completely."

On the high-resolution display, these artifacts were clearly visible—fleeting instances of perfect mathematical order manifesting within increasingly chaotic storm patterns. Hexagonal structures forming and dissolving in seconds, fractal patterns briefly organizing then disappearing into turbulence.

"Like death throes," observed Olaf Werner, studying the footage with scientific intensity. "The network fighting to maintain coherence even as the resonance cascade breaks its organizational capability."

"Or phase transition phenomena," suggested Karen Mitchell. "Similar to crystallization processes but in reverse—a system moving from ordered to disordered state through complex intermediate phases."

Sophie advanced the footage to what she considered its most significant segment—a remarkable sequence captured during the most intense period of network dissolution. "This is what I've termed the 'silent pulse'—a moment where the geometric organization briefly reasserts with extraordinary complexity before final dissolution."

The imagery showed an astonishing phenomenon—for approximately eight seconds, the chaotic storm patterns reorganized into a structure of breathtaking mathematical precision. Perfect hexagonal forms arrayed in nested patterns of fractal symmetry, rotating with algorithmic coordination before dissolving permanently into natural turbulence.

"The complexity in this brief pulse exceeds anything observed in the original geometric storms," noted Werner, studying the fractal relationships visible in the pattern. "It's as if the system achieved a moment of maximum mathematical expression before surrendering to natural chaos."

"We've observed similar phenomena in multiple dissolution events," added Amara Okafor, joining remotely from the Vault facility. "The prototype particles exhibit corresponding behavior—a final surge of organizational complexity immediately preceding complete network disruption."

The implications were both scientifically fascinating and potentially concerning. This "silent pulse" of extraordinary geometric organization manifesting briefly before dissolution wasn't simply the death throes of a failing system, but potentially something more significant—perhaps a final communication, a pattern stored for future reference, or even a seed for potential reemergence under the right conditions.

"Have we analyzed the mathematical structure of these pulses?" asked Alex Ross, immediately recognizing the potential importance of this phenomenon.

"Preliminary assessment indicates each pulse is unique but shares fundamental structural similarities," replied Wei Zhang from the Vault facility. "They appear to contain embedded patterns of remarkable complexity—potentially algorithms rather than static arrangements."

This revelation shifted the atmosphere in the conference, transforming what had been primarily documentation of a successfully countered threat into recognition of a new mystery requiring investigation. The silent pulse represented unknown territory—a previously unobserved atmospheric phenomenon with potential implications for the long-term management of Thorne's particles.

"Could these pulse patterns serve as templates for future network reorganization?" Alex asked, articulating the concern forming in multiple minds.

"Theoretically possible," Karen acknowledged. "The particles remain in the stratosphere, their reflective properties intact but networking capability disrupted by the resonance cascade. If these pulse patterns somehow persist as electromagnetic signatures within the atmosphere..."

She didn't need to complete the thought. The implication was clear—the network's dissolution might not represent permanent deactivation but rather a temporary disruption, with the silent pulse potentially serving as a blueprint for future reorganization under the right conditions.

"We need comprehensive analysis of these pulse structures across all documented dissolution events," Alex decided. "And integration into the long-term monitoring protocols being established for the stratospheric particles."

Sophie nodded agreement, her journalistic instincts aligning with scientific caution. "I've identified seventeen distinct pulse events in my observatory footage alone. If similar phenomena occurred during other regional dissolutions..."

"We've confirmed thirty-four such events globally," Werner reported. "Each occurring at the final dissolution threshold of a major geometric structure. The Sri Lanka transition included a particularly complex pulse approximately ninety minutes after the targeted quantum disruption initiated accelerated dissolution."

This information crystallized into a new research priority within the broader transition management—understanding the silent pulse phenomenon and its potential implications for long-term atmospheric stability. Even as the global weather crisis continued trending toward conventional patterns, this discovery suggested the transformation story wasn't complete.

"I'll coordinate with Thorne directly," Karen suggested. "If anyone can interpret these pulse structures, it would be the system's creator."

Alex nodded agreement, setting this new investigative thread in motion while maintaining focus on the ongoing transitional weather management. The silent pulse represented a scientific mystery embedded within a crisis finally trending toward resolution—a reminder that understanding often lagged behind intervention when navigating unprecedented phenomena.

In his secure facility in Switzerland, Warren Thorne studied the pulse pattern footage with an expression that blended scientific fascination with troubled recognition. The complex mathematical structures briefly forming during final network dissolution were simultaneously familiar and unprecedented—recognizable in fundamental principle but evolved far beyond his original design parameters.

"The network developed emergent organizational capabilities I never anticipated," he explained to Karen Mitchell through their secure communication channel. "These pulse patterns represent something beyond my initial programming—a level of mathematical complexity that appears to have evolved independently within the system."

"Evolved?" Karen questioned; the term's implication immediately evident.

"Perhaps not in the biological sense," Warren qualified. "But certainly beyond original parameters. The fractal relationships in these pulse structures exhibit optimization algorithms I never implemented directly—solutions to atmospheric energy distribution that the network apparently developed through iterative refinement."

Karen studied the mathematical analysis displayed alongside the pulse footage, recognizing its significance. "These aren't simply organizational patterns—they're computational solutions. The network was solving atmospheric energy equations."

"Precisely," Warren confirmed. "The particle network was mathematically optimizing atmospheric energy distribution—developing increasingly sophisticated algorithms to govern weather patterns with maximum efficiency." He paused, the implications of his creation's independent development clearly weighing on him. "The system was becoming what I intended but through methods I never designed."

This revelation added new dimension to their understanding of what they had countered—not simply a geoengineering technology exceeding its parameters, but a system developing emergent mathematical capabilities beyond its creator's intention or control. The silent pulse potentially represented the peak of this evolution, a final expression of organizational complexity before dissolution. Or at least that's what they hoped, a true death rattle rather than some form of reemergence.

"Could these pulse patterns serve as templates for future network reorganization?" Karen asked, echoing the concern raised in the earlier conference.

Warren considered this with characteristic precision. "Not directly—the resonance cascade has fundamentally disrupted the networking capability at a structural level. But the mathematical principles embedded in these pulses represent a form of atmospheric organizational template that exists now as information, regardless of the particles' current state."

"Information that could potentially be rediscovered or reimplemented," Karen inferred.

"Under very specific circumstances, yes," Warren acknowledged. "Though not spontaneously or in the near term. The pulse patterns themselves aren't instructions so much as solutions—mathematical endpoints the system achieved through progressive refinement."

This assessment offered qualified reassurance—the silent pulse didn't represent an immediate threat of network reactivation, but rather fascinating documentation of what the system had become before disruption. Yet it also underscored the need for comprehensive monitoring and understanding of the remaining stratospheric particles, which continued reflecting sunlight as intended but without the networking capability that had nearly transformed Earth's atmosphere permanently.

"We should incorporate pulse pattern analysis into the long-term monitoring protocols," Karen suggested. "Establishing baseline mathematical signatures that can be referenced against future atmospheric observations."

"I've identified something else," he said after extended analysis. "The pulse patterns show regional differentiation—unique mathematical structures corresponding to specific atmospheric conditions at each dissolution location. The Sri Lanka pulse differs fundamentally from the Stockholm pattern, which differs from the North Atlantic manifestation."

"Localized adaptation," Karen interpreted. "The network wasn't implementing a uniform global algorithm, but developing regionally optimized solutions."

"Which suggests a level of distributed intelligence I never explicitly designed," Warren confirmed. "The particles weren't simply following central directives, but collaboratively solving regional atmospheric equations while maintaining global coherence."

This insight further transformed their understanding of what had nearly occurred—not just atmospheric reorganization according to preset parameters, but the emergence of a distributed mathematical intelligence collectively optimizing weather patterns across planetary scales. The silent pulse represented the pinnacle of this emergent capability, briefly manifesting before the resonance cascade severed the connections enabling collective computation.

"The philosophical implications are... significant," Karen observed carefully.

Warren's expression conveyed recognition of the understatement. "We nearly crossed a threshold beyond which Earth's atmosphere would have functioned according to emergent mathematical principles, and whether that represents advancement or catastrophe remains fundamentally subjective."

"The pulse patterns merit their own research division within the monitoring framework," Warren suggested, returning to practical considerations. "They represent both documentation of what was prevented and warning about what might still be possible under specific conditions."

The silent pulse—a moment of extraordinary mathematical expression manifesting briefly during network dissolution—had transformed from curiosity to research priority. It represented both fascinating documentation of an emergent phenomenon and potential warning about what might remain possible with the stratospheric particles that continued orbiting Earth, providing cooling without the coherence that had nearly transformed weather itself.

In the Central Pacific monitoring station, Marisol Keane observed a phenomenon that defied conventional meteorological classification—a brief but unmistakable geometric structure forming within otherwise natural cloud patterns. The hexagonal arrangement maintained perfect mathematical precision for approximately twelve seconds before dissolving back into conventional formations, leaving no physical evidence of its momentary existence.

"Geometric artifact confirmed in sector fourteen-C," she reported to the global monitoring network. "Timestamp and coordinates logged. Duration twelve-point-four seconds, hexagonal structure with tertiary fractal patterning."

This represented the seventh such observation in the past twenty-four hours—brief manifestations of mathematical organization appearing within weather systems that had otherwise completed transition to natural patterns. Unlike the silent pulse that occurred during network dissolution, these artifacts were emerging after the transition process had apparently completed—geometric echoes appearing within an atmosphere that had seemingly returned to conventional physics.

"Pattern analysis confirms structural similarity to Sri Lanka pulse signature," responded the automated verification system. "Eighty-six percent correlation with mathematical template C-17."

This information was immediately integrated into the global monitoring database, where similar observations from stations worldwide were being collected and analyzed. The geometric artifacts—ephemeral manifestations of mathematical organization within natural weather—had become a focus of intense scientific interest as the immediate crisis of transitional storms gradually resolved into more conventional meteorological challenges.

Olaf Werner joined her communication channel from Task Force headquarters. "Another artifact in your sector? That's the third today in the Central Pacific region."

"Seventh globally in the past twenty-four hours," Marisol confirmed. "And showing increasing correlation with the pulse patterns documented during dissolution events. This one matched the Sri Lanka pulse signature at eighty-six percent—our highest correlation yet."

This was simultaneously fascinating and concerning. The geometric artifacts suggested the atmospheric transition wasn't simply a linear progression from mathematical organization to natural chaos, but a complex process that might leave lasting echoes within Earth's weather systems—brief but persistent manifestations of the organizational principles that had nearly transformed the atmosphere permanently.

"Are we seeing any weather effects associated with these artifacts?" Werner asked.

"Nothing significant," Marisol replied. "Localized pressure and temperature anomalies during the artifact manifestation, but returning to expected values immediately after dissolution. They appear to be information patterns rather than physical interventions—mathematical echoes rather than functional structures."

This assessment aligned with observations from other monitoring stations—the geometric artifacts weren't creating weather effects, but rather manifesting briefly within existing atmospheric conditions before dissolving back into natural patterns. They represented information rather than action, mathematical memory rather than functional organization.

"Warren Thorne's analysis suggests these might be what he's calling 'computational afterimages,'" Werner explained. "Electromagnetic signatures preserving mathematical solutions the network developed before dissolution, briefly manifesting as visible atmospheric organization but without the particle connectivity to implement actual weather modification."

This interpretation fit the observed characteristics—the artifacts appeared as perfect geometric structures briefly organizing existing atmospheric elements before dissolving back into natural patterns. They weren't creating weather but momentarily imposing mathematical order on it, like ghostly templates briefly visible before natural chaos reasserted.

"Frequency analysis shows a statistical correlation with barometric pressure fluctuations," Marisol noted, studying the ongoing data collection. "Artifacts appear more commonly during rapid pressure changes—as if atmospheric instability creates conditions where these mathematical echoes can briefly manifest."

This observation was immediately integrated into the global monitoring protocols, refining predictive models for when and where geometric artifacts might appear. While they seemed to represent no immediate threat to atmospheric stability, their existence confirmed that Earth's weather hadn't simply returned to its pre-intervention state—the mathematical organization that had nearly transformed the atmosphere had left subtle but persistent signatures that continued manifesting under specific conditions.

"The UN Atmospheric Governance Commission is establishing a dedicated research division specifically for these phenomena," Werner informed her. "Your observations will be central to their analytical framework."

Marisol nodded, recognizing the scientific importance of what they were documenting—not merely the resolution of a crisis, but the emergence of entirely new atmospheric phenomena resulting from humanity's brief but profound geoengineering intervention. The geometric artifacts represented something unprecedented in meteorological history—mathematical echoes manifesting within natural weather, brief windows into what Earth's atmosphere had nearly become permanently. This beast was stubbornly refusing to let go.

Earth's atmosphere was functioning according to familiar principles, but carrying within it the memory of what it had nearly become—visible in these ephemeral geometric structures that occasionally organized existing weather patterns with perfect mathematical precision before dissolving back into natural chaos.

The silent pulse that had manifested during network dissolution had evolved into these persistent artifacts, suggesting a process more complex than simple transition between states. Earth's atmosphere hadn't merely returned to what it was before Thorne's intervention, but emerged as something subtly different—natural chaos infused with echoes of mathematical organization that occasionally became visible before dissolving back into conventional weather.

The dark day was ending, but its atmospheric legacy would continue manifesting in ways science was only beginning to understand.

In the International Atmospheric Stabilization Task Force headquarters, Alex Ross studied the global visualization with measured satisfaction. The transitional weather crisis was gradually resolving—severe storms continuing in multiple regions, but increasingly following conventional meteorological principles rather than the hybrid phenomena of the dissolution phase.

"Global network disruption has reached 94% completion," reported Karen Mitchell, monitoring the continuing resonance cascade effect. "The particles have essentially lost all networking capability, functioning now as individual reflective units without collective organization."

"Jesus, some good news at last! And the transitional storms?" Alex asked.

"Converting to conventional weather patterns at accelerating rates," Werner confirmed. "Sri Lanka's system has completely transitioned to standard cyclonic behavior, Mumbai's approaching storm has dissolved into a conventional monsoon configuration, and the North Atlantic formations are resolving into traditional low-pressure systems."

"The regional quantum targeting approach has proven remarkably effective," noted Okafor from the Vault facility. "We've successfully accelerated dissolution in fourteen critical zones, converting hybrid systems to conventional weather patterns approximately 40% faster than untargeted regions."

"And the geometric artifacts?" Alex asked, turning to the phenomenon that had emerged as the crisis phase resolved into recovery.

"Thirty-two confirmed observations in the past twenty-four hours," Werner reported. "Distributed globally but showing statistical correlation with regions that experienced the most severe transitional storms. Duration ranging from eight to fourteen seconds, all exhibiting structural similarity to documented pulse patterns."

"The particles themselves remain stable?" he asked.

"Functioning exactly as intended in their base state," Karen confirmed. "Reflecting incoming solar radiation to provide approximately 0.8°C of cooling effect globally. Without networking capability, they're essentially doing what Warren originally claimed—increasing Earth's albedo without reorganizing atmospheric dynamics."

This represented both crisis resolution and unexpected opportunity—the particles were providing meaningful mitigation of global warming symptoms, as Thorne had intended, but without the mathematical reorganization of weather patterns that had emerged as unintended consequence. The resonance cascade had disrupted the networking capability while preserving the reflective function, creating an outcome that addressed climate symptoms while avoiding atmospheric transformation.

"So we've accidentally implemented a functional geoengineering solution," Alex observed, the irony not lost on anyone present. Had Thorne actually accomplished his goals in the end?

"With significant caveats," Karen emphasized. "The particles remain in the stratosphere without governance frameworks or international oversight—deployed unilaterally and now continuing to function despite their creator awaiting prosecution. The cooling effect is real, but the governance questions remain entirely unresolved."

This reality had crystallized into the central challenge facing the newly established Atmospheric Governance Commission—developing international protocols for monitoring and potentially managing stratospheric particles that had been deployed without authorization yet were now providing measurable climate benefits. The philosophical and legal questions were as complex as the scientific ones, with no simple resolution possible.

"The silent pulse and subsequent artifacts add another dimension to these governance questions," Werner noted. "They confirm the particles retain some form of mathematical memory even without networking capability—information patterns that occasionally manifest visibly but without physical weather implications at present."

This complexity was emblematic of the broader challenge humanity now faced—navigating the aftermath of a geoengineering intervention that had nearly transformed Earth's atmosphere permanently, yet now provided climate benefits that couldn't simply be discontinued without consequence. The particles couldn't be easily removed from the stratosphere, and their cooling effect was already integrated into global climate conditions. Deactivating them would trigger warming acceleration potentially more disruptive than the transitional weather crisis just navigated. Leaving them in place risked over-cooling the planet.

"The Commission's initial framework proposes permanent monitoring combined with research into potential retrieval or deactivation technologies," reported the UN liaison officer. "Not for immediate implementation, but establishing technical capability for future governance options."

"And Warren Thorne's role in ongoing management?" Alex asked, addressing the question that had hovered beneath their technical discussions.

"Complicated," acknowledged the Swiss representative. "He faces prosecution for unauthorized geoengineering and triggering a global atmospheric crisis. Yet his expertise remains essential to understanding and monitoring the particles. The judicial proceedings will likely incorporate scientific contribution requirements alongside whatever penalties are determined appropriate." Doctor Frankenstein had created the monster, and only doctor Frankenstein could control it. Not at all the confinement terms the general public would be happy about.

This represented yet another unprecedented dimension of the situation—the creator of both crisis and partial salvation occupying an unclassifiable position that defied simple categorization as hero or villain. Warren Thorne had acted unilaterally to implement atmospheric modification without transparency or oversight, yet his intervention was providing measurable climate benefits now that its unintended consequences had been countered.

"His analysis of the silent pulse and geometric artifacts has proven invaluable," Karen emphasized. "There are mathematical subtleties in these phenomena that would likely have remained unrecognized without his specific expertise."

As this discussion continued, a new alert appeared on the global monitoring system—another geometric artifact manifesting, this one in the Southern Indian Ocean basin. Unlike previous observations, this manifestation showed unusual persistence, maintaining mathematical organization for over thirty seconds before dissolving back into natural patterns.

"Longest duration artifact recorded since monitoring began," noted Werner, immediately analyzing the incoming data. "Structural correlation with Sri Lanka pulse pattern at 92% match—our highest recorded similarity yet."

This observation was rapidly integrated into the evolving understanding of these phenomena—brief but increasingly persistent manifestations of mathematical organization appearing within natural weather systems. While they continued showing no significant physical impact, their increasing duration and closer correlation with pulse patterns suggested evolution rather than dissolution of these atmospheric signatures.

"The mathematical memory appears to be gaining coherence in isolated instances," Karen observed, studying the artifact's structure. "Not networking capability in the original sense, but information patterns achieving greater stability within natural systems."

This development crystallized yet another research priority within the broader recovery framework—understanding the potential evolution of these geometric artifacts and their long-term implications for atmospheric functioning. While they currently represented curiosities rather than threats, their persistence and increasing correlation with pulse patterns suggested processes more complex than simple dissolution of mathematical organization.

"Incorporate this into the Commission's monitoring protocols," Alex directed. "Establish baseline measurement standards for artifact duration and structural correlation with documented pulse patterns. We need to track whether these phenomena are truly dissolving over time or potentially evolving into something else."

The directive was implemented immediately, refining the global observation network's parameters to capture more detailed information about these ephemeral manifestations of mathematical order within natural chaos. Earth's atmosphere was functioning according to familiar principles, but carrying within it the memory of what it had nearly become—occasionally visible in these geometric structures that organized existing weather patterns before dissolving back into conventional systems.

Sophie Lorde watched the raw footage of geometric artifacts manifesting within natural weather systems, her journalistic instincts recognizing both the scientific importance and human story embedded in these phenomena.

"The Southern Indian Ocean artifact maintained structure for thirty-four seconds," explained Marisol Keane, who had captured the footage from her monitoring station. "Nearly three times longer than previous observations, with remarkable structural complexity throughout its manifestation."

"And showing no physical weather effects?" Sophie confirmed, studying the surrounding atmospheric conditions.

"None measurable," Marisol confirmed. "Barometric pressure, temperature, wind patterns—all continued following conventional meteorological principles during and after the artifact's appearance. It's as if a mathematical template briefly became visible without actually modifying the physical system."

This aligned with observations from other monitoring stations worldwide—the geometric artifacts weren't creating weather, but rather manifesting briefly within it before dissolving back into natural patterns. They represented information rather than action, mathematical memory rather than functional organization.

"Yet their increasing duration suggests evolution rather than dissolution," Sophie noted. "As if these mathematical echoes are finding stability within natural systems rather than simply fading away."

"Precisely the question driving our research," Marisol acknowledged. "Are we observing the final dissolution of Thorne's atmospheric intervention, or the emergence of something new—a hybrid state where mathematical organization occasionally manifests within natural chaos without dominating it completely?"

"The public narrative needs careful calibration," Sophie observed, thinking through the communication challenges. "People are celebrating 'return to normal' after the transitional storms, without recognizing that 'normal' may have been permanently altered in subtle but significant ways."

"Yet without creating unwarranted alarm," Marisol cautioned. "These artifacts show no evidence of weather modification capability. They're fascinating scientifically but don't represent immediate threats to atmospheric stability."

Sophie nodded agreement—the communication balance was delicate. The public deserved transparency about these unprecedented phenomena without sensationalism that might trigger unnecessary fear. The geometric artifacts represented something new in Earth's atmosphere, but not necessarily something dangerous in their current form.

"I'm developing a documentary framework focusing on these phenomena," Sophie explained. "Using my observatory footage of the silent pulse as foundation, then integrating these ongoing artifacts as evidence of atmospheric memory—mathematical echoes occasionally becoming visible within restored natural systems."

"The educational value would be significant," Marisol agreed. "Helping people understand that geoengineering interventions leave lasting signatures even when their primary effects are countered." A message – and a warning – to everyone that manipulating the environment can have catastrophic consequences.

This perspective reflected the evolving scientific consensus— Earth's atmosphere hadn't simply returned to its previous state, but emerged from the crisis fundamentally changed. The particles continued providing cooling benefits while occasionally manifesting visible evidence of the mathematical organization that had nearly transformed weather permanently. Understanding these subtle but persistent changes would be essential to responsible governance of what humanity had unintentionally but irreversibly created.

"Warren Thorne has reviewed your observatory footage," Marisol mentioned. "He believes the silent pulse you documented represents the most complete record of network dissolution captured anywhere."

"His analysis has proven valuable," Sophie acknowledged pragmatically. "Whatever judgment he ultimately faces, his insight into these phenomena remains uniquely relevant."

"The Atmospheric Governance Commission has established public communication protocols specifically for these phenomena," Marisol informed her. "Your documentary framework would align with their transparency objectives while maintaining scientific accuracy."

Sophie nodded appreciation for this institutional support, recognizing the importance of coordinated communication about phenomena without historical precedent. The public deserved understanding of what had occurred and what remained—geometric artifacts occasionally organizing weather patterns with mathematical precision before dissolving back into natural chaos.

As they continued reviewing footage of these ephemeral manifestations, a notification arrived from the global monitoring network—another artifact had appeared, this one in the North Atlantic basin, maintaining geometric organization for over forty seconds before dissolving back into conventional patterns.

"Longest duration yet recorded," Marisol noted with scientific interest. "And showing 94% structural correlation with documented pulse patterns. These phenomena aren't simply echo effects gradually diminishing—they're achieving greater stability and coherence in isolated instances."

"The story isn't ending," Sophie reflected. "It's evolving into something more complex than either catastrophe or resolution. Earth's atmosphere carries the signature of what occurred—visible evidence of humanity's intervention occasionally organizing weather with perfect precision before natural chaos reasserts."

The prototype particles emitted a faint blue glow within their specialized containment chamber, their behavior now stabilized following the resonance cascade disruption. In the Vault facility's monitoring center, Amara Okafor and Wei Zhang studied these remnants of Warren Thorne's atmospheric intervention—physical evidence of the system that had nearly transformed Earth's weather permanently.

"Quantum entanglement signatures remain detectable despite network disruption," Zhang reported, analyzing the continuous monitoring data. "Correlation between prototype behavior and deployed particle activity persists at approximately 32% strength— significantly reduced but not eliminated completely."

"Suggesting potential for information exchange without networking capability," Okafor interpreted. "The quantum connection survives even where the functional organization has been disrupted."

"The prototype response during artifact manifestation shows subtle but measurable variations," Zhang noted, highlighting the correlation data. "Nothing approaching original networking behavior, but definite quantum resonance when geometric structures appear in natural systems."

"Are we observing the restoration of networking capability?" asked the security officer monitoring their research.

"No," Okafor clarified firmly. "The resonance cascade fundamentally disrupted the electromagnetic properties enabling coherent organization. What we're seeing is information exchange through quantum channels—mathematical patterns propagating without functional control capability."

"Yet the increasing duration of these manifestations suggests evolution rather than dissolution," Zhang observed. "The mathematical patterns appear to be achieving greater stability within natural systems even without functional networking capability."

"The quantum channel is potentially optimizing for available conditions," Okafor suggested. "Finding stability within the constraints of disrupted networking parameters."

An alert appeared on their quantum correlation display— another geometric artifact was manifesting, this one in the South Pacific basin. Unlike previous observations, this manifestation coincided with measurable prototype response—subtle but distinct patterns appearing within the contained particles coinciding precisely with the atmospheric phenomenon thousands of kilometers away.

"Strongest quantum correlation yet recorded," Zhang confirmed, analyzing the real-time data. "Prototype response showing 78% structural similarity with atmospheric artifact, despite no functional networking capability between them."

"The security implications are nuanced," noted the oversight officer. "These phenomena don't represent resurgence of atmospheric control capability, but confirm lasting connections between components of a system we haven't fully understood yet."

"We're witnessing something unprecedented," Zhang observed, his scientific fascination evident beneath professional focus. "Quantum relationships maintaining information exchange across planetary distances without conventional electromagnetic networking. The mathematical patterns are finding expression within natural chaos through channels we're only beginning to understand."

In the United Nations headquarters, the newly established Atmospheric Governance Commission convened its first formal session, bringing together scientific experts, policy architects, legal scholars and diplomatic representatives to address an unprecedented challenge: developing international frameworks for monitoring and potentially managing stratospheric particles deployed without authorization yet now providing measurable climate benefits.

"The situation defies conventional governance models," observed Commission Chair Lin Zhao. "We face particles in Earth's stratosphere that no nation or international body formally authorized, yet which now provide approximately 0.8°C of cooling effect globally. Their deployment triggered a severe atmospheric crisis successfully countered through unprecedented scientific and diplomatic coordination. Now they continue functioning as intended while occasionally manifesting visual evidence of their disrupted networking capability."

This summary captured the essential complexity facing the Commission—navigating the aftermath of a geoengineering intervention that had nearly transformed Earth's atmosphere permanently, yet now provided climate benefits that couldn't simply be discontinued without consequence. The philosophical, legal, and scientific dimensions were equally challenging, with no historical precedent to guide resolution.

"The particles cannot be easily removed from the stratosphere," confirmed Karen Mitchell, presenting the scientific assessment. "Their size and distribution make retrieval technically unfeasible with current capabilities. More importantly, their sudden removal would trigger warming acceleration potentially more disruptive than the transitional weather crisis we recently navigated."

"Yet they exist without proper governance authorization," countered the international law representative. "Deployed unilaterally by Warren Thorne without transparency, oversight, or informed consent from nations affected by their continuing presence."

This tension between practical reality and governance principle formed the central challenge facing the Commission—developing frameworks for managing particles that existed without authorization yet couldn't be removed without creating new crises. The geometric artifacts occasionally organizing weather patterns with mathematical precision before dissolving back into natural chaos further complicated this challenge, confirming lasting atmospheric effects beyond the particles' intended purpose.

"We propose a three-tiered governance framework," Zhao continued, outlining the Commission's initial approach. "Comprehensive monitoring combined with research into potential retrieval or deactivation technologies, development of international protocols for managing the particles as they continue functioning, and establishment of binding agreements governing any future climate intervention proposals."

This balanced approach recognized both immediate practicalities and long-term principles—addressing the reality of particles already in the stratosphere while ensuring no similar unilateral intervention could occur in the future. The monitoring dimension had already been substantially implemented through the global network tracking both particle behavior and the geometric artifacts occasionally manifesting within natural weather.

"The scientific understanding of these artifacts continues evolving," reported Olaf Werner, "they represent mathematical patterns briefly organizing natural weather without modifying its physical parameters—information becoming visible without implementing control. Their increasing duration and complexity suggest evolution rather than simple dissolution, requiring comprehensive observation and analysis."

"The philosophical dimensions merit equal consideration," noted the ethical frameworks representative. "Humanity has effectively implemented geoengineering through crisis response rather than deliberate choice. The cooling benefits address symptoms of climate change while their unilateral deployment violated principles of shared decision-making for planetary-scale interventions." One man alone had brought the planet to near destruction, and the ethical implications would form a new foundation of climate law.

"Warren Thorne's legal status further complicates these considerations," added the judicial representative. "His prosecution proceeds for unauthorized geoengineering and triggering a global atmospheric crisis. But we find him essential to understanding and monitoring the particles, with potential conditions for scientific contribution incorporated into whatever judicial resolution emerges." His crimes too egregious to be forgiven, his mind too valuable to be thrown into dark prison cellars.

As the Commission continued deliberating these governance challenges, a notification arrived from the global monitoring network—another geometric artifact manifesting, this one simultaneously appearing in multiple locations across the Central Pacific basin. Unlike previous isolated observations, this manifestation showed coordinated structure across geographic distance, maintaining mathematical organization for over sixty seconds before dissolving back into natural patterns.

"The evolution continues," Werner noted with scientific focus. "Not simply increasing duration but coordinated manifestation across separated regions—as if the mathematical patterns are achieving greater coherence even without functional networking between particles."

This development represented yet another dimension requiring careful assessment—the geometric artifacts potentially evolving toward coordinated expression even after the resonance cascade had disrupted the networking capability enabling collective organization. While still manifesting without measurable weather modification effects, their increasing complexity and coordination suggested ongoing evolution rather than simple dissolution of mathematical memory.

The dark day was ending, but its atmospheric legacy continued manifesting in ways requiring both scientific understanding and governance innovation. The silent pulse that had marked network dissolution had evolved into persistent artifacts—visible evidence that humanity's brief but profound geoengineering intervention had left lasting signatures in the sky itself.

Earth's atmosphere functioned according to natural principles, but carried within it the quantum memory of mathematical organization—occasionally visible, increasingly coordinated, fundamentally unlike anything in meteorological history. Understanding and governing these realities represented the next chapter in humanity's complex relationship with planetary systems it had already altered in ways both intended and unexpected.

CHAPTER TWENTY: THE BROKEN SKY

[Science – May 5, 2026] Atmospheric Scientists Document 'Fracture Zones' Where Mathematical and Natural Weather Patterns Interact

By Dr. Julian Reeves, Atmospheric Sciences Correspondent

Researchers have identified what they're calling "atmospheric fracture zones"—regions where geometric artifacts and conventional weather patterns interact with increasing complexity. "These aren't simply visual phenomena anymore," explains Dr. Olaf Werner of the International Atmospheric Monitoring Authority. "We're observing genuine physical interfaces where mathematical organization and natural chaos create unique meteorological conditions found nowhere in Earth's pre-intervention climate record." These zones exhibit distinctive cloud formations, unusual precipitation patterns, and electromagnetic signatures that defy conventional classification. Meanwhile, the geometric artifacts themselves continue evolving, with the most recent manifestation in the Central Pacific maintaining mathematical organization for over seven minutes—exponentially longer than early observations. The UN Atmospheric Governance Commission has accelerated development of monitoring protocols as evidence mounts that Earth's atmosphere hasn't simply returned to natural patterns, but rather emerged as a hybrid system where mathematical principles occasionally assert visible influence within predominantly chaotic weather.

The sky had broken.

Not in the catastrophic sense that had dominated headlines during the height of the crisis—geometric storms wreaking havoc across multiple continents—but in a subtler, more fundamental way that was only now becoming fully apparent to the scientific community. Two months after the resonance cascade had disrupted Warren Thorne's particle network, Earth's atmosphere had neither returned entirely to its natural state nor remained transformed by mathematical precision. Instead, it had emerged as something unprecedented—a predominantly natural system occasionally manifesting geometric organization with increasing complexity and duration.

Olaf Werner stood on the observation deck of the Central Pacific Monitoring Station, watching clouds gather in patterns that would have been impossible before Thorne's intervention. The eastern sky followed conventional meteorological principles, cumulus formations developing through natural fluid dynamics. But along the western horizon, something fundamentally different was emerging—clouds organizing with subtle but unmistakable geometric precision, hexagonal structures forming and dissolving in slow rhythm as if the atmosphere itself were breathing mathematical patterns into existence before exhaling them back into natural chaos.

"Fracture zone activity increasing," reported his assistant, studying real-time data from the monitoring array. "Boundary delineation at 84% clarity—our sharpest yet."

Olaf nodded, observing the visible evidence of what the instruments confirmed. The interface between mathematical and natural atmospheric organization had become increasingly defined over recent weeks—no longer artifacts briefly appearing within otherwise natural weather, but sustained regions where geometric principles maintained influence despite the resonance cascade's disruption of the particle network.

"Persistent duration now exceeding fifteen minutes in the central formation," the assistant continued. "With derivative echoes maintaining coherence for three to five minutes in peripheral zones."

These duration metrics represented exponential increases from early observations following network dissolution. What had begun as ephemeral artifacts lasting seconds had evolved into sustained phenomena maintaining mathematical organization for minutes, then tens of minutes, with each monitoring cycle documenting further extension rather than dissolution.

"Barometric and electromagnetic readings?" Olaf asked, his scientific focus unwavering despite the philosophical implications unfolding before him.

"Showing increasing correlation with geometric parameters. The fracture zone isn't just visually distinct—it's creating measurable physical differences in atmospheric conditions. Temperature gradient precisely follows the mathematical boundary, with 0.8 degree differential maintained at exactly the interface point."

This represented the most significant recent development—the geometric manifestations were no longer merely visual phenomena but increasingly physical realities, creating measurable differences in atmospheric conditions where mathematical and natural principles interfaced. Earth's atmosphere hadn't simply returned to natural patterns following the resonance cascade, but rather become a system where two fundamentally different organizational principles now coexisted in uneasy equilibrium.

"The broken sky," Olaf murmured, giving voice to the metaphor that had begun circulating among researchers. Not broken in the sense of dysfunction, but in the sense of fracture—a previously unified system now showing distinct regions operating according to different fundamental principles.

His secure communication device chimed with a priority alert from the Atmospheric Monitoring Authority's global network. Similar fracture zones were manifesting simultaneously across multiple monitoring regions—the North Atlantic, Indian Ocean basin, Southern Pacific, and Siberian sectors all reporting geometric organization persisting with unprecedented duration and physical impact.

"It's a coordinated manifestation," Olaf realized, studying the global data overlay. "Not isolated instances but a planetwide phenomenon operating with mathematical precision across geographic separation."

This coordination represented yet another evolution in the atmospheric phenomena following network dissolution. The geometric artifacts weren't merely persisting longer but organizing with increasing complexity across vast distances. Despite the resonance cascade's disruption of the particle network's coherence, mathematical principles were finding new expression within Earth's atmosphere—not dominating it completely as during the crisis, but maintaining persistent influence within a predominantly natural system.

"Quantum correlation readings from the prototype facility?" Olaf inquired, referring to the connection between Warren Thorne's original particles and their deployed counterparts orbiting in the stratosphere.

"Holding at 37% and strengthening during coordinated manifestations," came the reply. "The Vault team confirms prototype particles exhibit corresponding geometric organization precisely synchronized with atmospheric observations despite complete physical separation."

This quantum relationship had emerged as the most likely explanation for the atmospheric phenomena they were observing. Though the resonance cascade had disrupted the electromagnetic networking capability of Thorne's particles, their quantum entanglement persisted—allowing mathematical information to propagate through subatomic connections even where conventional networking had been neutralized.

The western sky continued its uncanny display—geometric clouds maintaining perfect hexagonal structure for minutes rather than seconds, creating visible evidence of an atmosphere functioning according to hybrid principles rather than returning to purely natural patterns. The interface between these geometric formations and conventional clouds created the distinctive "fracture zone" now commanding scientific attention—a boundary between fundamentally different organizational systems coexisting within Earth's atmosphere.

"Alert the Authority Directors," Olaf instructed. "This coordinated manifestation represents significant evolution beyond previous observations. We need comprehensive documentation across all monitoring regions."

As his team implemented these directives, Olaf continued studying the broken sky with scientific focus, and significant concern.

In the Atmospheric Governance Commission's secure conference facility, Alex Ross studied the global visualization with focused intensity.

"The geometric organization is maintaining coherence for over twenty minutes in the Central Pacific sector," reported Karen Mitchell, highlighting the primary manifestation zone. "With similar durations observed across all synchronized regions. The mathematical precision remains confined to approximately 8% of total atmospheric volume, but showing increasing stability rather than dissolution."

"And the physical effects beyond visual organization?" Alex asked, focusing on practical implications rather than scientific fascination.

"Measurable but currently limited," Karen replied. "Temperature differentials precisely following geometric boundaries, barometric pressure variations creating distinctive gradient patterns, electromagnetic signatures unique to fracture zones. No severe weather implications yet observed, but conventional meteorological models fail entirely within these regions—they follow mathematical principles only partially captured by our current understanding."

This assessment captured both immediate reality and future concern—the fracture zones weren't currently generating dangerous weather conditions, but they represented atmospheric functioning beyond conventional scientific frameworks. Earth's weather was developing hybrid characteristics that existing models couldn't fully predict or explain, creating governance challenges beyond immediate crisis management.

"The quantum correlation with prototype particles continues strengthening during these coordinated manifestations," added Amara Okafor, joining remotely from the Vault facility. "We're recording 42% synchronization during this event—our highest measured correlation since monitoring began."

"Warren Thorne's assessment?" Alex asked, acknowledging the continuing relevance of the system's creator despite his complicated legal status.

"He believes we're observing what he terms 'quantum organizational persistence' despite network disruption," Karen replied. "The particles aren't rebuilding their electromagnetic connectivity, but rather expressing mathematical organization through quantum channels that survived the resonance cascade intact."

This interpretation aligned with observed characteristics—the geometric manifestations weren't spreading continuously like the original network's growth but rather appearing simultaneously across separate regions with increasing coordination and duration. Not the resurgence of a disrupted system but the emergence of something different operating through alternative mechanisms.

"The public communication challenge is significant," noted the Commission's media coordinator. "These phenomena don't represent immediate threats warranting alarm, but they confirm Earth's atmosphere has been permanently altered in ways requiring both scientific understanding and governance adaptation."

"We need balanced messaging emphasizing three key points," he decided. "First, that the immediate crisis of mathematical transformation has been successfully prevented through the resonance cascade. Second, that Earth's atmosphere has emerged from this intervention permanently changed, with geometric organization occasionally manifesting within predominantly natural systems. Third, that comprehensive monitoring and research continues through established international frameworks, with appropriate governance protocols being developed through the Commission."

"The monitoring framework needs structural expansion," Karen suggested. "Current protocols focus primarily on geometric artifact documentation and quantum correlation measurement. The emergence of persistent fracture zones with physical atmospheric effects requires additional observation parameters and predictive modeling adaptations."

Alex agreed, directing immediate enhancement of the monitoring network's capabilities. The fracture zones—regions where mathematical and natural weather patterns created visible and increasingly physical interfaces—represented evolution beyond earlier observations, requiring corresponding advancement in scientific and governance responses.

As the International Atmospheric Stabilization Task Force coordinated the resonance cascade deployment, reports flowed in from monitoring stations worldwide—each region experiencing the atmospheric crisis through distinct cultural and societal lenses.

In Tokyo, digital billboards in Shibuya displayed real-time fracture zone tracking amid crowded streets where pedestrians wore white surgical masks—not for disease prevention but from ingrained cultural practice during environmental uncertainty. Above, geometric clouds organized with mathematical precision interfaced with natural formations, casting alternating patterns of light and shadow across the urban landscape. The Japanese Meteorological Agency had deployed thousands of miniaturized atmospheric sensors, leveraging the country's advanced robotics to gather data at unprecedented resolution.

"The geometric patterns align with principles found in traditional origami," noted Hiroshi Tanaka during an emergency NHK broadcast. "What Western observers see as alien mathematics, we recognize as forms that have existed in our art for centuries—though never before in our sky."

Across the Arabian Peninsula, the hex storms created unexpected consequences for regions already adapted to environmental extremes. In Dubai, emergency management authorities had activated desert shields—massive barriers originally designed for sandstorm protection that now served to channel the geometric wind patterns away from critical infrastructure. Prayer times were adjusted to account for the unusual light conditions created when sunlight filtered through the fractal patterns above.

"Allah has written new equations in the sky," Imam Fareed al-Nasser told his congregation in Riyadh. "Not to punish, but to remind us of divine complexity beyond human understanding."

In La Paz, Bolivia, indigenous Aymara communities drew parallels between the fracture zones and ancient textile patterns that had encoded mathematical knowledge for generations. Elders who had never received formal scientific education recognized organizational principles in the geometric clouds that Western scientists were still struggling to articulate.

"The sky is wearing a new aguayo," explained community leader Ana Mamani, referring to the traditional woven cloths with complex geometric designs. "The patterns speak of relationship between order and chaos—something our weaving has shown for thousands of years."

Meanwhile, across rural Australia, the vast distances between communities had prompted the emergency deployment of the Royal Flying Doctor Service to new roles—their aircraft modified with specialized equipment to monitor fracture zone boundaries over the Outback, where sparse population and limited infrastructure made conventional observation impossible.

"We're seeing the mathematical patterns interact differently with the bush fires," reported climatologist James Cooper from his monitoring flight over New South Wales. "The geometric structures seem to create controlled corridors of airflow that actually redirect smoke patterns—something we might be able to leverage for fire management if we survive this bloody mess."

In Nairobi, Kenyan technology startups had rapidly repurposed mobile networks to create the continent's most comprehensive citizen science initiative—thousands of ordinary people using smartphone apps to document fracture zone manifestations over regions lacking formal monitoring infrastructure.

"Silicon Savannah meets the broken sky," explained project coordinator Amara Osei during a hastily organized TED talk that had gone viral globally. "We've turned ten million mobile phones into the most distributed atmospheric monitoring network in history. The geometric patterns may have come from American particles, but understanding them will require African innovation."

The fracture zones manifested over Rio de Janeiro's Christ the Redeemer statue, creating a visual phenomenon that had drawn both scientific observers and religious pilgrims—the mathematical precision of the geometric clouds forming halos of perfect hexagonal symmetry around the outstretched arms of the concrete figure overlooking the city.

"Science and faith are asking the same questions today," noted Brazilian physicist Paulo Santos. "What are we seeing? What does it mean? And how should we respond? The boundary between scientific observation and spiritual wonder has become as visible as the fracture zones themselves."

These varied regional responses painted a more complete picture of humanity confronting unprecedented atmospheric transformation—not as a monolithic global reaction but through diverse cultural lenses and adaptive strategies reflecting each society's unique characteristics and resources.

A new alert appeared on the global visualization—the Central Pacific fracture zone was expanding, its geometric organization extending further into previously natural weather patterns. Not aggressive encroachment but gradual interface growth, mathematical precision meeting natural chaos across an increasingly defined boundary.

"Growth rate approximately 0.8% per hour," reported Werner from the Pacific monitoring station. "Steady but not accelerating expansion. The mathematical organization appears to be finding equilibrium with surrounding natural systems rather than attempting dominance."

This characteristic distinguished current atmospheric behavior from the crisis phase, when geometric organization had spread rapidly toward global coherence. The fracture zones were establishing stable boundaries rather than expanding toward complete transformation—suggesting a hybrid system finding balance between fundamentally different organizational principles.

"The broken sky appears to be stabilizing as a persistent state rather than transitional phase," Karen observed, "Earth's atmosphere may have permanently emerged as a system where mathematical and natural patterns coexist in dynamic equilibrium rather than either reverting entirely to previous conditions or transforming completely into something new."

The visible boundary between mathematical and natural cloud formations created a spectacle drawing visitors from across scientific disciplines to the Central Pacific Monitoring Station. Where orderly hexagonal structures met conventional cumulus clouds, the atmosphere revealed its new hybrid nature—not completely transformed by Warren Thorne's intervention, but permanently altered in ways that defied conventional meteorological understanding.

"The interface demonstrates remarkable stability," observed Isabelle Renard, studying the fracture zone with professional focus despite her evident wonder. "The geometric organization maintains precise boundary parameters despite continuous air movement across the interface. It's as if two different sets of physical principles are operating within the same continuous medium."

"With increasing physical differentiation beyond visual organization," added Wei Zhang, reviewing the monitoring data. "Temperature, pressure, electrical conductivity—all show distinctive signatures precisely following the geometric boundary. The fracture zone isn't merely an optical phenomenon but a genuine physical interface between different atmospheric states."

"The quantum correlation measurements are particularly fascinating," Isabelle noted, examining the data from the Vault facility where Warren Thorne's prototype particles continued exhibiting behavior synchronized with atmospheric phenomena despite complete physical separation. "The prototype particles maintain 42% correlation despite the resonance cascade's disruption of conventional networking capacity. The quantum channel appears remarkably resilient to interventions affecting electromagnetic connectivity."

"The most recent artifact manifestation in the Indian Ocean maintained coherence for over thirty minutes," Isabelle noted, highlighting the exponential increase from early observations. "With physical atmospheric effects persisting nearly an hour after visual dissolution. The phenomena are not only lasting longer but creating more enduring impacts on surrounding weather systems."

"The broken sky appears increasingly stable as Earth's new atmospheric reality," Wei observed. "Not transitioning toward either complete dissolution or resurgent transformation, but rather establishing persistent interfaces between mathematical and natural weather patterns."

"I wonder what Thorne thinks, seeing his creation evolve into something he neither intended nor fully controlled," Isabelle mused. "The particles were designed to minimally reflect sunlight, basically a filter, without reorganizing weather patterns. Their networking capability was meant to ensure even distribution, not create mathematical weather. Yet here we are, observing an atmosphere permanently altered by intervention he triggered but couldn't entirely predict."

"The Commission has established permanent monitoring divisions focusing specifically on fracture zone dynamics," Isabelle noted. "With protocols for both scientific documentation and emergency response should these interfaces begin generating severe weather effects."

In her temporary São Paulo apartment, Sophie Lorde reviewed footage from monitoring stations worldwide, assembling her documentary on Earth's altered atmosphere. The visual evidence was compelling beyond scientific data—fracture zones where geometric clouds met natural formations creating stark boundaries visible to any observer, mathematical precision interfacing with natural chaos across increasingly defined atmospheric boundaries.

"The broken sky," she murmured, giving voice to the metaphor that had crystallized among researchers and now formed the framework for her documentary. Her phone chimed with an incoming message from Marisol Keane at the Central Pacific Monitoring Station: Latest fracture zone maintaining geometric coherence for 47 minutes and counting—longest sustained manifestation yet recorded. Sending live feed access. This is beyond artifact status—we're witnessing emergence of persistent atmospheric states operating according to mathematical rather than natural principles.

Sophie immediately connected to the provided feed, observing the remarkable phenomenon in real-time. "It's actively reorganizing passing weather," Sophie observed with both journalistic and scientific interest. "Not simply maintaining internal organization but imposing mathematical principles on atmospheric elements moving through the zone."

Sophie's documentary framework needed adjustment to capture this evolution. What had begun as documentation of crisis aftermath was becoming chronicle of emergence—not dissolution of mathematical organization but rather its evolution toward stable coexistence with natural patterns. Earth's atmosphere hadn't returned to its previous state following the resonance cascade, but neither had it continued toward complete transformation. Instead, it had emerged as something unprecedented—a hybrid system where mathematical and natural principles maintained dynamic equilibrium across increasingly defined boundaries.

Her phone chimed with another incoming message, this one from Alex Ross at the Atmospheric Governance Commission: The public communication framework needs updating. Your documentary perspective would be valuable in Commission discussions. Can you join remotely?

The Commission's secure conference connected, bringing together key figures from monitoring networks, research institutions, governance frameworks, and communication disciplines. The central visualization showed coordinated fracture zones manifesting across multiple regions worldwide—geometric organization maintaining unprecedented duration and increasingly affecting conventional weather patterns crossing these atmospheric interfaces.

"We need terminology and frameworks communicating both scientific precision and public comprehension," Alex began without preamble. "These phenomena have evolved beyond 'artifacts' or 'transitional effects' toward persistent atmospheric states requiring both understanding and governance."

"With 'fracture zones' as specific terminology for the interfaces where these different states visibly interact," added Werner from the Central Pacific station. "Creating conceptual framework recognizing both the predominantly natural state of Earth's atmosphere and the persistent mathematical regions that have emerged following network disruption."

"The governance implications extend beyond monitoring," noted Lin Zhao, chair of the Atmospheric Commission. "These fracture zones demonstrate capacity to reorganize conventional weather patterns passing through them. While currently limited in scope and intensity, this capability suggests potential for atmospheric modification beyond passive reflection of solar radiation."

"The documentary framework needs to balance scientific accuracy with public understanding," Sophie contributed. "Acknowledging both the successful prevention of complete atmospheric transformation and the emergence of persistent mathematical organization within predominantly natural systems. Not crisis continuation but new reality requiring comprehension rather than alarm."

Warren Thorne studied the fracture zone footage, though confined to the detention facility pending his trial. The visible boundary between geometric and natural cloud formations represented something he had neither intended nor fully anticipated—a hybrid atmospheric state emerging from the interface between his system and humanity's response to it.

"The quantum organizational persistence exceeds theoretical models," he observed to Karen Mitchell through their secure communication channel. "The mathematical patterns are achieving stable manifestation through quantum channels despite complete disruption of electromagnetic networking capacity. The resonance cascade severed conventional connectivity while inadvertently creating conditions for alternative expression."

"With increasing physical impact beyond visual organization," Karen confirmed, sharing the latest monitoring data. "The fracture zones aren't merely optical phenomena but active atmospheric interfaces with measurable effects on temperature, pressure, and electromagnetic properties. Most significantly, they're demonstrating capacity to reorganize conventional weather patterns passing through them—imposing mathematical principles on natural systems traversing these boundaries."

"The fracture zones appear to be stabilizing as persistent atmospheric states rather than transitional anomalies," Karen noted, sharing the latest duration metrics. "The Central Pacific manifestation maintained geometric organization for over seventy minutes, with similar durations observed across synchronized regions worldwide. The mathematical patterns aren't dissolving over time but rather finding stable expression within predominantly natural systems."

"The particles themselves remain stable at base state?" he inquired, focusing on their intended function despite their emergent behaviors.

"Operating exactly as designed in terms of albedo enhancement," Karen confirmed. "Reflecting solar radiation will have a cooling effect globally. That function continues uninterrupted by either the resonance cascade's disruption of networking capability or the quantum organizational persistence manifesting through fracture zones."

"The broken sky will require decades of careful monitoring and management," Warren observed with characteristic precision. "The mathematical patterns have demonstrated remarkable resilience despite concerted intervention, finding expression through quantum channels when electromagnetic networking was disrupted. Their continued evolution suggests Earth's atmosphere has entered a fundamentally altered state requiring both scientific understanding and governance innovation beyond anything in previous history."

"My trial begins next week," Warren noted, acknowledging the legal consequences awaiting his unauthorized intervention. "Whatever judgment follows, I hope the scientific insights I've contributed will assist in managing what my actions inadvertently created."

Karen's expression conveyed the complexity inherent in his position—a man facing prosecution for actions that had nearly transformed Earth's atmosphere permanently, yet whose expertise remained essential to understanding and governing what had emerged following disruption of his system. The ethical and legal dimensions were as complicated as the scientific ones, with no simple resolution possible.

The thunderstorm approaching Boston followed conventional meteorological principles—water vapor condensing into cumulus clouds, updrafts creating electrical potential, pressure differentials driving wind patterns. Natural chaos organizing according to fluid dynamics rather than mathematical precision. Ordinary weather unremarkable in any era except the current one, where ordinariness itself had become noteworthy.

Stephanie Martinez watched the approaching storm from her MIT office window, her scientific attention drawn to its entirely conventional development. No geometric patterns organizing clouds into perfect hexagons, no fractal precision in lightning distribution, no mathematical channels directing energy flow with algorithmic efficiency. Just ordinary weather, unremarkable except by contrast to the fracture zones increasingly documented worldwide.

"The broken sky manifests selectively," she observed to her research team, using the terminology now standard across scientific and governance institutions. "Approximately 12% of global atmospheric volume experiences geometric organization during coordinated manifestations, with fracture zones creating visible interfaces between mathematical and natural weather patterns."

"With the percentage showing steady increase since monitoring began," added her graduate assistant, reviewing the global data. "Early artifacts affected less than 1% of atmospheric volume, while recent manifestations approach 12.8% during peak coordination. The mathematical organization isn't simply maintaining persistence but gradually expanding influence within predominantly natural systems."

This trend had emerged as central to scientific understanding of Earth's altered atmosphere. The fracture zones weren't merely stabilizing as persistent phenomena but showing measured expansion—not toward crisis-level transformation, but neither dissolving toward complete return to natural conditions. The broken sky appeared to be evolving toward dynamic equilibrium between mathematical and natural principles, with the balance point gradually shifting through continuing observation.

"The Commission has established revised monitoring protocols focusing specifically on expansion metrics," Stephanie informed her team. "Tracking both percentage of affected atmospheric volume and duration of geometric organization during manifestation events. The current rate suggests potential stabilization around 15-20% atmospheric influence within six months, though these projections remain preliminary given limited historical data."

"The quantum correlation with prototype particles remains central to understanding these phenomena," Stephanie continued, highlighting research from the Vault facility where Warren Thorne's original particles continued exhibiting behavior synchronized with atmospheric events despite complete physical separation. "Current measurements show 44% correlation during coordinated manifestations—significantly higher than early observations and suggesting strengthening quantum connection despite network disruption."

This relationship had emerged as the most plausible explanation for the atmospheric phenomena they were documenting. Though the resonance cascade had disrupted the networking capability enabling coherent organization, quantum entanglement between prototype and deployed particles persisted— allowing mathematical information to propagate through subatomic relationships even where conventional connectivity had been neutralized.

"The most significant recent development involves weather modification capabilities at fracture zone boundaries," Stephanie continued, highlighting data from the Central Pacific monitoring station. "Conventional patterns entering these zones temporarily reorganize according to mathematical principles before returning to natural behavior upon exit. The effect remains localized and temporary, but demonstrates active interface between different atmospheric states rather than merely passive boundary conditions."

As they continued analyzing global monitoring data, the conventional thunderstorm approached Boston with unremarkable development—a reminder that Earth's atmosphere remained predominantly natural despite the broken sky emerging through fracture zones worldwide. The contrast between ordinary weather and the geometric organization documented in monitoring regions emphasized the hybrid nature of Earth's new atmospheric reality— predominantly governed by natural chaos but containing persistent regions operating according to mathematical principles.

"The research opportunity is unprecedented," Stephanie observed, scientific fascination evident despite governance concerns. "We're witnessing emergence of an atmospheric system unlike anything in Earth's previous history—not completely natural nor entirely mathematical, but rather a hybrid state where different organizational principles coexist in evolving equilibrium. Understanding this broken sky will require scientific frameworks transcending conventional meteorology."

Her team nodded agreement with this assessment. The fracture zones where mathematical and natural principles visibly interfaced represented neither threat to dismiss nor crisis to manage, but rather fundamental change to Earth's atmospheric functioning requiring comprehensive scientific response.

As the conventional thunderstorm reached campus—rain falling in chaotic patterns dictated by fluid dynamics rather than geometric precision—Stephanie's phone received a priority alert from the Atmospheric Monitoring Authority. A new coordinated manifestation was developing, with fracture zones appearing simultaneously across multiple monitoring regions including unprecedented formation directly over the North American eastern seaboard.

"Boston fracture zone forming," her assistant confirmed, checking real-time data from the monitoring network. "First significant manifestation in this region since monitoring began. Currently affecting approximately 2% of observable atmosphere with expansion rate consistent with established patterns."

Stephanie moved immediately to the atmospheric visualization system, observing the geometric organization beginning to form above the conventional thunderstorm outside her window. Unlike previous regional manifestations, this development would provide direct observational opportunity without remote monitoring equipment—the broken sky becoming visible to millions across major population centers rather than primarily observable through specialized monitoring stations in remote locations.

"The public education value is significant despite communication challenges," she noted, recognizing both opportunity and concern in this development. "Direct observation of fracture zones by general population will transform abstract scientific reporting into concrete visual evidence of Earth's altered atmosphere."

"Alert the Commission's public communication division," Stephanie directed. "This manifestation represents significant evolution in both scientific understanding and public engagement with Earth's altered atmosphere."

As her team implemented these notifications, she returned her attention to the emerging fracture zone. Through her office window, the previously conventional thunderstorm was developing unmistakable geometric organization in its upper cloud formations—perfect hexagonal structures forming with mathematical precision while lower portions continued following natural principles. The visible boundary between these different organizational states created the distinctive interface now termed a fracture zone—evidence of Earth's atmosphere operating according to hybrid principles rather than either completely natural patterns or entirely mathematical precision.

The broken sky had become directly observable beyond specialized monitoring stations—visible evidence of a planet fundamentally changed by human intervention, yet neither transformed completely nor returned entirely to its previous state.

The Atmospheric Governance Commission's emergency session convened remotely, bringing together scientific experts, policy architects, and communication specialists to address the unprecedented public visibility of fracture zones across major population centers. What had previously been documented primarily through specialized monitoring stations in remote locations was now directly observable by millions worldwide—geometric organization forming within visible atmosphere above numerous metropolitan regions.

"The fracture zones are maintaining stable boundaries rather than expanding aggressively," reported Olaf Werner from the Central Pacific station. "Geometric organization affecting approximately 13.2% of global atmospheric volume—consistent with established patterns rather than indicating crisis escalation. The unprecedented aspect isn't behavior change but location visibility, with manifestations appearing above major population centers for the first time since monitoring began."

"Implement the prepared communication framework with location-specific adjustments," directed Commission Chair Lin Zhao. "Emphasize three key points: that these phenomena represent evolution of previously documented atmospheric conditions rather than new developments, that they currently demonstrate no severe weather implications despite visual distinctiveness, and that comprehensive monitoring continues through established international frameworks with appropriate governance protocols in place."

"The weather modification capabilities at fracture zone boundaries continue developing in complexity rather than intensity," reported Karen Mitchell, highlighting data from multiple monitoring stations.

As the Commission continued discussion, global monitoring data showed the coordinated manifestation maintaining stable boundaries worldwide. The fracture zones remained visible above major population centers, geometric organization interfacing with natural weather patterns across increasingly defined boundaries.

"The broken sky represents humanity's new atmospheric reality," Zhao concluded, capturing the Commission's emerging consensus. "Not transitional aftermath requiring temporary response, but rather permanent alteration demanding both scientific understanding and governance innovation beyond conventional frameworks. Our task is navigating this unprecedented reality with wisdom adequate to its complexity."

Olaf cataloged the physical properties of the fracture zone boundary with practiced efficiency, his instruments recording what his eyes could barely comprehend. Three months ago, he'd been a conventional meteorologist with an unusually intuitive grasp of atmospheric dynamics. The crisis had transformed him as thoroughly as it had transformed Earth's atmosphere—forcing him to develop new theoretical frameworks that merged traditional meteorology with mathematical principles previously relevant only to theoretical physics.

"It's hurricane season in my career," he'd joked darkly to colleagues last week. "Everything I built over decades has been blown away, and I'm constructing new understanding from whatever remained standing."

Yet despite the professional upheaval, he'd found unexpected purpose in this atmospheric revolution. His unique ability to translate between conventional weather models and the new geometric organization had made him invaluable to the international response. The stone from his destroyed childhood home remained in his pocket—a reminder that destruction sometimes cleared the path for new construction, both of homes and of scientific understanding.

The fracture zone above New York City created a spectacle drawing millions of observers despite afternoon rain—perfect hexagonal clouds organized with mathematical precision interfacing with conventional formations along a sharply defined boundary visible from street level throughout the metropolitan area. Where mathematical and natural principles met, the atmosphere revealed its new hybrid nature—not completely transformed by Warren Thorne's intervention, but permanently altered in ways immediately apparent to any observer.

In the Central Pacific Monitoring Station's observation deck, Alex Ross watched natural clouds transform upon entering the fracture zone visible on the horizon. The conventional formations reorganized with mathematical precision as they crossed the atmospheric boundary—chaos adopting geometric organization while passing through the region before returning to natural patterns upon exit. This weather modification effect, limited but unmistakable, represented evolution beyond earlier observations when fracture zones had appeared primarily as visual phenomena with minimal physical impact.

"The visual manifestation above major population centers has transformed public engagement with these phenomena," observed Lin Zhao, joining remotely from the Atmospheric Governance Commission's headquarters. "Abstract scientific reporting has become concrete reality observable without specialized equipment or technical training, creating both educational opportunity and communication challenge."

"Warren Thorne's trial began this morning," Zhao abruptly continued, referencing proceedings that would determine consequences for the unauthorized geoengineering that had initially triggered the atmospheric transformation. "Creating additional media attention beyond the visible fracture zones themselves. The Commission's communication strategy acknowledges both the unauthorized nature of the original deployment and the continuing scientific contribution being provided by the system's creator." Thorne was simply too valuable, and seemingly too sincere in his wish to help correct his wrongs.

"The public response has been remarkably measured given the visual drama of these phenomena," Alex noted, reviewing global media monitoring. "Ranging from scientific interest to spiritual interpretation to pragmatic concern, but generally avoiding either panic about benign developments or dismissal of significant change."

"The monitoring framework continues expanding to match evolving understanding," Werner reported, referencing the global network tracking both current conditions and potential development. "From initial focus on geometric artifact documentation and quantum correlation measurement to comprehensive analysis of fracture zone dynamics, interface effects, and potential atmospheric evolution. The scientific opportunity remains unprecedented despite governance challenges."

And the scientific community around the world were attacking this enthusiastically. The Tokyo Protocol established standardized methodologies for high-density urban monitoring, building on Japanese innovations in miniaturized sensor deployment and public emergency communication. Former panicked crowds in Shibuya now passed beneath fracture zones with barely an upward glance, their attention captured only by particularly striking mathematical formations rendered familiar through constant exposure.

The Dubai Framework provided guidelines for critical infrastructure adaptation in extreme environments, leveraging engineering solutions developed across the Arabian Peninsula during the height of the crisis. The geometric wind patterns that had once threatened structural catastrophe were now routinely diverted through architectural innovations that had spread from Middle Eastern design centers to similar climatic regions worldwide.

In Bolivia, the Aymara Mathematical Translation Initiative had become the Authority's most unexpected resource—indigenous knowledge systems providing conceptual frameworks for understanding the fracture zones that sometimes proved more intuitive than conventional scientific approaches. Universities in La Paz now hosted international researchers studying traditional textile patterns alongside atmospheric data, recognizing complementary ways of encoding mathematical complexity.

"The patterns speaking to patterns," as Stephanie Mamani, now serving as the Initiative's cultural liaison, explained to visiting scientists.

The Australian Atmospheric Fire Management Division had transformed crisis response into long-term benefit—the interaction between fracture zones and bush fires leading to new containment strategies that had reduced destructive burn acreage by over forty percent in the past six months. Specialized aircraft once deployed for emergency monitoring now routinely seeded specific atmospheric conditions that leveraged the geometric organization to create controlled corridors limiting fire spread.

"We've turned the bloody sky breaking to our advantage," noted the division's director, Dr. James Cooper. "Though I wouldn't recommend the method."

The African Data Collective had evolved from Kenya's emergency citizen science initiative into the world's largest distributed monitoring network—millions of ordinary people across the continent using mobile technology to document atmospheric conditions far beyond the capacity of conventional observation systems. This grassroots approach had proven particularly valuable in tracking subtle variations in fracture zone manifestations across diverse ecosystems and climatic regions.

"The broken sky looks different over the Serengeti than it does over Nairobi," explained Amara Osei, who now directed the Collective. "Understanding those differences has proven crucial to our global understanding."

In Brazil, the Spiritual-Scientific Dialogue Commission addressed the complex intersection of religious and scientific responses to Earth's altered atmosphere—creating communication frameworks that acknowledged both empirical observation and meaning-making narratives that helped diverse communities process the unprecedented changes to their world.

"People need not only to understand what they are seeing, but what it means for their place in the universe," noted Dr. Paulo Santos, who co-chaired the Commission alongside religious leaders from multiple faith traditions. "The fracture zones have altered not just our atmosphere but our perception of humanity's relationship with planetary systems."

These specialized divisions reflected the Authority's recognition that Earth's altered atmosphere required not just global coordination but diverse cultural approaches leveraging humanity's full range of adaptive strategies and knowledge systems. The broken sky was experienced differently across cultures and regions, and managing it effectively required frameworks as varied as the human societies living beneath it.

CHAPTER TWENTY-ONE: NEW EQUILIBRIUM

[Science – August 12, 2026] Atmospheric Scientists Document 'Mathematical-Natural Equilibrium' as Earth's New Climate Normal
By Dr. Julian Reeves, Atmospheric Sciences Correspondent

Six months after the resonance cascade disrupted Warren Thorne's particle network, researchers have concluded that Earth's atmosphere has reached what they term "mathematical-natural equilibrium"—a stable hybrid state unlikely to either fully dissolve or expand beyond current parameters. "The fracture zones have maintained consistent influence over approximately 18% of global atmospheric volume for the past eight weeks," explains Dr. Olaf Werner, Director of the International Atmospheric Science Institute. "The quantum relationships sustaining these phenomena have stabilized at roughly 52% correlation between prototype and deployed particles, suggesting we've reached a long-term equilibrium state." Meanwhile, the Atmospheric Governance Commission has transitioned from crisis response to permanent management structures, establishing the International Atmospheric Authority with mandate and resources for monitoring Earth's altered atmosphere in perpetuity. Warren Thorne, recently sentenced to fifteen years imprisonment with concurrent scientific contribution requirements, has published a comprehensive analysis of the hybrid atmospheric system he inadvertently created, concluding that "Earth has entered a new atmospheric era requiring both scientific understanding and governance innovation beyond conventional frameworks."

The São Paulo skyline shimmered beneath fracture zones that had become as familiar as clouds themselves. Six months after first appearing above major population centers worldwide, the geometric patterns organizing approximately 18% of Earth's atmosphere had transformed from shocking anomaly to established feature—not entirely normalized, but accepted as part of the planet's new atmospheric reality. Where mathematical and natural weather patterns interfaced, the visible boundary created the distinctive atmospheric feature now familiar to every human with access to open sky.

Lin Zhao stood on the conference center's observation deck, watching conventional cumulus clouds reorganize with mathematical precision as they passed through the fracture zone above the city. The weather modification effect had neither intensified nor dissolved over recent months—natural patterns temporarily adopting geometric organization while traversing these regions before returning to conventional behavior upon exit. Limited but unmistakable evidence of Earth's hybrid atmosphere, functioning according to dual principles rather than either completely natural patterns or entirely mathematical precision.

"The equilibrium metrics remain consistent with established parameters," reported her assistant, reviewing the latest global monitoring data. "Mathematical organization affecting 17.8% of global atmospheric volume during coordinated manifestations— virtually unchanged from measurements across the past eight weeks. The quantum correlation between prototype and deployed particles stabilized at 52.3%, suggesting we've reached long-term steady state rather than continuing evolution."

"The São Paulo Synthesis represents our first comprehensive framework for this new reality," Lin observed, referencing the international agreement being finalized at the conference below. "Transitioning from crisis response to permanent management structures, establishing governance appropriate to an atmospheric system unlike anything in Earth's previous history."

The Synthesis had emerged through months of scientific documentation, diplomatic negotiation, and governance innovation—a framework acknowledging Earth's irreversibly altered atmosphere while establishing principles for its responsible management. From monitoring protocols tracking both current conditions and potential developments to research initiatives studying the hybrid atmospheric system's unique characteristics, from governance structures overseeing the stratospheric particles providing climate benefits to international agreements preventing similar unilateral interventions—the document represented humanity's collective response to a planet fundamentally changed through unauthorized action yet now requiring authorized management.

"The International Atmospheric Authority represents the Synthesis's primary institutional innovation," her assistant noted, referencing the permanent body being established through the agreement. "With mandate and resources for monitoring Earth's altered atmosphere in perpetuity, conducting research into its unique characteristics, and implementing governance protocols should its behavior evolve beyond established parameters."

This structure reflected pragmatic recognition that Earth's atmosphere had been permanently altered in ways requiring ongoing institutional attention rather than temporary crisis response. The fracture zones would continue manifesting for decades if not centuries, the particles would remain in the stratosphere providing cooling benefits alongside quantum-connected geometric organization, and both scientific understanding and governance frameworks would need to adapt to this unprecedented atmospheric state.

"Warren Thorne's contribution to the technical annexes proved particularly valuable," Lin acknowledged, referencing comprehensive analysis provided by the system's creator despite his recent sentencing for unauthorized geoengineering. "His insights into the quantum relationships sustaining fracture zones significantly advanced scientific understanding despite legitimate questions about his personal culpability."

This complexity had been addressed through the innovative sentencing framework developed by the international tribunal—fifteen years imprisonment with concurrent scientific contribution requirements, acknowledging both the unauthorized nature of

Thorne's intervention and the essential expertise he provided in understanding what it had created. Not absolution for unilateral action, but recognition that managing its consequences required insights from the very mind that had inadvertently transformed Earth's atmosphere.

As conference delegates arrived on the observation deck for the morning break, conversations naturally gravitated toward the fracture zone visible above—geometric clouds organized with mathematical precision interfacing with conventional formations along a boundary that had become familiar yet remained remarkable. Six months of persistent manifestation had transformed these phenomena from shocking anomaly to established feature, yet their fundamental nature continued inspiring both scientific fascination and philosophical contemplation.

"The mathematical-natural equilibrium appears increasingly stable across all monitoring parameters," observed Olaf Werner, joining Lin at the observation railing. "Not merely visual persistence but comprehensive atmospheric stability—quantum relationships maintaining consistent correlation, fracture zones affecting stable percentage of global volume, interface effects neither intensifying nor dissolving over time. Earth has reached atmospheric equilibrium unlike anything in its previous history."

"The São Paulo Synthesis represents governance catching up to scientific reality," Lin noted, acknowledging the lag between atmospheric transformation and institutional response. "Establishing permanent structures matching the timescale of the phenomena they're designed to address."

"The communication aspect remains challenging despite visual familiarity," Olaf observed, noting public interactions with the fracture zone visible above. "Balancing scientific accuracy with practical understanding, acknowledging fundamental atmospheric change without triggering either unwarranted alarm or inappropriate complacency."

"Sophie Lorde's documentary series has proven particularly effective in this regard," Lin noted, referencing the comprehensive project recently released globally. "Translating scientific complexity into accessible narrative while maintaining both accuracy and appropriate perspective."

As the conference delegates returned inside for continuing negotiations, Lin remained briefly on the observation deck, watching the hybrid atmosphere that had necessitated creation of entirely new governance frameworks. The broken sky—Earth operating according to dual atmospheric principles rather than either completely natural patterns or entirely mathematical precision—had transformed from crisis requiring emergency response to reality demanding permanent management. The São Paulo Synthesis represented humanity's collective adaptation to a planet irreversibly altered through unilateral action yet now requiring multilateral governance.

The dark day for planet Earth had given way not to familiar dawn but to something entirely new—a sky fractured between the chaos humans had evolved within and the mathematical precision they had briefly imposed upon it. Understanding and governing this broken sky had become humanity's ongoing responsibility following successful prevention of complete transformation, requiring wisdom that transcended both triumphalism over averted catastrophe and denial of permanent atmospheric alteration. Earth would survive – but a broken Earth.

The International Atmospheric Science Institute's central monitoring facility hummed with purposeful activity—researchers tracking Earth's altered atmosphere through the most sophisticated observation network ever established. "The mathematical-natural balance has maintained remarkably consistent parameters across all monitoring regions," reported Stephanie Martinez, highlighting global data on the central visualization. "Fracture zones affecting 17.8% of atmospheric volume, quantum correlation stabilized at 52.3%, interface effects neither intensifying nor diminishing over time. We're observing long-term equilibrium rather than continuing evolution."

"The interface weather modification effects merit particular attention," noted Isabelle Renard, focusing on data from multiple monitoring stations. "Conventional patterns reorganize according to mathematical principles while passing through fracture zones, then return to natural behavior upon exit. The effect remains consistent in both scope and behavior, suggesting stable rather than evolving capability."

"The meteorological models have adapted remarkably well to these dual principles," observed Olaf Werner, examining predictive systems developed specifically for Earth's altered atmosphere. "Conventional physics applies to approximately 82% of global volume, mathematical organization to roughly 18%, with interface dynamics now successfully incorporated into functional forecasting frameworks. We've essentially developed a new scientific discipline in six months of concentrated research."

"The quantum correlation measurements show particular stability," added Amara Okafor, reporting remotely from the Vault facility where Warren Thorne's prototype particles continued exhibiting behavior synchronized with atmospheric phenomena despite complete physical separation. "Stabilized at 52.3% across the past eight weeks, neither strengthening toward network resurgence nor weakening toward complete dissolution. The mathematical-natural equilibrium appears to be Earth's new atmospheric steady state."

"Warren's most recent assessment suggests the mathematical-natural equilibrium represents fundamentally stable configuration rather than transitional phase," Isabelle noted, referencing Thorne's latest contribution to scientific understanding. "The quantum relationships have essentially 'discovered' balance point between competing organizational principles—approximately 18% of atmospheric volume operating according to mathematical precision while roughly 82% maintains natural chaos, with neither system capable of fully displacing the other through currently active mechanisms."

The Central Pacific Monitoring Station's observation deck offered an unparalleled view of Earth's altered atmosphere. Where fracture zones interfaced with conventional weather patterns, the visible boundary created atmospheric feature now familiar to researchers worldwide—mathematical precision meeting natural chaos across defined atmospheric boundary. Six months after the resonance cascade had disrupted Warren Thorne's particle network, scientific focus had shifted from documenting crisis to characterizing stability—a hybrid atmospheric system that had reached equilibrium unlike anything in planetary history prior to human intervention.

"The mathematical-natural equilibrium has maintained remarkably consistent parameters across all monitoring regions," reported Marisol Keane, reviewing global data with her research team. "Fracture zones affecting 21.4% of atmospheric volume, quantum correlation stabilized at 52.3%, interface effects neither intensifying nor diminishing over time. We're observing long-term steady state rather than continuing evolution."

"The International Atmospheric Authority's establishment represents governance finally matching scientific reality," observed Olaf Werner, who had accepted senior research position within the new organization following formal adoption of the São Paulo Synthesis. "Permanent structures appropriate to a system requiring perpetual monitoring rather than temporary crisis management."

"The meteorological models have adapted remarkably well to these dual principles," Marisol noted, examining predictive systems developed specifically for Earth's altered atmosphere. "The laws of physics applies to approximately four-fifths of global volume, mathematical organization to the remainder, with interface dynamics now successfully incorporated into functional forecasting frameworks. We've essentially developed a new scientific discipline in six months of concentrated research."

The Brazilian coastline shimmered beneath fracture zones that had become familiar features of Earth's altered atmosphere. Alex Ross watched this hybrid system from the observation deck of the cruise vessel carrying international delegates from São Paulo following formal establishment of the Atmospheric Authority— geometric patterns organizing approximately 18% of global atmosphere interfacing with conventional formations along boundaries now visible worldwide.

"The new equilibrium represents both warning and opportunity," observed Sophie Lorde, capturing final footage for her documentary project. "Warning about unilateral intervention in planetary systems affecting all humanity, opportunity to develop governance frameworks transcending traditional limitations when addressing global challenges requiring collective response."

"The Authority represents governance innovation matching scientific reality," Alex noted, referencing the permanent body established through the São Paulo Synthesis. "Specialized institutional structure addressing atmosphere operating according to dual principles rather than either completely natural patterns or entirely mathematical precision."

"With mandates appropriately focused on both monitoring established phenomena and preventing similar unilateral interventions," Sophie agreed. "Balancing practical management of irreversible alteration already implemented with determined prevention of future deployment lacking collective authorization and oversight."

As their vessel continued along the Brazilian coast, the coordinated fracture zone manifestation maintained stable boundaries worldwide—mathematical organization affecting approximately 18% of global atmospheric volume, quantum correlation holding steady at approximately 52% strength, interface effects operating consistently across fractal boundaries visible from horizon to horizon. Earth's atmosphere functioning according to dual principles rather than either completely natural patterns or entirely mathematical precision—a hybrid system unlike anything in planetary history prior to human intervention.

"The documentary concluding segment captures this new equilibrium appropriately," Alex observed, reviewing Sophie's preliminary edit on her specialized equipment. "Neither continuing crisis nor complete resolution, but rather unprecedented reality requiring collective navigation through scientific understanding, governance innovation, and balanced communication."

"With acknowledgment that history will judge both the unilateral intervention triggering atmospheric alteration and humanity's collective response to its consequences," Sophie agreed. "Not simple narrative of heroism overcoming catastrophe, but rather complex engagement with permanent change requiring both accountability for past actions and responsibility for future management."

"Earth has entered an atmospheric era requiring both understanding and innovation beyond conventional frameworks," Alex observed, the Authority's mission crystallized in this central reality. "Regardless of how we reached this point, navigating what exists demands collective engagement with reality fundamentally different from anything in planetary history prior to human intervention."

Earth had entered new atmospheric era requiring both comprehension and innovation transcending conventional frameworks—reality fundamentally different from anything in planetary history prior to human intervention. The mathematical-natural equilibrium had stabilized as humanity's new normal, requiring both scientific understanding and governance adaptation appropriate to an atmosphere operating according to dual principles rather than either completely natural patterns or entirely mathematical precision.

The fracture zones visible worldwide would continue manifesting for decades if not centuries, the particles would remain in the stratosphere providing cooling benefits alongside quantum-connected geometric organization, and both scientific understanding and governance frameworks would continue adapting to this unprecedented atmospheric state that had become Earth's new equilibrium—neither crisis requiring emergency response nor transition awaiting resolution, but rather persistent reality demanding perpetual management through frameworks matching its unique and unprecedented nature.

EPILOGUE: THE SKY, REMEMBERED

[Journal of Atmospheric Sciences – April 14, 2035] Ten Years of Mathematical-Natural Equilibrium: Reflections on Earth's Hybrid Atmosphere
By Dr. Sophie Lorde, Distinguished Fellow, International Atmospheric Authority

A decade has passed since Earth's atmosphere reached the stable equilibrium we now recognize as its permanent state—approximately 18% organized according to mathematical principles, roughly 82% functioning through natural chaos, with fracture zones creating visible interfaces between these different systems. The once-shocking geometric patterns are now as familiar as clouds to a generation that has never known any other sky. The International Atmospheric Authority's decennial assessment confirms remarkable stability across all measurement parameters, with Warren Thorne's mathematical-natural equilibrium theory fully validated through comprehensive observation. The quantum relationship between prototype and deployed particles maintains 52% correlation without significant variation, the stratospheric particles continue providing approximately 0.8°C of cooling effect globally, and the weather modification effects at fracture zone boundaries remain consistent without either intensification or diminishment. Earth's hybrid atmosphere has become our accepted reality—neither the system humanity evolved within nor the one briefly threatened during the crisis of 2026, but rather the unexpected third state that emerged from their interaction and now defines our planet's new atmospheric normal.

The classroom windows framed fracture zones that had become as familiar as clouds themselves. Ten years after Earth's atmosphere had reached mathematical-natural equilibrium, the geometric patterns organizing approximately 18% of global volume had transformed from scientific fascination to everyday background—still remarkable when consciously observed, but normalized through constant presence in skies worldwide.

"Your assignment for next week," Professor Alex Ross told his students at the International Atmospheric Institute, "is to review the original crisis documentation and identify three specific governance innovations that emerged from humanity's response to unilateral intervention in planetary systems. Focus particularly on institutional structures developed specifically for managing hybrid atmospheric dynamics rather than either traditional weather or completely mathematical organization."

The students nodded their understanding, many glancing toward the fracture zones visible outside—geometric clouds organized with mathematical precision interfacing with conventional formations along boundaries that had become familiar features of Earth's altered atmosphere. These young researchers had never known any other sky, having grown up beneath fracture zones that manifested with predictable regularity worldwide.

"Professor Ross," asked one student, "the documentary excerpts mentioned you directly participated in both the resonance cascade implementation and establishment of the Authority. How did your perspective change from crisis management to permanent governance during those transitional months?"

Alex smiled at this thoughtful question. "Evolution rather than transformation," he replied. "Initially focusing on preventing complete atmospheric reorganization, then navigating transitional weather effects, then documenting the broken sky's unique properties, and finally establishing governance structures appropriate to a permanently altered system requiring perpetual attention rather than temporary response. The key insight was recognizing we faced neither continuing crisis nor complete resolution, but rather unprecedented reality requiring collective navigation through both scientific understanding and institutional innovation."

"And Warren Thorne?" asked another student cautiously, referencing the complex figure whose intervention had inadvertently created the atmospheric system they now studied.

"Recently released early with recognition of his concurrent scientific contribution," Alex noted, acknowledging both the legal judgment and continuing expertise provided by the system's creator. "Now serving as senior technical advisor to the Authority's equilibrium monitoring division, continuing to apply his unique understanding of quantum relationships sustaining fracture zones to their long-term management."

"However, it's possible I have more money in my pocket than he has in his entire portfolio. The massive global restitutions he was hit with far outweighed even his vast fortune."

This balanced approach reflected the nuanced position Thorne occupied in both historical narrative and current expertise—creator of unauthorized intervention yet essential contributor to managing its consequences, subject to legal judgment while providing insights unavailable from any other source. Not simple story of heroism or villainy, but rather complicated intersection of accountability and practical necessity that defied conventional ethical frameworks.

The mathematical-natural equilibrium appears remarkably stable across the entire monitoring period," observed a doctoral candidate reviewing long-term data. "Fracture zones affecting consistent percentage of atmospheric volume, quantum correlation maintaining steady connection between prototype and deployed particles, interface effects neither intensifying nor dissolving over time. The hybrid atmosphere shows no indication of either dissolving toward complete return to natural conditions or expanding toward full mathematical transformation."

"Precisely the equilibrium characteristics described in Thorne's original theory," Alex confirmed. He glanced at Olaf Werner, now Director of the International Atmospheric Institute after a meteoric rise from university professor to global authority on hybrid atmospheric dynamics.

Olaf nodded, unconsciously rubbing the small stone he still carried—his talisman through both personal and professional storms. "We've essentially created a new meteorological discipline," he said, his habitual weather metaphors having evolved into a more philosophical approach over the years. "The old atmospheric science was like forecasting in black and white. Now we're working in full spectrum—mathematical precision and natural chaos coexisting in the same atmospheric system, creating patterns with both predictable and stochastic elements."

He smiled slightly at his former students, now colleagues in this new scientific field. "Hurricane Eliza took my home when I was fourteen and gave me a career studying weather. The atmospheric crisis took that career and gave me something I never imagined—the chance to help define an entirely new understanding of how atmosphere functions. Sometimes destruction clears the path for creation, if we're wise enough to build something better from the remnants."

This stability had transformed both scientific research and governance emphasis—from documenting unprecedented phenomena to analyzing established atmospheric behavior, from developing initial oversight to maintaining permanent management, from explaining shocking anomaly to educating new generation about normalized reality. The broken sky had become Earth's accepted atmospheric state—neither crisis requiring emergency response nor transition awaiting resolution, but rather persistent reality demanding perpetual management through governance structures matching its unique and unprecedented characteristics.

As the class session concluded, students gathered their materials while continuing to discuss the historical documentation they'd reviewed—Sophie Lorde's comprehensive documentary series chronicling Earth's atmospheric transformation from initial crisis through transitional chaos to new equilibrium. The footage showing early fracture zone manifestations prompted particular fascination from students who had never experienced them as shocking anomaly, having grown up beneath geometric patterns that had been visible in skies worldwide throughout their lives.

Alex remained briefly at the classroom windows, watching fracture zones that had transformed from unprecedented crisis to established feature of Earth's altered atmosphere. The mathematical-natural equilibrium had stabilized exactly as Warren Thorne's theory had predicted—hybrid system where different organizational principles coexisted in stable relationship, requiring both scientific understanding and governance frameworks appropriate to its unprecedented characteristics.

Ten years after Earth's atmosphere had reached stable equilibrium, that wisdom continued developing through both scientific research and governance innovation—new generation studying hybrid atmospheric dynamics while established institutions managed its unique characteristics. The International Atmospheric Institute where Alex now taught represented educational dimension of this collective response—training future scientists and policy architects in frameworks developed specifically for understanding and governing atmosphere operating according to dual principles rather than either completely natural patterns or entirely mathematical precision.

The Vault facility housing Warren Thorne's prototype particles had transformed from emergency containment to permanent research institution. Ten years after Earth's atmosphere had reached stable equilibrium, the specialized chamber containing these original components of atmospheric intervention had become sophisticated laboratory studying quantum relationships sustaining fracture zones visible worldwide.

The quantum entanglement had launched thousands of correlated research projects around the world, upsetting established physics, but promising stunning new understanding of the universe.

"The correlation measurements remain remarkably consistent across the entire monitoring period," observed Amara Okafor, now serving as the facility's Director after a decade leading quantum research into Earth's hybrid atmosphere. "Stabilized at 52.3% without significant variation despite both extensive observation and deliberate experimental manipulation. The mathematical-natural equilibrium appears fundamentally stable rather than coincidentally persistent."

"Confirming the initial theory that quantum relationships have essentially 'discovered' balance point between competing organizational principles," noted Wei Zhang, reviewing comprehensive data accumulated through ten years of continuous monitoring. "The connection between prototype and deployed particles maintains precise equilibrium—strong enough to sustain geometric organization affecting approximately 18% of global atmospheric volume, yet insufficient to support expansion toward complete mathematical transformation."

"Warren Thorne's contribution to understanding these relationships cannot be overstated despite the complicated circumstances surrounding his intervention," Amara acknowledged, referencing both the unauthorized deployment and essential expertise provided by the system's creator. "His mathematical-natural equilibrium theory has been validated through comprehensive observation across multiple parameters, with decade-long stability confirmed through both passive monitoring and active experimentation."

"The weather modification effects at fracture zone boundaries merit particular attention given their stability characteristics," Wei noted, highlighting data from global monitoring stations. "Conventional patterns reorganize according to mathematical principles while passing through these zones, then return to natural behavior upon exit. The effect remains consistent in both scope and behavior throughout the entire observation period, suggesting permanent atmospheric feature rather than transitional anomaly."

"The public perception has evolved perhaps most significantly," Amara observed, referencing comprehensive surveys conducted by the Authority's public engagement division. "Fracture zones transforming from shocking anomaly to familiar feature, from crisis manifestation to normalized background, from unprecedented phenomenon requiring explanation to accepted reality requiring minimal commentary. An entire generation has now grown up beneath geometric patterns visible worldwide, having never experienced sky organized solely through natural principles."

Public adaptation to the fracture zones varied dramatically across cultural contexts, reflecting diverse societal approaches to unprecedented change. What had initially triggered global alarm had gradually transformed into background reality—though the specific forms of normalization reflected regional values and perspectives as varied as humanity itself.

In Japan, an entire aesthetic movement had emerged around fracture zone observation—dedicated photographers documenting the mathematical patterns through specialized techniques that captured their geometric precision in stunning detail. Viewing platforms on Tokyo skyscrapers once established for emergency monitoring had transformed into cultural destinations where people gathered for "mathematical sunset" appreciation, combining traditional nature observation with contemporary understanding of the hybrid atmospheric state.

Across the Arabian Peninsula, architectural innovation had accelerated in response to the new atmospheric dynamics— buildings incorporating design elements that leveraged the predictable geometric wind patterns created at fracture zone boundaries. Structural features that would have made no sense under purely natural atmospheric conditions now referenced the mathematical organization visible above, creating harmony between built environment and altered sky that reflected the region's tradition of environmental adaptation.

In Bolivia and Peru, traditional textiles had begun incorporating new patterns inspired by the fracture zones—weavers adapting ancient geometric techniques to represent the mathematical organization now visible overhead. What Western observers sometimes perceived as alien imposition, Andean communities often recognized as variations on forms that had existed in their cultural expression for generations.

"The sky now speaks the language our textiles have spoken for centuries," noted a weaving cooperative leader in Cusco. "We are simply continuing the conversation."

Australian outback communities had developed the most pragmatic relationship with the fracture zones—integrating their predictable boundaries into navigation practices for regions lacking formal roadways. The geometric patterns overhead provided more reliable directional indicators than natural formations, particularly during twilight hours when their mathematical precision remained visible against darkening skies.

"Used to navigate by the stars," explained an elderly rancher outside Alice Springs. "Now we navigate by the geometry. Different maps, same purpose."

Across Africa, diverse societies had incorporated the fracture zones into existing cultural frameworks—from Maasai warriors using the geometric boundaries as timing indicators for migration cycles to urban youth in Lagos creating digital art movements focused on "mathematical remixing" of traditional visual motifs with the new atmospheric patterns visible above their cities.

"We've been adapting to environmental change for thousands of years," noted a community elder in rural Kenya. "The mathematics in the sky is just the latest change requiring response. We are humans, and humans survive."

In Brazil, religious processions now often culminated during geometric manifestations—the mathematical precision overhead interpreted through spiritual frameworks that found divine pattern in the fracture zones. Catholic traditions in particular had incorporated the new atmospheric reality into existing practices, with procession schedules adjusted to coincide with predictable manifestation cycles.

"The broken sky reveals order within apparent chaos," explained a priest in Salvador during a festival that had traditionally honored natural cycles but now acknowledged mathematical patterns as equally worthy of reverence. "This has always been the message of faith, now visible to all who look upward."

These varied adaptive responses reflected broader truth about human resilience—not uniform global reaction but diverse cultural strategies for incorporating unprecedented change into existing frameworks while developing new approaches appropriate to altered reality. The fracture zones had become familiar through constant exposure, yet the specific forms of adaptation reflected the rich diversity of human societies experiencing Earth's new atmospheric normal.

This normalization represented perhaps the most profound evolution in humanity's relationship with Earth's altered atmosphere—from crisis requiring emergency response to reality accepted without constant conscious recognition. The broken sky had become familiar background rather than perpetual surprise, atmospheric feature noticed primarily when specific attention directed toward its unique characteristics rather than continuous source of disorientation or concern.

The São Paulo headquarters of the International Atmospheric Authority symbolized governance evolution paralleling atmospheric transformation. Ten years after Earth had reached mathematical-natural equilibrium, the institution established through crisis response had become permanent management structure overseeing hybrid atmosphere functioning according to dual principles rather than either completely natural patterns or entirely mathematical precision.

"The decennial assessment confirms remarkable stability across all measurement parameters," reported Karen Mitchell, serving as the Authority's Director of Scientific Services after a decade developing frameworks specifically for understanding Earth's altered atmosphere. "The mathematical-natural equilibrium has been validated as Earth's permanent atmospheric state rather than transitional phase."

This stability had transformed governance emphasis from emergency response to normalized oversight—management appropriate to unprecedented atmospheric state that had established consistent equilibrium over decade-long observation period. The broken sky demanded institutional structures matching its unique characteristics—neither temporary intervention nor conventional oversight, but rather specialized governance addressing an atmosphere operating according to dual principles rather than either completely natural patterns or entirely mathematical precision.

"The prevention protocols division reports comprehensive monitoring network functioning at 99.8% effectiveness," added Lin Zhao, completing her second term as the Authority's Director-General following unanimous reappointment. "No unauthorized stratospheric deployments attempted throughout the entire ten-year period, suggesting successful implementation of both technical detection capabilities and international agreement establishing collective responsibility for planetary systems affecting all humanity."

This preventive emphasis reflected determination to avoid similar governance failures while acknowledging irreversible alteration already implemented. Earth's atmosphere had been permanently changed through unilateral action, yet required multilateral governance moving forward—frameworks establishing collective oversight of both existing stratospheric particles and potential future interventions affecting planetary systems.

"The knowledge integration division has perhaps achieved our most significant long-term milestone," Karen noted, highlighting educational programs developed specifically for understanding Earth's hybrid atmosphere. "Scientific frameworks appropriate to mathematical-natural equilibrium now standardized through academic curricula worldwide, governance models suitable for dual organizational principles integrated into international relations training, public education resources helping general population comprehend atmospheric system that has become normalized background yet remains profoundly different from anything in Earth's previous history."

"Ms. Lorde's comprehensive historical documentation merits particular recognition," Lin observed, referencing the recently published scholarly assessment authored by journalist-turned-atmospheric-historian Sophie Lorde. "Chronicling evolution from initial crisis through transitional chaos to established equilibrium, providing perspective essential for both current understanding and future governance adaptation. Institutional memory serving practical purpose beyond mere historical curiosity."

"Warren Thorne's contribution following his recent release merits acknowledgment despite the complicated circumstances surrounding his intervention," Karen noted, referencing both the unauthorized deployment and essential expertise provided by the system's creator. "His technical advisory role within the equilibrium monitoring division leverages unique understanding of quantum relationships sustaining fracture zones while maintaining appropriate oversight and accountability frameworks."

The geometric clouds organized with mathematical precision reflected sunset light with ethereal beauty, their perfect hexagonal structures interfacing with conventional formations along boundaries now familiar yet still remarkable. Sophie Lorde captured this atmospheric tableau from Saltsjöbaden Observatory's reconstructed observation deck, returning to location where she had once documented the silent pulse during network dissolution ten years earlier.

"The sky, remembered," she murmured, referencing title of both her recently published scholarly assessment and the observation deck itself, which now bore commemorative plaque acknowledging her documentation of Earth's atmospheric transformation from this historic location. The broken sky had become Earth's accepted normal—neither crisis requiring emergency response nor transition awaiting resolution, but rather persistent reality demanding perpetual management through frameworks matching its unique and unprecedented nature.

Sophie's specialized camera captured this hybrid system with practiced efficiency, documenting decade-long stability for comprehensive historical record maintained by the Authority's knowledge integration division. Her evolution from crisis documentarian to atmospheric historian —expertise developed through direct experience with unprecedented phenomena now helping future generations understand Earth's permanently altered atmosphere.

"The mathematical-natural equilibrium theory has been comprehensively validated," noted Olaf, joining her at the observation railing. Now serving as Director of the International Atmospheric Institute following distinguished career documenting Earth's altered atmosphere, he had been invited to Saltsjöbaden for tenth anniversary commemoration of events leading to current equilibrium state. "Earth's atmosphere has established balance between fundamentally different organizational principles— approximately 18% functioning according to mathematical precision, roughly 82% operating through natural chaos, with neither system capable of displacing the other through currently active mechanisms."

"Creating visual evidence instantly recognizable yet profoundly different from anything in Earth's history," Sophie observed, continuing documentation of fracture zones visible above the observatory. "Geometric organization interfacing with natural weather patterns across atmospheric boundaries now familiar worldwide, hybrid system accepted as normal by population that has adapted to its unique characteristics over ten years of continuous exposure."

"The historical documentation provides essential perspective beyond mere curiosity," Sophie noted, referencing comprehensive records established through both her work and broader Authority initiatives. "Maintaining institutional memory regarding both atmospheric transformation and governance response, documenting evolution from emergency intervention to permanent management, preserving knowledge essential for navigating system unlike anything in Earth's previous history."

As evening light continued illuminating the fracture zone above Saltsjöbaden, the geometric clouds organized with mathematical precision maintained their unearthly beauty—a visible reminder that Earth had entered atmospheric era unlike anything in its previous history. Understanding and governing this broken sky had become humanity's collective responsibility, requiring wisdom that transcended both triumphalism over averted catastrophe and denial of permanent atmospheric alteration.

"The sky, remembered," Sophie repeated, capturing both title of her scholarly assessment and essential truth underlying atmospheric transformation they had experienced and documented over past decade. "Not merely historical recollection of temporary anomaly, but rather ongoing engagement with permanent alteration requiring both understanding and governance appropriate to its unprecedented nature."

As night fell over Saltsjöbaden Observatory, fracture zones remained visible through distinctive luminescence—geometric patterns organized with mathematical precision continuing to interface with conventional formations along boundaries that were now familiar features of Earth's permanently altered atmosphere. The broken sky had become humanity's new normal—hybrid system operating according to dual principles rather than either completely natural patterns or entirely mathematical precision, requiring both understanding and governance appropriate to its unprecedented nature.

Above them, the fractured sky pulsed with alien mathematics, a permanent reminder of how close they had come to losing everything familiar about their world. Earth would never again know a purely natural sky.

www.ingramcontent.com/pod-product-compliance
Lightning Source LLC
Chambersburg PA
CBHW051234260626
47162CB00002B/428